SECRET JUSTICE

SECRET JUSTICE

A NOVEL

PAUL GOLDSTEIN

ANKERWYCKE

Cover design by Elmarie Jara/Ankerwycke.

Printed in the United States of America

18 17 16 15 14   5 4 3 2 1

Library of Congress Cataloging-in-Publication Data

Names: Goldstein, Paul, 1943- author.
Title: Secret justice : a novel / Paul Goldstein.
Description: Chicago, Illinois : American Bar Association, [2016]
Identifiers: LCCN 2015043731 | ISBN 9781634252775 (alk. paper)
Classification: LCC PS3607.O4853 S43 2016 | DDC 813/.6--dc23 LC record available at http://lccn.loc.gov/2015043731

Discounts are available for books ordered in bulk. Special consideration is given to state bars, CLE programs, and other bar-related organizations. Inquire at Book Publishing, Ankerwycke, American Bar Association, 321 N. Clark Street, Chicago, Illinois 60654-7598.
www.ShopABA.org

For Carl Yorke

"It is emphatically the province and duty of the judicial department to say what the law is."

—*Marbury v. Madison* (1803), wall inscription inside the United States Supreme Court Building

At 6:00 a.m. on the second day of his Senate confirmation hearings, Richard Davenport has the "Y" swimming pool to himself. For the better part of his life he has trained in echoing, chlorine-steeped rooms like this one, and in minutes he is benumbed by the black line that inscribes the bottom of the pool. Memories stream past like water.

Davenport remembers a summer evening in 'Sconset on the eastern tip of Nantucket. At seven, the Atlantic is evident only by indirection: the day's fading light reflected off the water's surface; the clean and temperate air; the vast, ambient silence. A dozen or so neighbors and friends gather on the back lawn of Davenport's—really his wife Olivia's—summer home, all of them of an age and time in which flannels and blazer are de rigueur for the men, cotton skirt and cashmere cardigan pulled over trim shoulders for the women. The Adirondack chairs are dark green against the purple light. Sparky—their daughter Nola's dog; Nola is studying in France this summer—scurries about, making a pest of herself, jumping onto the lap of any guest who makes the mistake of petting her. The first round of drinks has been consumed and the chatter in the air is agreeable. It is summer, and any differences among the guests have been swept beneath the hedgerows.

Olivia, the perfect host, is everywhere, shooing Sparky off comfortable laps, overseeing the drinks table, and filling glasses. (Was this the year that people started taking wine instead of cocktails before dinner?) Always careful of her fair skin in summer, Olivia is not tanned like the others, and, watching her move among their friends, Davenport is amazed at how little her beauty has changed over the more than two decades since their undergraduate days. She is the smartest person here. Despite an indifferent education—she once told Davenport that she drank and drugged her way through Chapin, and she didn't have to tell him that she did the same at Harvard—Olivia has the fiercest intelligence he knows.

"See what you can do with Sparky, will you, Richard? She's such a pest!" Rough-coated and whiskery, Sparky is a Jack Russell terrier, with all the aggressiveness of the breed and a mind of her own. Davenport makes a feint in the dog's direction, but the animal runs off, and he resumes talking with his occasional tennis partner, Paul McConnell, about the challenges of his firm's new office in Budapest.

"My husband!" Olivia cries. "Useless!" With much arm-waving, she chases after Sparky, snatching the terrier up to her chest just as the dog is about to jump onto yet another lap. "Bad, bad girl! You know what we do with bad girls, don't you?" Olivia looks around to confirm that her little drama has drawn the attention of the small crowd and, placing her hands under the dog, throws her perilously high into the air before catching her. The second toss is even higher. The startled looks of the guests mirror that of Sparky herself. Olivia's color is high, and Davenport recognizes the barely controlled hysteria behind her voice and gesture. It is an easy guess that she started on her cocktails—no wine for Olivia, only well-iced martinis—hours before their company arrived.

Memory distorts time. At one point in the evening it seems to Davenport as if the cocktail hour has gone on too long, and he looks around for Olivia to collect their guests for dinner. Seconds or minutes pass before an awareness of her presence turns him toward the house, and there she sits, legs dangling from the sill of a flung-open second-floor window, silently observing the crowd, a cocktail glass in one hand, the other hand resting on Sparky's back. By this time in their marriage, Olivia has attempted suicide twice. Both attempts were private and bloodless—once with a car idling in the closed garage, the other time with gin and sleeping pills—and it is inconceivable that she has a third attempt in mind, for the act would be too public and the fall too short to accomplish anything more than some broken bones. Davenport is confident that, even in Olivia's inebriated state, the prospect of pain terrifies her.

Then he sees her intentions. Cues pass between a long-married couple that are invisible to outsiders—the tilt of a head, a contained smile—and in the same instant that he realizes what is about to happen, Davenport tears across the lawn, arriving below the second-story window just in time to catch the falling dog. A tiny heart hammers in a fragile chest; it feels as if the dog has swallowed whole some small, frantic beast. The next day, Olivia denies the incident. But Sparky remembers. The dog skitters off whenever Olivia approaches, and in Davenport's mind, he does the same.

Why did he marry Olivia? If asked at the time, Davenport would have spoken of her beauty and intelligence. But, if caught in a candid moment, he would have added something about the enchantment of her recklessness. And why did Olivia choose him? Although she never said this, Davenport believes that Olivia married him because, forced to decide between saving her and rescuing a falling dog, even then it would surprise her which he chose.

1

Under the high, wide ceiling, the hearing room could be one of Europe's grand railroad terminals, a place where great crimes can be committed and concealed in full public view. When Senator Oren Nyquist pushes back from the long table for a whispered conference with the aide who crouches behind him, Richard Davenport takes the moment to reflect that, after two days of mostly hapless questioning from the senator's fellow committee members, he has told no lies, but also given up no secrets.

"You can relax, Mr. Davenport. I am your last inquisitor." The senator's narrow, coarse-featured face is a preacher's and not constructed for levity. His attempt at a smile gives the impression of a man biting down on pain. "As the committee's most junior minority member, it falls to me to pick through the table scraps. That's not to suggest, sir, that you offered my colleagues much to chew on. You give new meaning to the phrase 'stealth candidate.' You are a blank slate."

Davenport is the first Supreme Court nominee since Lewis Powell, decades ago, to be chosen directly from private practice, and he lacks the history of appellate opinions, law review articles and Justice Department memos that encumbers the typical nominee picked from the judiciary, academe, or public service. He doesn't know Nyquist well enough to make a joke—indeed he doesn't know him at all—so he keeps his answer plain. "If my record looks like a clean slate, Senator, it's only because—"

Nyquist leans into the microphone and the back of his suit jacket separates from his shirt collar as if an unseen hand is trying to restrain him. "I said a blank slate, Mr. Davenport, not a clean one."

The remark must sound like a punchline to the two dozen or so photographers squatting in front of the committee table, for electronic flashes explode in unison to capture the nominee's reaction. In fact, the senator's distinction strikes Davenport as odd, too mean-spirited for the venue, and too esoteric even for public television, which is broadcasting the hearings from a booth along a side wall.

"I'm sure, Mr. Davenport, that your handlers over there, Mr. Jaffe and his team, have thoroughly instructed you so that you won't have to give the American people even the smallest clue as to your personal affairs or your views on the great social and moral issues that will come before the court. Let's see how good a student you were."

Bennett Jaffe sits in the first row, directly behind Davenport. The rest of his team is dispersed around the room along with several partners from Davenport's law firm. The seat on the aisle next to Bennett, the one traditionally reserved for a member of the nominee's family, is empty.

"Let's turn to your finances," Nyquist says. "When Chairman Mandeville questioned you yesterday, your answers were regrettably not as complete as the American people deserve from a Supreme Court nominee."

As Davenport himself would do in preparing a witness for trial, Bennett instructed him not to speak other than to answer a question. Nyquist has not asked a question, but still Davenport hears himself say, "Incomplete in what respect? As I explained to the committee yesterday, if the Senate confirms my nomination, I will sell all of my investments in publicly held companies and invest the proceeds in either treasury bills or well-diversified mutual funds, even though to do so will require me to pay significant capital gains taxes to both the federal government and New York State."

"I congratulate you on your financial acumen, Mr. Davenport. Not many Americans today have capital gains on which they can pay taxes." A thin crackle of amusement threads through the row of aides and committee hangers-on seated behind the senators, but Nyquist ignores it and uses the eraser on his pencil to flip through the pages of the nominee's financial report.

Davenport recognizes the poise and gestures of an experienced trial lawyer. Senators are more at home giving speeches than cross-examining witnesses, but Bennett has warned Davenport about Nyquist's skill at framing questions. The senator built his political career in North Dakota, first as a district attorney locking up methamphetamine dealers for unprecedented prison terms, and then as the state's attorney general, prosecuting large eastern banks that he cast as the villains behind the mortgage frauds impoverishing the state's farmers and homeowners.

Davenport fills his questioner's silence. "Unfortunately, my remaining investments—principally my holdings in four small companies founded by friends and clients—cannot be so easily liquidated, and in the unlikely event that one of them becomes the subject of a dispute before the court, I would of course recuse myself." Again, he asks himself how the senator has contrived to put him so off balance that he should make these rookie mistakes.

Nyquist's eyes are deep-set behind black half-frames, and when he looks down, as he does now, they disappear into shadow. "What in fact interest me, Mr. Davenport, are not the documents that your handlers provided to the committee, but the documents they chose not to provide—documents that my own staff were forced to discover on their own."

Without turning, Nyquist reaches a hand back over his shoulder and accepts a file folder from his aide. The hand-off sounds an alarm, and Davenport feels a moment's panic, but for what? His accountants delivered every scrap of his financial materials to Bennett's team. He cannot connect the sheaf of papers that the senator places on the table in front of him to any known records. He has no Swiss bank accounts, no interests in offshore companies. Unlike other lawyers in his income bracket, he has no financial secrets.

Nyquist leans back, and for an instant the television lights turn the lenses of his half-frames into fiery orbs. "Your wife—"

Olivia. "You mean my late wife—"

"Forgive me. Of course, Mrs. Davenport has gone Home."

The remark is so indecorous, so monstrous, that the other senators look down or busy themselves with papers to hide their embarrassment from the cameras. Were she alive today and in this room, Olivia, an atheist descended from a long and unwavering line of Rhode Island Episcopalians, would have arched an eyebrow, stared straight at Nyquist and, even stone sober, told him to go to hell.

"But, you see, I raise this unfortunate subject because it is Mrs. Davenport's passing over that occasions my inquiry." Nyquist glances though the papers, although Davenport is sure that he has already absorbed their content. "According to these records, Mrs. Davenport left a fortune more than ten times the size of yours."

"My wife left most of her estate in trusts. Some are charitable trusts. Others name our daughter, Nola, as their sole beneficiary. Friends and household employees received gifts and she also left Nola some cash and stock. But most of my wife's bequests to Nola are tied up in trusts."

"And your wife left no cash or stock to you? She didn't make you the beneficiary, or even the trustee, of one or more of these trusts?"

Davenport wonders why Nyquist is implying that he has withheld information when the charge can so easily be refuted. "I received nothing from my wife, in or out of trusts."

"And you have no control over these assets, in or out of trusts?"

"None."

"No influence, over the trusts for your daughter?"

This time Davenport tries for humor. "Who today has any influence over his children?"

A wave of laughter starts up, but when Davenport turns to the row of seats behind him, silence drops over the room like a radio being switched off, and he realizes his mistake at once. The spectators think, wrongly, that he has turned for help from Bennett, when in fact he was glancing at the chair on the aisle, the chair that Bennett reserved for Nola. It is still empty.

"Isn't that unusual, Mr. Davenport?" Nyquist's expression reveals nothing; his words lack even the dullest edge. "For a wife to leave nothing in her will to her husband?"

"I haven't made a study of the question, Senator. My wife certainly knew that I have assets of my own."

The hearing room stirs alert. This is a Washington crowd, keen to the slightest nuance of a legislator's question and the weakness of a witness's response, and they smell blood. This is why Bennett was scowling when Davenport looked past him to the empty chair. Nyquist is asking not why he withheld assets from the committee, but why his wife would withhold them from him. Committee Chairman Mandeville looks over Davenport's shoulder at Bennett and shoots him a worried frown.

Under the television lights, the chairman's snowdrift of carefully sculpted hair glows above a broad, pink face. Well-cut gray flannel lends his bulk the presence of statuary. Mandeville takes his instructions from the White House—from Bennett—but Bennett has withheld the details of these conversations from the nominee. "Do you remember the old Westerns, Richard? You know, when the doctor arrives at the homestead to deliver the baby and orders the husband into the kitchen to boil lots of water? Well, your job is to stay in the kitchen and boil water."

Nyquist's aide hands the senator a gray paperbound volume sprouting dozens of yellow Post-its from its pages. The book has the look of a government document, and Davenport tries to place it among the financial filings of the corporations past and present that he has represented.

Because Mandeville is looking at Bennett, he doesn't see the gray volume. But Bennett sees it, and the sudden alarm on the chairman's face when he turns his gaze to where the document is now on the table in front of Nyquist is surely a reflection of Bennett's own. Mandeville pulls the microphone to his lips. "If I may interrupt, Senator, we have been going now for two and a half hours. I believe it's time for a short recess."

"I've only just started, Mr. Chairman." Nyquist's voice has a breathless, strangled quality. "I have been allotted a mere fifty minutes for my questions. It seems only fair to let me continue."

Next to the eighteen other senators, the lank-haired junior senator from North Dakota looks raw, unfinished. His complexion is sallow, and his expression at rest is sorrowful. The others at the baize-draped table—twelve Democrats and six Republicans, fifteen men and three women—are coiffed, buffed, and powdered for the cameras, and the banks of television lights illuminate them like saints in a Renaissance painting.

"Maybe there are some others here whose constitutions are less robust than yours, Senator, and they may need a break." The chairman's gavel comes down even before he finishes the sentence. "We will recess for ten minutes."

Before the echo of the gavel dies, the senators are out of their seats and Bennett's hand is on Davenport's shoulder. "Come into my office," he says.

At the long cafeteria-style tables in the back, the reporters rise to stretch. Their presence in the hearing room is an artifact from an earlier time, for today they observe the proceedings on wide-screen monitors hanging from the walls. They could as well be watching television at a downtown bar. Davenport follows Bennett past the press to the alcove in a far corner that has become the site of their hurried recess conversations. On the ornately carved telephone table that fills half of the small space is a Senate phone with no dial.

Bennett is a Washington warhorse. A stranger would guess that he is in his sixties, even though at forty-nine, he is only a year older than Davenport. He is paunchy, has wiry gray hair, a worried, always moist brow, and dark fleshy pads beneath his eyes. His dissolute appearance is not from drink or drugs, but overwork. The raggedness about him is such that, the first time they met, Davenport expected to find a food stain on his tie or cigarette ash on his lapel, but Bennett's dress is always crisp and immaculate. When he leans in to talk, Davenport smells the mint of the nicotine gum that has replaced the cigarettes. "Is the gray binder what I think it is?" The mint fails to mask his breath, which has turned rank.

Davenport nods. "It's a sealed document. Nyquist isn't going to open it."

The 517-page volume is the transcript of the coroner's inquest into the death by drowning of Olivia Ives Davenport, Davenport's wife, in stormy November waters off Nantucket Island. The inquest left no witness unexamined, including the two pathologists who confirmed each other's estimate of Olivia's blood alcohol level at the moment she slipped over the railing, and the three psychiatrists, including Olivia's own, who guessed at her state of mind. And of course Richard Davenport, her companion on the last ferry of the day from Nantucket Harbor to Hyannis. Weeks later, after the Barnstable district attorney determined that there was no cause for charges to be filed, the transcript was permanently sealed and only four numbered copies made: one for the coroner; one for the clerk of the court; and one each for the immediate family. Davenport doesn't know how Nyquist obtained a copy.

Bennett says, "You should have shown me the transcript when I asked. I'm your lawyer."

"You're the president's lawyer, not mine. There's nothing in it that's relevant to my fitness to serve."

"Then why did you have it sealed?"

"I didn't. The request came from Olivia's family lawyers."

"What were they trying to hide?"

"The Iveses aren't people who hang out their wash."

The alcove is open to the hearing room floor, and during these rushed conversations Davenport feels like an actor forced to change costume in public. But this is professional Washington, not the tourist version, and no one intrudes or even loiters nearby.

Bennett says, "If there's nothing in there, what are the Post-its for?"

"It's what trial lawyers do to intimidate a witness when they have nothing on him." Bennett is a lawyer, but he has spent his career in politics. He doesn't know that a litigator will lard a witness's deposition or financial statements or business diary with these scraps of yellow paper, then place the volume on counsel's table directly in the line of sight from the witness stand in order to worry the witness—everyone has something to hide—that his opponent has succeeded in locating the most damning evidence against him.

Bennett's cellphone rings, a tinny rendition of "The Star-Spangled Banner." He turns away to take the call, and Davenport realizes that the man now guiding his future is so complete a stranger that he doesn't know if his choice of ringtone was an act of patriotism or of irony. After a brief, whispered conversation, Bennett turns back to Davenport. "That was Mandeville. He's worried about the Post-its. He thinks Nyquist is going to use your transcript to wreck the nomination."

The *your* confirms for Davenport where Bennett's loyalty lies. "Tell him there's not a single word there to connect me to the drowning. Law enforcement in Nantucket studied the transcript like it was scripture."

"They didn't have the motive to go after you that Nyquist has."

"If the senator thinks he's found something, I need to hear it now. I don't want him harassing me after I'm on the court."

"My job is to get you confirmed, not to worry that someone's going to blackmail you."

The statement is so reckless, Davenport wants to grab Bennett by his roostery throat and shake him, but he believes that he has himself gone too far down Washington's path of expedience to act on principle now. He says, "You're missing the point. Nyquist knows that if he wrecks my confirmation, the president will just nominate someone else."

Bennett draws closer. "Do you want to be a Supreme Court justice or not?"

"More than anything."

"Then let me do my job. Nyquist thinks McWhorter's seat belongs to him."

Charles McWhorter, whose place Davenport has been nominated to fill, was until his death in July the court's most conservative member and, like Nyquist, a hero to the Religious Right. Nyquist's name, along with Davenport's, had been on the short list leaked by the White House to the media, but Davenport believes Bennett himself had put the senator's name there to placate these voters and donors. "The president would never nominate Nyquist."

Bennett says, "Then you don't know your old friend. If you go down in flames, the president is going to need someone he can get through the Senate without a challenge, and no one's more confirmable than one of the Senate's own."

In the days leading up to the hearing, Nyquist had been alone among the Judiciary Committee members of both parties in declining Bennett's request for the customary office visit from the nominee, or so Bennett told Davenport.

Davenport says, "There are senators he could appoint who aren't right wing Republicans."

"But none with the Southern Democrats behind him. The whole country is moving to the right. And when Nyquist goes on the court, we have a conservative Democrat in North Dakota who has a shot at winning his seat in the Senate."

When, not *if*. "Mandeville would never let Nyquist through."

"If your confirmation falls apart, I promise you the Judiciary Committee will have a new chairman by the time Nyquist comes before it."

"I don't want Mandeville to bury the transcript."

"Fortunately for this administration," Bennett says, "that's my call, not yours." He turns and elbows his way through the reporters to wherever Mandeville has gathered his committee. A spasm seizes Davenport's neck and, as secretly as he can, for he is returning to the witness table and imagines the television cameras are on him again, he rotates each shoulder to relieve the strain.

Staffers drift back into the hearing room in groups of two or three, talking and laughing with the self-consciousness of workers who conduct their lives in a public venue, close to genuine power but lacking it themselves. The senators file in and, like their aides, talk among themselves, though without the laughter. Davenport looks over his shoulder, but Bennett has not yet returned and the chair on the aisle reserved for family is still empty.

For weeks before the hearings, more to placate Bennett than with any hope of success, Davenport left telephone and email messages for Nola. She returned none, but must have talked with someone on Bennett's staff because yesterday morning, just moments after Davenport began reading his prepared statement to the committee, she slipped into the hearing room and took the seat beside Bennett. The movement, so close by, caught Davenport in mid-sentence. He turned, and for a heart-stopping moment mistook for Olivia the slight-figured woman taking the seat on the aisle—so closely does fair-skinned Nola with her dark, unruly mass of hair resemble her mother. The tricks that sorrow plays on us! Twenty rushed minutes later, when he had finished his statement and turned to greet her, the chair was again empty. Bennett later told him that she left before he was half-way through.

Chairman Mandeville exchanges whispers with the ranking member, Lloyd Heffernan, who sits next to him, then gavels the hearing to order. At the far end of the table, Nyquist swings the arm of the microphone toward himself, its arc evoking the self-confidence of a hangman. The gray transcript is gone. Bennett has struck a deal, and Davenport wonders what price he himself will have to pay.

The buzz in the room trails off and Nyquist clears his throat. "Mr. Davenport, I'd like to turn, if we may, to New York's Susie Briscoe Act. As I'm sure you know, the Act protects physically or mentally challenged individuals from the harvest of their organs for the purpose of transplantation in others."

When President Anthony Locke was New York's governor, Davenport, as his counsel, had steered the unsuccessful effort in the legislature to sustain Locke's veto of the bill. Nyquist's question puzzles him because the senator knows what his answer must be. "The senator is evidently not aware that the Susie Briscoe Act is presently the subject of litigation now on appeal to the Second Circuit, and as such, may eventually come before the Supreme Court. In the—"

"Yes, Mr. Davenport, I'm fully aware of both the *Straubinger* case pending in the Second Circuit and of your … disinclination to let the American people know how you might actually vote on a particular issue. My question is, in light of your involvement in the passage of that law, how could you possibly vote on it when it comes before the court?"

Over Nyquist's shoulder, his aide studies Davenport. The young man's expression betrays none of the enmity that Davenport anticipates, and an eager sweetness, if not humor, frames the bright eyes and open, apple-cheeked manner. Another evangelical. Davenport imagines that it was young men like this who went off to fight the Crusades while their dour-faced masters plotted and issued orders from home. Before returning his gaze, Davenport drops the curtain behind his eyes.

"*If* it comes to the court, Senator, not *when*. At this point there is only a district court decision. No one knows what the Second Circuit will do, or if there will be an appeal."

"Would you recuse yourself when it comes to the court?"

"If it comes to the court, I would have to consider that as a possible option."

"But, given the court's present line-up, your recusal would result in a 4–4 vote. Don't you think the American public is entitled to a more decisive result than that? Don't you think the Straubinger family is entitled to a real decision? You have a mother and father here"—Nyquist consults the note card in front of him—"working folks from Buffalo, New York, and their twin boys, one sick, the other ...... well... … in an institution. Win or lose, after all the hopes they have invested in this case, don't you think they deserve a definitive decision?"

"Senator, I respect the independence of Supreme Court justices too much to presume to know how they will vote in a particular case, so I don't buy your hypothetical 4–4 vote as an inevitability."

"Isn't that asking a good deal—" Nyquist suddenly breaks off and makes a show of consulting his wristwatch before continuing. "As a matter of fact, this is not why I bring up the Susie Briscoe Act today. The Act was passed by the New York legislature over the veto of then Governor Locke, was it not?"

"It was."

"That must have been quite a battle."

"Was there a question, there? I heard a statement, Senator, but was there a question?"

"My question is, as Governor Locke's counsel, what role did you play in his campaign against the override of his veto?"

"I talked with the leaders of the legislature. Other members of the senate and assembly, as well. I communicated the governor's views to them."

"The governor who was your Harvard roommate—"

"Teammate. We swam together at college."

"Did you advise Governor Locke on the constitutionality of the Susie Briscoe Act?"

"No, I did not, Senator. That was the job of the state attorney general."

"Well, in the course of your jawboning the New York legislature, did you happen to form any views of your own on the Susie Briscoe Act, on the appropriateness of scavenging spare body parts from mentally and physically disabled people as if they were wrecked cars in some rusty junkyard?"

According to Bennett, Nyquist's financial support comes less from North Dakota than it does from Washington-based political action committees funded by conservative donors, and the senator can expect his constituents and financial backers to cheer his public evisceration of this New York lawyer. But Nyquist's contempt for the president's agenda has seduced him into committing a mistake. "As I said, Senator, in light of the pending litigation it would be inappropriate—"

"Truly, Mr. Davenport, you are a frustrating witness." Nyquist's tone is aggrieved. "If you had been listening, you would know that my question did not concern the substance of your views. As legitimately interested in them as the American people may be, I was not asking about your substantive views for or against the Susie Briscoe Act. I was merely asking if you in fact entertained any views of your own on the bill."

Davenport thinks back to the question, and Nyquist is of course correct. Yet again, he has violated one of the most fundamental rules for a witness on cross-examination: don't answer a question unless you are sure you understand it. He knows what Nyquist's follow-up will be, and frames his answer to anticipate it. "My job as counsel to the governor was to carry his message where it needed to be carried. There was no need for me to form a view of my own on the Susie Briscoe Act."

"Well that's our dilemma, isn't it, Mr. Davenport? We all know what the president's views are on the great issues of consequence for the American people, but after two days of testimony, we still haven't a clue as to what your views are or, indeed, if you have any views at all. Now that Governor Locke is President Locke, can we expect you to continue to carry these messages that he whispers into your ear onto the United States Supreme Court in the event you are confirmed?"

The implication of the question is absurd, but a cold rivulet of sweat streams down Davenport's side. "If you are asking, Senator, do I go duck hunting with the president, the answer is no. I don't even go duck hunting with the vice president." This brings the expected ripple of laughter from the Beltway crowd. For some reason, out of all proportion to the quip, it heartens Davenport that several of the senators at the table, both Democrats and Republicans, laugh too.

"What do the American people know, Mr. Davenport, of the moral compass that will guide your decisions?"

Until this moment, Davenport believed that Nyquist's exasperation with him was for show; that it was for his constituents and his conservative supporters. But the huskiness he now detects in the senator's voice, a roughness, really, comes from a deep well of emotion. And, now that Davenport can finally see them, the eyes that examine him when Nyquist pulls down on his half-frames are bloodshot and haggard. This is a man under tremendous strain. His passion has exposed his vulnerability and Davenport imagines that, if only he looked hard enough, he could peer into the soul of this man who would labor to construct a dark and disturbing story from between the innocent lines of a gray-bound coroner's transcript. How seriously he has misjudged his adversary! In this shallow and political city, here is a man who has not only skin in the game, but blood and sinew too.

Mandeville shoots a worried look over Davenport's shoulder. Bennett has apparently returned to his seat behind the nominee, and the nervous eye play between the handler and the chairman resumes. Whatever deal Bennett, Mandeville, and Nyquist made over the coroner's transcript, Davenport makes a quick decision that he wants no part of it. The one hope he has of surviving his memories of that night on the ferry is that their force will diminish over time. He despairs that blackmail will stoke the fires forever. He needs Nyquist to show his hand right now. "If the senator has a question about my past, I invite him to ask it. Do you have something specific on your mind, Senator?"

Mandeville, in high color, places a hand over the microphone, leans past Heffernan, and whispers harshly to Nyquist. Davenport cannot make out the words. From across the vast railway terminal of a room, Nyquist's eyes stay locked on Davenport's.

"That depends on whether there is something in your past that you wish to disclose to the committee."

"Senator Nyquist—" Mandeville sees that his hand is over the microphone, lifts it and starts again. "Senator Nyquist, this is not—"

If Nyquist hears the chairman, he does not acknowledge him. "In light of your past, in light of things you have done or not done, would you characterize yourself as a moral relativist—"

Wham! The chairman's gavel strikes the knob of wood in front of him. "Senator, you must—"

Nyquist pays no heed. "— as a nihilist, a man without moral direction on the life and death issues that inevitably will come before the court—"

Wham! "The witness has no obligation—"

Nyquist's voice rises. "He is my witness, Mr. Chairman—"

Mandeville, whose hand has been resting on the top of the microphone for minutes now, leans into it once more. "The committee has been very forbearing, Senator Nyquist. Our witness has been very forbearing. Surely the time—"

"We had an agreement, Mr. Chairman—"

Wham! Wham! Wham!

Before the gavel snaps in two, which it surely will, Davenport raises his voice just enough to be heard over the clamor, "It's perfectly fine, Mr. Chairman. I am prepared to answer the senator's question."

Reluctantly, Mandeville sits back, and Nyquist leans even further over the table.

"The law," Davenport says. "If you want to know what my judicial philosophy is, it will be to follow the law."

Mandeville says, "That is a splendid answer, Mr. Davenport." The Chairman gives no sign that he has in fact heard the answer or that he has anything on his mind but to end the day's questioning.

"Of course, the law," Nyquist says. "But few cases get as far as the Supreme Court of the United States if the law that governs them is as clear as your answer implies it will be."

"With all due respect," the Chairman says, "you are now several minutes beyond your allotted time, Senator Nyquist."

Nyquist doesn't hear him. "Can you tell the American people, Mr. Davenport, what compass will guide you as you go about discovering the law in the great many cases where the law's command is not as crystal clear as you suppose it will be?"

"Why, the facts, of course. The facts of the case in front of me."

"I don't understand."

"It has been my experience as a trial lawyer that there is no better guide to the correct legal result in a case than a proper understanding of its facts."

Nyquist says, "I'm sure that as a lawyer, you made an artful use of facts and law, Mr. Davenport, but as a justice you are going to need some larger principle to guide you." Nyquist removes his half frames and plays with one of the plastic stems, flicking it back and forth like a light switch. At the corners of his mouth are the beginnings of a smile. This must be the intimacy that a condemned man and his executioner feel toward each other. "The great principles that separate us as sentient beings from God's lesser creatures."

"No, Senator, I'll stick with the law and the facts. They're a far sounder guide to correct results than your moral abstractions and pieties."

"And if the law is unclear and the facts cannot be found?" The shadow of a smile reaches Nyquist's eyes, and the wooden features give no sign that he is offended.

"I suppose in that case, Senator, I will just have to look harder." The room is entirely still. Mandeville looks across at Nyquist, whose eyes are still on the witness, his hand with the glasses frozen in its movement. The chairman raises his gavel. Davenport resists the urge to look one by one at the other eighteen men and women who sit across from him, as he would with a jury, and instead fastens his gaze on Nyquist alone. It dismays him that his daughter, the one person he wishes would hear his words, is not in the room.

"So you are comfortable looking just to the facts and the law?"

"Senator, for those of us who lack an unerring moral compass, which is to say for all of us, it is not some rarefied notion of justice that offers hope for resolving our hardest choices, but the law and facts of the case before us." The words come closer to the truth than any Davenport has spoken in these two days. In any event, they have had their effect, for even his inquisitor turns silent. Without another glance in his direction, the chairman lets his gavel fall.

2

On Davenport's first full day in chambers, the court is already four weeks into its term. Letters, thousands of them, fill the postal bins stacked two and three high behind his secretary's desk.

"They brought them up from the basement yesterday." Anne Hirsch was Davenport's secretary at his law firm in New York, and on the day his nomination was announced, she offered to come with him to the court. Glad to have her, he didn't ask the reason. Her husband, a New York City policeman a year away from retirement, has begun taking the train down to Washington on weekends and will move here permanently when he leaves the force. "Justice Bricknell's secretary said the mail is about the assisted suicide case."

"*Chief* Justice Bricknell," Davenport says. As skilled as she is, Anne has always been a degree or two more self-confident than her talents warrant. In New York she paid no more deference to the senior partners at the law firm than she did to the bike messengers in the reception area, and a client who made the mistake of putting her on hold when she was making a call for Davenport would invariably discover that she had hung up on him. Most bosses would consider Anne's inattention to rank and politesse a fatal defect, but Davenport rarely corrects her. The rudeness is mild, and if it discomfited his clients, particularly the more pompous ones, that wasn't necessarily a bad thing. She will accept his correction about Bricknell's title, or she won't, and it will be interesting to watch the Chief Justice's reaction if she doesn't.

The court will hear argument in the assisted suicide case, *Clark v. Pennsylvania*, at the end of the week. Davenport carries one of the postal bins into his office, sets it next to the rocking chair, and takes an already opened envelope off the top. In three typed paragraphs the letter implores him in the most urgent terms—Say no to death panels!—to vote for Pennsylvania's ban on assisted suicide. He returns the letter to its envelope and considers what to do with the countless others. Until Anne hires a second secretary, she won't have the time to sort through this mail herself. His already over-burdened law clerks would view the task as beneath them.

Davenport leans back in the rocker and takes in the office, formerly Charles McWhorter's, that will be his for the rest of his career. The meticulously paneled and corniced oak walls have a golden hue but, at ten in the morning, the light in the room is a silvery gray. One tall window looks out onto Second Street and the other offers a postcard view of the Library of Congress's grand and sprawling Jefferson Building. No sounds intrude from the street nor, even with the door open, from the adjacent messenger's alcove or from Anne's desk down the hall. The profound silence is from more than the thick walls and heavy drapes. Olivia, though an atheist, believed in angels and spirits and, were she alive, she would tell her husband that at least a century's worth of ghosts guard the quiet.

Piles of briefs overflow the work table, and on Davenport's desk is a no less daunting stack of bench memos—the tightly reasoned summaries prepared by his law clerks to guide him through the week's arguments. He has read the memos for this week's cases and knows that he should start now on the briefs, but instead he reaches for another envelope from the bin, and then another. After a half-hour of this, twenty or so letters are open on the floor on one side of the rocker, all urging affirmance of the assisted suicide ban in terms—often in words—that are identical from one letter to the next. On the other side of the chair are three letters, each different in argument and phrasing, pleading for him to vote to overturn the ban. In one, which is handwritten, the author has underlined in red crayon her plea that every minute the court delays its vote is another minute of agony for Mr. Clark and his family.

"Reading your fan mail?" Justice Madeleine Cardona is large-framed, and the high heels and a mannish suit make no concession to her size. Black hair pulled back in a bun and a face that is almost Aztec in its smooth planes and sharp edges add to the overall impression of severity.

She has been on the court seven years and Davenport knows her from their service together on the board of the New York Legal Aid Society.

She hands a ribbon-tied box to Davenport. "From Justice Keane. Your secretary said his son just delivered it."

Davenport removes the envelope attached to the package. Inside is a card cut to the figure of a dancing leprechaun in top hat, suspenders, and green trousers. On the reverse side, in a broad, bold hand, are the words "Welcome to Magh Meall" and the signature *Bernie Keane*. Davenport knows nothing of Magh Meall, but Keane's gesture surprises, even touches him. Bernie Keane's politics diametrically oppose those of President Locke, and presumably his appointee; and Keane's public image is not of a boisterous hard-drinking Irishman, nor even of a cheery leprechaun like the one on the card, but an almost frail, scholarly wisp of a man, pale and dry as paper, one whose observations from the bench, to colleagues and advocates alike, can etch like acid.

Davenport shows Madeleine the card and guesses at the pronunciation. "Magh Meall?"

Madeleine shrugs. "Maybe it's the dark place under the bridge where trolls hang out."

Madeleine's dislike of Keane is no secret. Last term Keane wrote an opinion refusing to hear the final appeal from a death row inmate because the man's lawyer had filed the papers three days late. It made no difference to Keane that the missed deadline was the fault neither of the inmate nor his lawyer, but of the court clerk. Rules are rules, Keane wrote, and if we make an exception in this case, where do we draw the line? Madeleine's dissent attacked Keane so vehemently that the three other dissenting justices refused to join her opinion and wrote their own.

Madeleine says, "I was stunned when I heard you hired one of Keane's clerks—"

"Former clerk—"

"You really should have talked to me before you hired him."

Davenport reminds himself that he is here to build bridges, not burn them. "Harold came highly recommended. I like him."

"See if you're still so happy with him at the end of the term. This is going to be a hard year for you. You don't know the shortcuts yet. My first term, I was here nights and weekends until ten, eleven o'clock. And, remember, I already had four years' experience on the Second Circuit.

"What does this have to do with Harold?"

"You're going to fall behind, which means you're going to have to rely on your clerks more than you thought you would. You won't have the time to check their work as thoroughly as you want, so you're going to find yourself trusting their judgment. And it's Harold, who has the experience, who's going to take the most dangerous issues for himself. The right wingers didn't have to plant a mole in your chambers. You opened the door and invited him in."

"I thought it would be useful to have his point of view. Provide balance."

"If you're planning to be the justice who makes this a unanimous court, you can get all the point of view you need from the Op-Ed page of the Washington Post."

Davenport's surprise at Madeleine's intuition about his plans must be evident, because she says, "Every one of us has that fantasy when we arrive here. That we're going to be the one who unites the court. For some it's more realistic than others."

"But not me."

"Trial lawyers aren't good at bending. You're going to have to learn how to do that."

"So long as no one asks me to bend over." The remark is crude, but Davenport doesn't like being told what to do, and Madeleine might as well know that from the start.

Even more than her physical presence, it is Madeleine's silences that intimidate, and she falls into one of them now. Davenport argued a white collar securities case before her when she sat on the Second Circuit, and all the time the other two judges on the panel fired questions at him, not letting him utter a single complete sentence, Madeleine remained stone silent. Then, in the last minute of his allotted time, she asked the one question that cut like a scalpel to the heart of his defense. She was like that at meetings of the Legal Aid board too. Only in rare unguarded moments was it possible to glimpse a mind that silently weighed, balanced and re-balanced tactics and strategy.

It seems like minutes before Madeleine finally speaks. "Clerks can only help you to a point, and then you need someone you can truly trust. Family. Without Phil that first year, I don't know what I would have done."

Madeleine had evidently watched the confirmation hearings on television and observed the empty family seat next to Bennett Jaffe. Davenport says, "My daughter is at school."

"She's at Barnard, isn't she?"

"Columbia." He looks down and sees that the card from Keane is still in his hand. "But this isn't why you stopped by."

"I thought you might want a lift home tonight."

"Thanks, but I'm going to be late." Since last week, Davenport has been Madeleine's downstairs neighbor at Harbour Square in southwest Washington where her husband Phil, a retired real estate developer, found a condominium for him. He glances over at the mail bin. "What do you do with the letters?"

"I don't spend any more time with my fan mail than I do reading amicus briefs. They're all bought and paid for by interest groups. The only difference is that the letter-writing is better organized."

"And the other justices?"

"Some have their secretaries or their aides read through them. You know, looking for death threats or anything like that."

"But not you."

"I have life tenure. I'm not afraid to die."

. . . .

"Justice Bricknell is here to see you." It is Anne's voice on the intercom, and as the Chief Justice strides into the office, Davenport is sure that he detects on the fleshy, handsome face a small wince at Anne's amputation of his title.

"I hope I'm not disturbing you." Even as he reaches to shake the new justice's hand, the Chief Justice's dark eyes dart about, picking out the few personal items—the rocker, three small antique rugs, a high back desk chair from the New York office—that Davenport has added to the furnishings Justice McWhorter left behind. He has met the Chief, as the justices refer to him, at bar association events and of course at the swearing-in, but this is the first time he has been alone with him. Bricknell's examination of the room gives Davenport the liberty to study him, and he decides that, under the wavy silver hair and wide brow, the Chief's eyes, though shrewd, betray neither intelligence nor wisdom.

"Ah, I see that Bernie Keane has brought you a welcome gift." The Chief glances at the leprechaun card and opens the lid of the ribbon-wrapped box. When he lifts out the quart bottle of Jameson's eighteen-year-old Irish whiskey, the label is the same emerald green as the leprechaun's trousers. The Chief replaces the bottle on the desk. "Is this a good time for our little tour of the building?"

"As good as any." Keane's former clerk, Boyce Harold Williams III—Harold—had shown Davenport around when he was here last week, and today the new justice lacks the patience for what he expects will be a painfully unhurried, lecture-filled tour. But, whatever Madeleine says, Davenport hopes to unite the court, and so follows Bricknell out of his office.

Without looking, the Chief waves in the direction of the alcove where Davenport's messenger Edward Cunningham sits, and lifts his other hand tentatively, as if to rest it on the new justice's shoulder, then quickly withdraws it. Proceeding down the corridor, the Chief's stride is brisk, his observations rote. Even though name plates are affixed to the doors, the Chief recites the name of each justice as they pass by chambers. In a grave baritone he describes the changes commissioned for the building's interior spaces by predecessors going back to Chief Justice Charles Evans Hughes, as if architecture were a Chief Justice's principal responsibility. Of his own essays in interior design, completed or planned, he says nothing, and Davenport does not ask.

Their circuit takes them through the vaulting, red-carpeted conference room with its oil portraits of the earliest Chief Justices—"Ah, yes, of course, I swore you in here"—and its green-carpeted twin across the hall with portraits of the more recent Chiefs, and then the justices' dining room. Unlike the court's public spaces, where the cathedral-high ceilings and marble-clad walls magnify the slightest echo and the cold smell of stone is everywhere, the court's private quarters have a casualness, even randomness about them, except when interrupted by the brass gates that the Chief must unlock with a code punched into a small keypad.

On the second floor, where each justice has been allotted extra office space, it seems to Davenport that he could be wandering the back halls of a grand country home. Turning a corner, he comes face to face with life-sized photographs of four of his new colleagues, each in the uniform of the justice's hometown baseball team, swinging a bat or throwing out the first pitch of the season. Other justices have hung prints and paintings on the walls outside their second offices. The Chief takes Davenport to corners of the building that Harold did not: the gym and basketball court directly above the courtroom ("The highest court in the land," the Chief says with a practiced chuckle); the small movie projection room from the days when pornography was regularly on the court's docket. Up a winding staircase, a bibliophile's dream of a library, an oak forest, occupies the building's entire third floor. Reference librarians are at their desks and cloth-bound statutes and leather-bound volumes of decisions fill the shelves. Not a single patron is in sight.

The visit to the library turns the Chief buoyant, and he remains so while an elevator attendant takes them down to the cafeteria thronged with tourists, and then to the basement, bustling with a carpenter shop, print shop, and offices assigned to the court police. The Chief anticipates Davenport's thought. "One could live very nicely here for days," he says. "I suspect that some of our clerks do." Again, the lines are well-rehearsed; the mayor of this little town has given this tour many times. "What do you think of the place?"

It is an odd, even buffoonish, question that Davenport decides to take seriously. He thinks of the cavernous halls and empty library; the new term's crew of clerks picking up the assignments from their predecessors; the assisted suicide case waiting to be argued, and *Straubinger,* the transplant case which, despite his parries with Nyquist at the confirmation hearing, is doubtless on its way here. He says, "It feels like the building is holding its breath."

"Ah, yes. I meant the architecture. What do you think of it?"

"Very grand," Davenport says.

At the entrance to Davenport's chambers, the Chief waves off the justice's half-hearted invitation to come in, but draws close and, as he does, Davenport is aware of the faint, not unpleasant aroma of tobacco.

Where in a United States government building does the Chief Justice get to smoke a cigar? "I understand that you swam at Harvard."

The Chief has done more research on his new colleague than Davenport has done on him. "Freestyle."

"But not synchronized swimming, I suppose." The laugh is hearty, and this time the Chief touches Davenport's back, but speculatively, to see if I he objects. "Girls' stuff, isn't it? Synchronized swimming."

Davenport thinks he knows where this is leading, considers whether and where to move the conversation, and decides that establishing some distance from the Chief may not be a bad way to start their relationship after all. "We had relay teams."

"I'm sure you did, but no one would call swimming a team sport. You know, men putting their shoulders together."

"Or women," Davenport says, to maintain the boundary.

"Football was my sport in college. Not Big 10 or anything like that, of course, but the important thing was teamwork."

Although Davenport remembers that Northwestern was the Chief's law school, he doesn't know where he went to college. But he was right about the direction of the observation on swimming.

"Eleven men on the field, all working from the same playbook. Every one of us on the same page."

"And now you have nine." He may not know where the Chief played, but it isn't hard to guess his position. "Teamwork is a lot easier when you're the quarterback."

"I didn't say that teamwork was easy. Only that it's important."

The Chief half-turns to leave, and Davenport decides not to ask why, if teamwork is that important, he has let his court divide 5–4 on so many life-and-death issues. Instead he says, "What do you do with all the mail? The letters from people who want you to vote one way or another on a case."

The clever eyes turn dumb for a moment, then sharpen. "Oh, you mean the letters about assisted suicide." He laughs in a distracted way. "We get so much mail here at the court. Everyone wants to tell us what's on their mind. Can you believe it, Carl Shell"—one of the justices—"reads every one." As he walks off, Davenport concludes that the Chief Justice of the United States is not a man who would let bins of mail obstruct his forward movement down the field.

* * * * * * * * * * * * * * * * * * * *

Davenport is reading Harold's bench memo for the assisted suicide case when his messenger, Edward Cunningham, comes in. A light-skinned African-American, as tall as the justice but narrow as a split rail, Edward worked for Charles McWhorter during the late justice's entire fourteen years on the court, starting at a time when every chamber had a messenger. Aides have since replaced messengers, and most of them are young women, a fact that, when he related it to Davenport, seemed for Edward to be a source of genuine regret. If the justice chose to keep him on, Edward said that he preferred for the justice to call him his messenger, not his aide. When Davenport asked what his duties were, Edward told him that when he arrives at chambers at 8:00 in the morning, he has nothing to do, and by five o'clock, he has half of it done.

Edward's gray hair is brushed straight back and his dress is impeccable—well-pressed tweed suit, white shirt, dark silk tie, old-fashioned aviator framed glasses. "Is there anything else, Justice Davenport?" It is now after six, and the justice hears only the faintest reproach in the messenger's voice. Davenport has decided to keep Edward on, at least for the present.

"Just one thing, Mr. Cunningham." The messenger's deportment makes any other form of address seem incorrect. The *Mr. Cunningham* appears to please the messenger, for he allows himself a small smile.

"The mail." Davenport indicates the plastic bin. "There are more in Mrs. Hirsch's office. I'd like you to sort through them."

"Sort through them, how?"

There is a movement in the doorway, and Edward turns to the voice behind him. "I'm sure you'll figure out a fine way to do it, Edward." It is Bernard Keane. "That's why Justice McWhorter found you indispensable." Keane comes into the office. "Before you go, perhaps you can remember where Justice McWhorter left his tea set."

Edward goes to the antique cabinet next to the sofa, opens the double doors, and removes a silver tray on which are four china cups and saucers.

"Thank you, Edward. Now if you leave me alone with Justice Davenport, perhaps he will open that bottle of Jameson's over there and I'll explain to him how fortunate he is to have you as his messenger."

Edward closes the door behind him, and Davenport pours a dollop of whiskey into the justice's cup and another into his own. Keane takes the upholstered chair across from the rocker and studies the teacup in his hand. "Camouflage. The ideal ruse if my oncologist should happen by."

The indecipherable glint in Keane's eyes dismisses any inquiry, so Davenport thanks him for the gift and asks about Magh Meall.

"Oh, that! Magh Meall is an Irishman's fantasy of paradise, a place open only to deities and the occasional worthy mortal." The slightest hint of a brogue inflects his voice.

"But never more than nine."

"Including the occasional rogue."

Davenport lets the whiskey roll over his tongue. How is it possible for so transparent a liquid to embody this many layers, notes and rhythms, one succeeding the other? Smoke, peat, tobacco, wood, even leather fill his senses.

"Did you meet my boy Kevin when he delivered this?" When Davenport shakes his head, Keane says, "Kevin and I watched your testimony on the television in my chambers. Kevin gave your performance a straight A."

"And you?"

The wiry gray eyebrows rise a fraction. "If I were in a generous mood, I'd give you a B+."

The tone is light, and again, there is the touch of brogue behind it, but the remark stings. "Where did I let you down?"

"I'm a great admirer of trial lawyers, Richard—may I call you that? We all use first names here. My law practice for the Church before I went on the bench was mostly counseling. You know, keeping the Cardinal out of court. But I sat through enough trials to know that there are few creatures on earth as fearless as a fine trial lawyer."

"But?"

"I thought your answer to Nyquist about following the facts and the law, wherever they take you, was a bit slick."

"I've always found it to be the safest course."

"If you're a lawyer, maybe, or even a trial judge. But not a Supreme Court justice."

It may be the excellent whiskey, and perhaps this was Keane's intention in making the gift, but Davenport unexpectedly finds himself drawn to the slight figure sitting across from him. "Madeleine says I should be prepared to bend."

"That's good advice, but only if you're careful about in which direction."

"You mean left or right?"

"No, and I don't mean bending to the views of the other justices." The pleasant countenance instantly turns cold and Keane's features sharpen. "You do that only if you're a fool like the Chief and think that anything less than a unanimous vote is a moral failure."

"Then what?"

"You bend to your heart. Your moral core. If you are a spiritual man, to your soul."

Before Davenport can respond, Keane says, "Working for the Cardinal, I had occasion to attend inquests all up and down New England, so I'm familiar with coroners' transcripts. I know that your wife died under sufficiently questionable circumstances that an inquest was required. And, most important, I know that Senator Nyquist will stop at nothing to achieve his political ends."

The observation and the warning are too glib. If the gray transcript had even appeared within the television camera's frame, it would hardly have been visible on Keane's screen. If Keane thought Davenport's performance at the hearings was slick, then Keane's own performance now is even more so. With McWhorter gone, Davenport wonders at the relationship between the man who is now the court's most conservative justice and Oren Nyquist the most conservative member of the United States Senate.

"The assisted suicide case is going to be quite a chivaree, don't you think?" The harsh mentor of just a moment ago has disappeared and Keane is once again the amiable colleague. But Davenport is wary, and after a few more minutes of this, he drains his cup and suggests to Keane that he do the same.

. . . .

After Keane leaves, Davenport takes a handful of envelopes from the plastic bin and opens one. If despair has an odor, it is the sour smell of paper that has been stored too long. Yet Davenport cannot leave the envelopes alone, for he knows too well what he is searching for among these letters from strangers: a message, the smallest gesture, from his daughter. Nola had drawn away from him long before Olivia's death, even before she moved out of their apartment on Manhattan's East Side for a dormitory at Columbia. It seemed that, for its lifeline, their small family had been allotted a single length of rope, and the closer Nola drew to Olivia, the greater her distance grew from him. But no day passes for Davenport without the anticipation of a phone call or email from his daughter, and although no sane person would search these bins for a letter from his only child, the busyness of the effort numbs the persisting ache.

Sifting through a haystack of letters is not the worst of Davenport's humblings. Last weekend, he flew to Nantucket to secure the 'Sconset house for winter, his first time there since Olivia's death. He knew that Nola had been at the house the week before, but only because Anne told him that his daughter had called the office to make sure he wouldn't be there at the same time. Nola had left no visible evidence of her stay and, between draining pipes and hanging storm windows, Davenport ransacked the rooms like a burglar, first downstairs, and then the upstairs bedrooms, searching for some recent sign of her—a note, a book turned page down on the table, even a fast food wrapper in the garbage pail under the sink. But all that he could find in this house where Nola had spent almost every summer of her young life was a bathing suit, a pair of well-worn jeans, some old running shoes, and a folded T-shirt imprinted with the faded image of a schooner. This last, when he pressed it to his face, had the musty smell of beachfront damp.

Of Olivia, there was no sign at all. Davenport speculates that Nola will put the house on the market next spring, and that she had come the previous week to scrub the place clean of any mark of her mother's existence, and in so doing to erase almost three decades of her father's life.

3

They are on Route 16, a few miles from the Home, and Junior hasn't said a word. He just stares out the passenger window. Gloria Straubinger guesses that he's thinking about his brother. She says, "Did Mr. Bossio give you a court date? Unless your father's going to drive you, I need to know when your hearing is." Junior has a license, but the DMV suspended it. "What did Mr. Bossio tell you?"

"He said the charges are bullshit."

Gloria starts for the horn, as if that would silence her son, but catches herself. "You're talking to your mother, Junior, not to one of your friends. Not to your father either." She knows the way the two of them talk.

"Do you really think I'm going to jail for hanging out with my friends?"

"You're under age, Junior. You were drinking."

"It was just a six-pack. We weren't even driving. We were just sitting in the car."

"They said there were drugs."

"Drugs? That's bullshit. We had some weed. Weed's not drugs."

Talking to Junior is like popping corn, Gloria thinks, the way he jumps around, but at least he's talking. If he's not in the mood, he can give her the freeze for the whole trip out to the Home and back. Not that Junior's dumb. When he was still in school, the assistant principal told her he was in the top 25% on the IQ test, as if he got all the brains, and poor Denny got none. "You can't carry on the way your friends do."

"You think I'm different." His breath fogs the front window. "I'm not."

"You come home late, all doped up and can't get to work in the morning. That's why you got fired."

"From the food bank? They made that up. It's bullshit. I told them I wanted to work the counter, up front. They let me go because I'm sick and they don't want to pay benefits."

Junior is 5'10", taller than his father, and muscular from working out at the "Y." It's easy to see that he has a physique, even through the flannel shirt, and it's hard for anyone to believe that he's as sick as he is, that because of his kidneys he's got a tube sticking out of his stomach and has to hook himself up to a machine every night. Gloria got him the job stocking shelves at the food bank so he'd have something to put on his resume when he gets better and can get a job with a future.

"I told them, 'Who wants to spend their life in a stockroom?' But they wouldn't give me the counter. They said they had a problem with my attitude."

"Your attitude? You don't think it was that shirt?"

"What shirt?" He knows what she means. "Oh, that. That's a goof. No one fires you for wearing a T-shirt."

The shirt is black, and it was all balled up when Gloria put it in the wash, so she didn't see the words. But when she shook it out to put in the dryer, there they were, bright as a neon sign, yellow letters four, five inches high: FUCK YOU. That's it. Nothing else there. Right on the front of the shirt. FUCK YOU. She felt physically sick when she saw the words. Her first thought was to throw it away, but she didn't know what Junior would do if she did. Junior can be dangerous when he's upset. Or he'd just get another shirt, even if Gloria can't imagine the kind of store where you can buy something like that. She thanks God Junior doesn't have tattoos, only the skull and crossbones on his right leg, which is a joke, really, because he used to dress up like a pirate on Halloween.

"It's just a food bank, for God's sake. In East Jahungaland—"

This time Gloria's hand flies off the steering wheel and smashes into her son's jaw. It amazes her that she has struck him, something that she has never done to either of the boys. The food bank is on the city's mostly black East Side. "Don't you ever talk like that!"

Junior turns to stare out the side window again, and when Gloria slows the car to pull onto the shoulder, she knows he thinks she's going to kick him out and let him hitch a ride or walk the rest of the way. But in fact she has pulled over to call Dr. Burroughs's office so that the superintendent, who likes a heads-up when Gloria is ten minutes from the Home, can come down and greet her in person.

After Gloria puts the phone away and is back on Route 16, she says, "All this drinking and smoking has to be bad for you."

Junior shakes his head. "I researched it on the Web. Weed doesn't hurt your kidneys."

"It will if it makes you so stupid you forget to hook yourself up to your machine."

"How would you know?"

"You don't know it, Junior, but your mother still looks in on you."

"What do you want from me?"

He has turned to face her, and when she glances over, she doesn't know if the tears in his eyes are because he's angry or sad. "I want you to stay well until we know what Denny wants. The transplant."

That silences Junior, and they finish the trip without another word.

Dr. Burroughs is coming down the stairs when they pull into the parking lot. "Dr. Ice," Junior says.

This is what Leonard calls the superintendent. "You can stay in the car if you're going to talk like that. Just because your father is rude doesn't mean you have to be." Gloria knows this will keep him quiet because Junior looks forward to these visits with his brother even more than she does.

The Freedom Home for the Developmentally Disabled is three stories of ivy-covered red brick, and to Gloria it looks more like the high school she went to than it does a place for people like Denny. Some days, three or four cars are in the visitor lot at the end of the gravel drive, but this morning Gloria and Junior are the only ones here. A rail fence separates the parking lot from the adjoining pasture, and by the time they leave a dozen or so cows will be grazing there. But at this hour there are no cows, and rime frosts the patchy grass. The sour odor of freshly spread manure mixes with the acrid smell of paper smoldering in a garbage fire at the far side of the pasture. The sky is gray, as it always is in Western New York from October through March.

Dr. Burroughs waits at the bottom of the stairs, as erect as a dancer. Gloria's first thought when she met Dr. Burroughs was that the superintendent could be a movie star, for she has that glow about her. Plain herself, Gloria believes that looks are an indelible part of a person's character, and she has to fight her habit of deferring to attractive women like Dr. Burroughs. The superintendent doesn't wear a wedding band, and there are no photographs of a husband or children in her office. Gloria wonders why a woman this stunning doesn't have a family, and she thinks this may be how she stays so perfect-looking.

"Mrs. Straubinger." The superintendent's fingers are cool when she takes Gloria's hand and nods to Junior. Then Gloria notices the one flaw that she will again forget as soon as she leaves. On the bridge of Dr. Burroughs's fine, straight nose, where the bone should form an edge, there is the tiniest flat spot, shaped like a diamond, as if for a second God had rested just the very tip of his little finger there. It puzzles Gloria that a professional woman wouldn't get a flaw like this fixed, and she thinks that maybe it's because some men might find it sexy.

At the guard's desk in the lobby, Gloria signs in for Junior and herself, and Dr. Burroughs escorts them down the wide corridor. As always, the off-white walls look freshly painted. There's a cleanliness and simplicity about the Home, a feeling of order and quiet that lifts Gloria's spirits even as it reminds her that she's a visitor here. Dr. Burroughs, in her pumps, khaki skirt, and a nice Kelly green cardigan thrown over the shoulders of a white cotton shirt, is so much a part of the place that it could have been built around her.

This is the first time since they got in the car that Gloria is face to face with Junior, and when she sees that he's wearing a black T-shirt under the plaid flannel, her heart shrinks. Junior has two black T-shirts, one with the name of some band on it, and the other one. If it's the other one, and he takes off his flannel shirt in there, Gloria worries they won't let him visit any more.

At the metal door with the glass and chicken wire window, Dr. Burroughs punches in numbers at a keypad. There is a small video camera above the door, and it swivels back and forth so that it sweeps the entire corridor. Below the keypad is a printed sign that Gloria can't help thinking about every time she sees it: CAUTION: ELOPEMENT

RISK. The word always stops her. She has never seen a female patient here but, even if there is one, who is she going to elope with?

Dr. Burroughs opens the door to a room as wide and bright as a school classroom. Besides Denny, there are a half-dozen or so men at the tables stacking blocks or sorting cards, some of them swaying in place, some standing still. Two of the men must be in their sixties, one wandering around, the other crouching and rocking on his heels, and Gloria doesn't know why, but seeing them makes her sadder than seeing the others, even Denny. The attendant is in a corner reading a book. In a low voice, Dr. Burroughs asks Gloria to come to her office after she says hello to Denny.

If Denny is aware of the three of them at the door, he gives no sign. Gloria should know better by now, but when she hasn't visited the Home for a while, she still expects Denny's face to light up, and sometimes she even thinks he'll raise his arms for a hug. The expectation is so entirely physical that she can actually feel his hands press on her back. But of course this never happens. When they were babies, Junior would gurgle and grin and stick out his arms for her to hold him, but Denny was stiff and still as a log, and she would ask herself how it was possible that twins could be so different.

Denny doesn't acknowledge Junior either, but if this bothers Junior, who pulls up a stool across the table from his brother, he doesn't show it. Denny has arranged a neat row of toothpicks on the table and when Junior carefully selects one, Gloria instinctively draws back. Once, when she was visiting, another resident picked up one of Denny's toothpicks like that and Denny exploded. He lifted the tower he had built from the toothpicks and, after smashing it on the floor, threw himself against the walls repeatedly until the attendant had to call for help. It took three men to get him to his room, Denny is that strong. But he doesn't object when Junior picks up the toothpick, or when his brother dips each end of it into the glue jar and carefully places it on the top of the new tower that Denny is building.

From a distance, Gloria inspects Denny for bruises and is glad to see that the old black and blue marks have faded and there are no new ones. The scariest part when Denny lived at home was that when he threw himself against the wall with all his force, he made no sound. He didn't cry or even grunt, so the only sound Gloria heard was the "Bam!" when his body struck the wall, and sometimes "Crack!", the sound of his head hitting. It seemed to her as if he wanted to escape from his own body, like those movies of baby birds struggling to break out of their shells. Denny's tantrums terrify her and are the reason why, after years of arguing with Leonard, she gave in and they brought him to the Home.

Gloria hands Junior a box of multi-colored toothpicks that she bought at the A&P to add some color to Denny's dull, wood-colored towers, and takes the elevator to Dr. Burroughs's office on the third floor. She considers why the superintendent wants to talk to her, and thinks it may at last be the expected good news.

. . . .

Entering the superintendent's office for only the second time, Gloria feels the way she does when she goes to the doctor's and has to undress and put on the flimsy gown with the open back, so that when the doctor in his tie and white jacket comes in, she might as well be naked. The office is bigger than she remembers, with two whole walls of shelves packed with books. Framed degrees and awards fill the another wall. Dr. Burroughs is behind the desk, her back to the windows that look onto the parking lot.

"Denny's bruises look better," Gloria says, even though she hopes that what the superintendent wants to talk about is that her son has started speaking. "Isn't it something, the way he builds those towers out of toothpicks? I see the others with their blocks, but Denny can work with something as small as toothpicks."

"As a matter of fact," Dr. Burroughs says, "we're trying to wean him from his towers. Just because self-stimulation engages Denny doesn't mean it's good for him. We'd like to see some progress in his interpersonal skills."

"You mean like talking."

"Talking's certainly important. But there are other skills we want Denny to master."

Gloria says, "We spend all this time fighting in court, and we still don't know if Denny wants the operation."

The superintendent lifts a pencil off the desk and twists it one way, then the other, between the tips of her index fingers. "I would imagine the court case has disrupted your lives. How are you and Leo handling it?"

"Leonard," Gloria says. No matter what Gloria wants to talk about, the superintendent is always two steps ahead of her, crawling around in her thoughts. It was a mistake to mention the case, because now Dr. Burroughs is going to want to talk about it.

"What I meant was, I can understand your ambivalence about the case."

Gloria knows what she meant. "Whatever you think, I don't favor Denny over Junior."

"Of course not. But before anyone cuts into him, you want to be sure you know what he wants."

"Do you think that's wrong?"

"That's not my decision to make."

"But you're telling me you can't teach him to talk."

"That's not what I'm saying—"

"If you can't teach him, why I should keep him here?" Gloria doesn't know why she said that. She doesn't want to remove Denny from the Home.

Dr. Burroughs says, "You shouldn't believe what you see on television news shows."

The superintendent thinks Gloria is worried because of the Channel 7 series about conditions in the state's homes. Abusive guards. Neglected patients. Filthy bathrooms. In fact Gloria is just trying to figure out a safe way to ask the superintendent a question. The office is warm with the baking smell of old radiators, like in the room downstairs, and Gloria imagines Junior unbuttoning his flannel shirt. What if the attendant takes a break from reading his book and sees those two words on the front of Junior's T-shirt?

Dr. Burroughs takes a TV remote control off her desk and hands it to Gloria. "Look at the monitor. Go ahead, change channels."

The screen, which is set into a bookshelf above the doorway, shows an empty corridor. After a few seconds, without Gloria pushing any buttons, the screen shifts to a room like the one Denny was in. Teenagers are in a circle on the floor with a grown-up sitting in the middle.

"Where's Denny's room?" She wants to see if Junior has taken off his shirt.

Dr. Burroughs takes back the remote and, after fumbling a few buttons, finds the one for the room where Denny sits across the table from Junior. Junior's flannel shirt is still on.

Finally, Gloria has the question organized in her mind. "If only one of us, Leonard or me, decides to remove Denny, do we both have to sign the forms?" Gloria is afraid that if they lose their case, Leonard is going to take Denny to a state that will allow the operation, even if Denny hasn't said that he's willing to give his kidney to his brother.

"Who signed Denny's admission papers?"

"I did." Gloria's heart races. "Only me."

"Then you're the only person who can sign him out."

The relief is immense. "I have to do what's best for my family."

"We also want what's best for your family, Gloria. If Denny is ever going to have a chance of living in society, he's going to have to start learning the necessary skills here."

"Like speaking."

"With severe autism, it's impossible to make promises about a patient's progress, but I can tell you that if we don't make an effort, Denny has no chance of managing on his own. Have you thought about his future after you and your husband are gone?"

"Junior," Gloria starts to say, but she can't finish the sentence. She is thinking of the old men, of the one in Denny's workroom, rocking in the corner. "But it's my decision if he stays here or not?"

"Whenever you're ready to care for Denny at home, you can sign him out. Of course, if you change your mind later, I can't promise we'll still have a place for him. With the budget cuts in Albany, the waiting list is only getting longer."

Absently, Dr. Burroughs picks up the pencil again, and Gloria wonders why the superintendent is so nervous.

. . . .

When Gloria goes into the big room, not even the attendant reading his book looks up. Junior is hunched over the table across from Denny, the two of them taking turns adding to the toothpick tower. Gloria wonders what it's like for Denny to sit across from someone whose face and features are identical to his own. Does he understand that Junior is his brother? His twin? Why does it always startle her that, except for the blankness in his eyes and the soft grunts that come from somewhere in his throat, Denny looks and moves like someone who is completely normal? His eyes do not connect with Junior's. Does he know that they are building this tower as a team? Anyway, she's glad to see the two boys together, even if she has to admit that she is jealous of Junior being so close to his brother. She remembers the colored toothpicks she gave Junior and asks where they are.

Junior takes the box from his shirt pocket and hands it over his shoulder to her. "Denny doesn't want these. He likes the ones he always uses." Still looking at Denny, not her, Junior says, "Denny's not dumb, you know. You always act like he's dumb, but he's not. He knows what he wants."

Gloria says, "We need to go. I have to get to work."

Back in the van driving home, Gloria says, "It was nice watching you with Denny. You have a special way with him. You're the only person that does. You're the only one he's ever talked to." Denny has spoken to Junior three times that she knows—just a word or two, no more—and Gloria also knows that Junior won't tell her unless she asks. "Did he say anything today?"

"Why do you keep asking? It's all you ever think about."

Gloria cannot explain this to him as she did to Dr. Burroughs, and when she doesn't answer, Junior goes silent again and looks out the side window. Under the gray sky, abandoned farm implements and the carcass of a pickup truck rust in a weed-choked field. Finally, Junior says, "We should bring Denny home."

"Who would take care of him? I work six days a week. Sometimes twelve hours a day. Your father's never home, except for meals."

"I would."

They have talked about this before. "You'll take care of your brother the way you took care of those tropical fish I bought you." Junior may have a high IQ, but he thinks if a pinch of fish food is good, a handful is better, and he killed them all.

"Denny's not a fish!"

"How can you take care of him if you can't even take care of yourself?" Or, she thinks, what if you go off on one of your adventures, not telling anyone where you are, and without your machine.

"I don't know what you're talking about."

"You know very well what I mean—all this time we're spending in court, and you can't even take responsibility to keep yourself healthy."

"I'm not going to be on that machine forever. After the transplant—"

"Don't get ahead of yourself, Junior. You don't know what's going to happen with the appeal."

"Bossio says we're going to win."

"Let's wait and see what happens."

"I feel like a freak attached to that machine all the time."

"It's only at night."

"You don't know what it's like. You don't know anything."

"Anyway, if there's a transplant, the next thing is for you to get a real job and get your life on track. You can't stay at home with Denny."

Gloria wonders if it's Junior's thinking that's like popcorn, or her own. She feels as if in the nineteen years since the boys were born, she still hasn't caught up on her sleep. She's like those women with their screaming children at the checkout counter at the Tops Market, so distracted that they hand the cashier their driver's license instead of a credit card, or they forget to pick up the change. That's how she knows Dr. Burroughs has no children. She always has that focus, that sharpness about her.

Yesterday, on the sidewalk outside Tops, Gloria saw a nice looking woman with a little boy, no more than a year old, learning how to walk on his own, the way toddlers do—tipsy, barreling around like a little drunk man, but by some miracle staying upright.

"This must be a very special time in your life," Gloria said to the mother.

The woman thanked her. "Do you have any children?"

"No," Gloria heard herself say. "We haven't been blessed."

Now, in the van with Junior, this disloyalty to her boys horrifies her. "I'm sorry," she says to Junior, but he's off in his own world again.

4

A voice booms from the doorway to Madeleine's chambers, stopping Davenport on his way to the robing room. "Richard! Come on in! Madeleine will be out in a minute."

Phil Bronson, Madeleine's husband, backs his wheelchair away from the door to make room for his visitor. Robust and thick-chested, he is one of those naturally gregarious people who, even though he is paralyzed from the waist down, centers the energy in a room. With him in Madeleine's anteroom are her two secretaries, her aide, and Davenport's messenger, Edward Cunningham.

Phil says, "Did you know that Edward here has a grandson working at an aerospace company in Paris? I'm giving him places for the boy to visit. I suggested the Musée d' Orsay and Sainte-Chapelle. Do you have any ideas?"

Davenport looks for some sign of Madeleine. "The Carnavalet," he says.

When he lived in New York, Davenport would see Phil at Legal Aid affairs and the Manhattan charity events that so occupied Olivia's crowd. The real estate developer's sociability and self-earned wealth helped to ease his more reserved wife through the political turnstiles that guard appointments to the federal judiciary. Last night, to welcome Davenport to the court, the couple gave the obligatory party for all the sitting justices at their Harbour Square penthouse. While giving Davenport a tour of the apartment, Phil described the crippling accident that occurred on a bicycle tour of Provence as lightly as another man might describe a collision on the tennis court.

Choices. Do you go to Sainte-Chapelle or the Carnavalet? Do you heed the caution of age or, reaching to recapture for an instant the fearlessness of your youth, do you release the hand brakes on your rented bicycle so that in one moment you are racing through a rush of air, and in the next you are sprawled on the hard ground, numb with the knowledge, as true as the burn of salt in your eyes, that your life has irreversibly altered course? Bracing yourself on the deck of the Hy-Line ferry as it rises and plunges into the heaving sea, your wife perched on the seaward rail, do you step forward or do you step back?

Madeleine comes into the anteroom, leans down to kiss Phil on the cheek, gives instructions to a secretary, and continues with Davenport down the corridor to the robing room. Davenport considers the complications for Phil of life married to a Supreme Court justice, living half-in, half-out of the cocoon, acting is if you know nothing of the court's confidential business when inevitably you do. He imagines how Olivia would have handled the role and decides that, with her appetite for alcohol and high drama, not well. If she were still alive, Locke would probably not have nominated him.

"Does Phil miss working?"

"You mean entertaining my staff looks like less fun than building shopping centers? He had to retire. He puts on a good front, but the accident changed him. He can be doing fine, like you saw him just now, and then something—or nothing at all—will happen, and he drops into a pit so deep, no one can reach him. It can last for days."

Davenport thinks this is going to be a prelude to one of Madeleine's long silences, but she says, "Have you ever seen Christine argue?" Christine Corbett, Madeleine's former clerk, is the lawyer for Randall Clark, the terminally ill fireman who is challenging Pennsylvania's ban on assisted suicide. "You're in for a treat. In another three or four years she's going to be the most sought-after lawyer in the Supreme Court bar. Watch our male colleagues when she's at the lectern. You wouldn't believe she has three children at home. Two girls and a boy."

They arrive at the door to the robing room, and again Madeleine shifts abruptly. "What we talked about last week—this magnificent majority you want to create. Forget about getting Bernie Keane on your side. The others? Maybe they'll fall into line." She doesn't say if she is one of the others.

* * * * * * * * * * * * * * * * * *

The very idea of a robing room strikes Davenport as overwrought, as do the nine individual closets, each with a brass name plate, his the shiniest. The carpet is maroon, as in so many other rooms in this part of the building sequestered from the public. The desktop photocopier tucked in a corner is a surreal intrusion of the workaday world. Conversation in the room is spare and, unlike last night at Madeleine and Phil's penthouse where they were lubricated by cocktails and the company of spouses, the justices this morning seem like an assemblage of strangers, all of them ill at ease.

As the Chief pulls on his robe, Davenport observes on each ample sleeve the broad gold chevrons introduced by Chief Justice Rehnquist, but later abandoned, to distinguish the Chief from the associate justices. Davenport helps Madeleine on with her robe, and she helps him with his while the others form a line and wait. As the most senior justice, Herb Bauman is first in line, and the Chief shakes his hand, then Bernie Keane's, and as he passes down the line toward Donna Cippolone and Davenport at the end, the other justices do the same with each other. At a nod from Madeleine, Davenport follows the ritual himself. For the first time since arriving at the court, the possibility that he will succeed in drawing this odd group together seems remote, and the fact that as a trial lawyer he regularly won unanimous verdicts from twelve strangers seems suddenly irrelevant.

From somewhere, a buzzer sounds and the justices follow the Chief's chevroned sleeves, billowing like spinnakers, down the short distance to the back entrance to the courtroom. The velour drapery through which they pass possesses the same deep nap as theater curtains, and as Davenport brushes by the heavy material, its stale, closeted smell pulls him back for an instant to those grade school auditorium pageants whose possibilities to a child's imagination seemed boundless. On the other side of the curtain, after the dark of the passage, the courtroom dazzles and the people filling it are already on their feet.

* * * * * * * * * * * * * * * * * *

Carl Shell leans across Donna Cippolone and says to Davenport, "Webster's Unabridged." When Davenport doesn't understand, Shell nods in the direction of the Chief's chair. Cippolone says, "The Chief's wife embroidered the pillow case for him, but his aide puts the Webster's dictionary underneath it." Davenport sees that Bricknell does in fact sit higher at the bench than the other justices, even Alex Palfrey, the tallest of the nine. Then he observes that the back of the Chief's chair is lower than the others, adding to the impression of the occupant's height. Davenport had turned down the offer of a custom-built chair from the foreman in the court's carpentry shop, telling him that McWhorter's chair was fine, but Bricknell had obviously taken up the offer.

The Chief pulls the thumb-sized microphone to his lips and his baritone rumble fills the hushed courtroom. "We will hear argument in Number 15-783, *Clark v. Pennsylvania*. Ms. Corbett."

Christine Corbett has the poise of a rock star and brings no notes with her to the lectern. "This will just take a moment," she says, and leans forward to turn the old-fashioned mechanical crank on the side of the lectern to raise it to her level.

Madeleine was right, for, looking down the bench, Davenport is aware of a flexing and straightening among the male justices. The reason is at first hard to discern, for Corbett is plain, her figure blockish. Her eyes, a startling green, are her strongest feature, and she has performed some magic with makeup to draw attention away from a beaky nose and narrow lips. But, neither beautiful nor even pretty, she carries herself like a queen, and that makes her impossible not to look at. Davenport straightens, too, for Corbett is looking directly at him. He is the court's swing vote, and she is prepared to align her argument with his questions. What she doesn't realize is that he has made his own plans for her too.

"Mr. Chief Justice, and may it please the court. I represent petitioner Randy Clark, a fireman, from Lebanon, Pennsylvania who, even after rising to the rank of lieutenant, was always the first one off the truck and into the burning building. For almost a year after 9/11, Mr. Clark volunteered his days off to help remove debris at the World Trade Center site. According to medical experts at the trial, it was the toxins he encountered there that caused his cancer. Mr. Clark is in full possession—too full possession—of his senses. He lies at the threshold of death, with no prospect of recovery, and he asks this court only to let him cross that threshold."

It is unusual to begin a Supreme Court argument with a statement of facts, much less a biography, but Corbett has apparently studied the transcript of Davenport's confirmation hearings and takes seriously his concern for the facts of a case. Davenport does indeed have a fact in mind, one calculated to build bridges, but in the corner of his vision the Chief leans in to speak, so for the moment he defers.

"This court has regularly rejected challenges to state prohibitions on assisted suicide, Ms. Corbett. What makes your client's case different?"

"In the precedents you refer to, Mr. Chief Justice, the patient had died by the time his case reached this court. Mr. Clark is still alive and he asks that his plea be heard."

Looking past Corbett into the packed courtroom, the confluence of monumentality and intimacy is dizzying. The ceiling vaults as high as a cathedral, but the floor below is no larger than the nave of a neighborhood church. The Chief sits barely six feet from Corbett, and if instead of a question he tossed her an egg, and she caught it carefully, it wouldn't break.

"The fact that the patient is still alive no doubt distinguishes your case from the others," the Chief says, "but what legal difference can it possibly make? The doctors pursued the earlier cases vigorously. They kept the cases alive."

"They kept the cases alive, Mr. Chief Justice, but not the patient. We have not just doctors here, but a man suffering grievously, one who is asking this court to let him decide for himself how he is going to die—peacefully or in unbearable pain."

Carefully, Davenport picks the words he needs to keep the argument's focus on the fireman, not the doctors. But, before he can speak, a chain saw starts up, Bernie Keane's public voice. "Counselor, you—your Mr. Clark—aren't asking us to let him decide how he dies. You are asking us to let him decide whether he dies, and when, and with what kind of help."

The back rows of the courtroom stir. These are not only Oren Nyquist's supporters, the senders of letters and demonstrators on the courthouse steps. They are Bernie Keane's people too, and within the constraints of decorum, they are here to cheer on their hero. Have they come to celebrate their faith, Davenport thinks, or just to glory in the blood of gladiatorial combat?

"We are not asking the court to recognize a free-ranging right to assistance at end of life, Justice Keane." Corbett's pace has picked up. She has consumed almost ten of her allotted thirty minutes, and her eyes travel between Keane, at the Chief's other side, and Davenport, who as the most junior justice sits at the far end of the bench. "We accept that not even the loosest interpretation of constitutional standards would justify such an open-ended right."

Keane says, "Then, where would you have us draw the line between your client and everyone else? How would you have us measure the kind of pain that would justify assistance to suicide in one case but not another? Your client is, I gather, in crippling physical pain. But what about the next petitioner who comes before us, one whose pain is only in his mind? A woman suffering depression, say? Would you allow assisted suicide for that person?"

What is Keane doing? Surely, in his own long life Keane has seen someone fall into a depression so dark and agonizing that death actually appears to be salvation. At the end, not only had Olivia's emotional pain consumed her, but there had been no palliative to offer even the most transient relief. No, Keane knows very well that when it comes to pain, there is no difference between body and mind; it is all the same. Keane knows about Olivia's madness. He had asked the question to goad the new justice into making a mistake.

"I don't think, Justice Keane ... I believe—" The flawless advocate falters and she glances at Davenport again. The lectern is so close to the bench that Corbett must turn in order to do so, and when Davenport turns to meet her eyes, he sees that Keane is looking at him too. He sets aside the earlier question he had prepared to bring Corbett back to the fireman and grapples instead for a response to Keane.

The racketing chain saw persists. "Surely, counselor, mental illness is curable in a way that your client's physical illness evidently is not." Two fingers under his chin, Keane cocks his head and offers a thin-lipped smile. "We wouldn't want to be killing off people who might someday get their health back, would we? Who among us hasn't at some low point in his life felt such sadness that, even just for an instant, he wished for oblivion? But a patient suffering mental illness may recover and enjoy a fulfilling life for the rest of his years."

Again Davenport misses the beat, and before he can stop her, Corbett says, "If the court finds it necessary to draw a line for the kind of pain that will justify assistance at death, certainly the line between physical and mental illness would be one place to draw it."

Even as Davenport wishes that Corbett hadn't accepted the too-easy logic of Keane's distinction, he understands her strategy. If she can't get the court to take the giant step she wants, then she will accept a more modest advance. The tactic will not disserve her client, whose pain is demonstrably physical, and although the organization paying Corbett's fee supports assisted suicide regardless of the nature of the victim's suffering, her ethical duty is to win the case on whatever terms will serve her client. But the move is a strategic mistake, for Keane was only baiting her. Wherever Corbett draws the line, Keane will never vote to support assisted suicide.

Before Keane can push her further, Davenport says, "Surely, Ms. Corbett, we have a century's worth of legal evolution in which the law has come to embrace the teachings of modern science that mental and physical pain are often indistinguishable."

At the other end of the bench, Madeleine glares at him, and Donna Cippolone whispers, "What are you doing?" Thick-featured, Cippolone is as plain as Madeleine is elegant. Unlike Madeleine, who wears a white frill at the collar of her black robe, Cippolone chooses no decoration.

A moment's panic crosses Corbett's face before her self-possession returns. She realizes that she has erred, perhaps fatally, in thinking that her acceptance of Keane's distinction would win his vote and, even more troubling, that it would not lose the vote of the new justice. Behind the alert green eyes, she weighs and balances the alternatives, much as Davenport has observed her mentor, Madeleine, do. "Perhaps I misspoke, Justice Davenport. I didn't mean to give the impression that a hard and fast line can be drawn between mental and physical illness as an occasion for assistance at death."

Keane lets his thin smile settle on Davenport for a long moment to let him know how much he dislikes being challenged. "Are you sure you don't want to reconsider your rejection of the distinction between physical and mental suffering, counsel?" Keane's words are a taunt. "Retract your retraction?"

Herb Bauman, who as the most senior justice sits at the other side of the Chief from Keane, says, "I don't see why you're spending so much time on the record, counsel, or on these hypothetical questions. It isn't our role to retry this case. I haven't yet heard a word about the larger constitutional principles at stake here. Due process. Privacy. Individual choice."

"We fully address those principles in our brief, Justice Bauman."

Corbett is now worried about time and must decide, to the extent the decision is hers, between addressing Bauman's abstractions, on which she cannot expect the justices to move from their longstanding ideological positions, or spending the ten minutes that remain focusing on the facts that interest the new justice.

Madeleine makes the decision for her. "Has Mr. Clark executed a health care directive?"

"Yes, Justice Cardona. He has designated his wife to make health care decisions for him, so that—"

"So that means we can stop talking about doctors, doesn't it?" Madeleine's tone is final. "It is the family that gets to decide."

"Yes, Justice—"

"You don't mean the family," Alex Palfrey says. "You mean the wife." He flings his long arms forward to grasp the far edge of the bench. His voice is mocking and his red-and-white striped bowtie nests like a gaudy bird on the black collar of his robe. "As long as we are diving into the record, what does the record tell us about Mrs. Clark—the family member who is now making the life and death decisions for this fireman? What are her motives in all this? I'm curious, counselor, is there any evidence in the record of the size of Mr. Clark's life insurance policy? The identification of its principal beneficiary?"

The question is outrageous, and dismay registers even in the front rows reserved for members of the bar. The court's most conservative justice after Keane and Park is telling his colleagues that the newest justice's passion for facts can lead the court and its petitioners into dark and twisted corners no less than illuminating ones. Corbett's voice remains steady. "No, Justice Palfrey, there is nothing in the record about life insurance."

"Well, then," Palfrey pulls back from his perch and lets his voice drop, "There is evidence in the record, isn't there, that Mr. and Mrs.

Clark were already living separate and apart more than five months before he was hospitalized? That a divorce was in the works before he was diagnosed?"

"Living apart, yes, Justice Palfrey, but there is no evidence they were planning to divorce—"

"Or, for that matter to reconcile," Palfrey says. "How confident can we be, Ms. Corbett, about the presumed motives of the person who, if your position on assisted suicide prevails, becomes the family executioner?"

Davenport wonders why Harold hadn't mentioned the Clarks' separation in the part of his bench memo where he summarized the trial record. The court's term has only just started, and he remembers Madeleine's warning about this clerk, formerly Keane's, he has brought into his chambers.

Palfrey isn't done. "Have you considered, counselor, where a decision investing a family member with this life-and-death power would take us? Today you would have us sanction assisted suicide—"

"Not assisted suicide, Justice Palfrey. End of life decisions—"

"How do we know that next term you won't be back here asking us to uphold euthanasia?"

"There is a world of difference, Justice Palfrey—"

"Not when you lift the bar on assisted suicide, there isn't. A patient asks for help in dying, so you would give it to him. If his illness makes it impossible for him to communicate, you let his family speak for him and to ask for help in ending his life. You apparently would do so even though the family may benefit from the patient's early death."

"Not so, Justice Palfrey—"

"What if the family decides that an elderly or disabled parent costs more than he is worth to them? Do we let the family just kill him off?"

"The government would never let them do that," Corbett says.

"But isn't that what the government is trying to stop the family from doing here?"

The small red light on the lectern flashed on seconds ago and the Chief says, "You are out of time, Ms. Corbett, but I am sure the court will indulge your taking a moment to confirm my understanding of a point you made earlier." To Davenport's ear, the Chief still smarts from

Keane's interruption of his questioning at the start of the argument. "You told us that this case differs from others that have come before us because in those cases, the patient had already died and it was only the physicians who were making a claim. I just want to confirm that there is no question but that the physicians are still in this case. They are making a claim too."

"That is exactly right, Mr. Chief Justice. The physicians are objecting to the state's interference with their ability to practice medicine as they see fit."

The prod from the Chief puzzles Davenport, but it is Keane's questions that stick in his mind. Why would a justice whose opinions have for decades consistently rejected any place for assisted suicide in the court's jurisprudence veer so sharply off-path and suggest that it might be acceptable in some circumstances? And why would he make physical pain the dividing line? And that look of his when Davenport opposed him. Davenport has no illusions that Keane's welcome-to-the-court gift or the shared drinks held any promise of a true friendship, but he cannot remember when anyone other than Olivia regarded him with such cold disdain.

Corbett takes her chair, and the Chief says, "Mr. Gormley, you may proceed when you are ready."

5

Pennsylvania's attorney general, James Gormley, is sleek as a seal. The shaved head glistens under the courtroom lights, and an American flag pin occupies the buttonhole of his three-piece navy suit. "Mr. Chief Justice, and may it please the court." Gormley looks down at the small stack of index cards he brought with him to the lectern. "We are here today on behalf of the people of the great state of Pennsylvania to defend the wisdom and judgment of their elected representatives in categorically outlawing assisted suicide in our state."

The people of Gormley's great state would be better served this morning by a lawyer drawn, like Christine Corbett, from the priesthood of the Supreme Court bar. Having one of these advocates represent you is no guarantee of success at the court, but not having one vastly magnifies the risk of disaster, and it is a mistake for a state attorney general to assume that the highest court in the land requires the attendance of the state's highest legal officer. When a judge or justice asks a question, he wants to hear facts, law and analysis, not a politician's platitudes.

Cippolone speaks into her microphone. "Can you tell us, Mr. Gormley, what Pennsylvania's constitutional authority was to enact this law?"

Gormley adjusts his tie and glances at the warning light on the podium as if he could will it to turn red. Seated next to him, his co-counsel, a middle-aged man with a bad haircut and the harried look of a bureaucrat, elbows forward to help, but the attorney general recovers. "The authority, Justice Cippolone, is the same as that for any of our state's criminal laws—to secure the values of a civilized society."

"Of course." Cippolone says, "What of Mr. Clark's values? Is there anything in the record to reflect that?"

"Well," Gormley pauses to tug on his lapels, "we know that he is a fireman and a family man—"

"Would it surprise you, Mr. Gormley, if the record revealed that petitioner Clark is an atheist? An agnostic?" Cippolone's years in Washington, first on the court of appeals and now on the Supreme Court, have not softened the serrated edge that, twenty years ago when she was an assistant district attorney in Brooklyn, dispatched a succession of sex offenders into that borough's criminal justice system. "Would it surprise you to learn that Mr. Clark is a man who doesn't believe in the hereafter and thus doesn't share the worries of the good people of your state that he will suffer eternal damnation for taking his own life?"

The question is a prosecutor's trick, a hypothetical with no support in the trial record—at least, Davenport thinks, if Harold hasn't hidden this part of the record from him too.

"Well, it's a balance, Your Honor—"

"Are you sure of that, Mr. Gormley? What about the constitutional principle that prohibits one group of Americans from forcing their religious beliefs on some other group or individual?"

"What I meant to say, Justice Cippolone, is that before its enactment, this law, like all legislation in my state, received the most careful constitutional scrutiny—"

"We also do some of that here at the Supreme Court, Mr. Gormley. Examine legislation for constitutional defects."

The laughter from the lawyers in the front rows creates an opening, and Herb Bauman seizes it. "On this subject of the Constitution, Mr. Gormley, can you tell us how the State of Pennsylvania distinguishes between the act of assisting an individual in taking his own life and the act of merely advising him on end-of-life possibilities? Would you stop a doctor—or anyone, for that matter—from giving a patient a self-help book on suicide? I believe this is what the Hemlock Society did at one time. Isn't there a matter of free speech at stake here?"

Bauman was a law professor at Yale before coming to the court, and it is rumored that he gets the brightest Yale Law graduates to clerk for him by promising them a free hand in writing his opinions, just as when he was on the faculty there, he got the best students to write his law review articles.

"We address that in our brief, Your Honor—"

Bauman's thick eyebrows lift and meet to form an obtuse angle. "I'm sure you do, counselor, but why don't you tell us what the difference is between advising and assisting?"

"Death is what's different!" Keane's chain saw rips through his impatience with the fumbling attorney general. "Handing someone a lethal dose is what's different. Not handing him a book or a pamphlet. Not whispering in his ear. What's different is handing him a dose that will kill him."

Keane had measured every beat of the attorney general's response and timed his own entrance with precision. And not just Keane. Davenport realizes that Bauman, Cippolone, and the others are attuned to rhythms that so far remain silent to him. Only Gilbert Park, if he follows form, will ask no questions, but instead will wheel back and forth in his high-backed recliner, eyes on the ceiling, hands steepled beneath his chin as if in the deepest thought.

Looking out into the courtroom, Davenport encounters a deeply hooded pair of eyes staring back from the second row. Of course Oren Nyquist would be here, his apple-cheeked aide at his side. The senator's supporters in the back rows would be expecting him, and after the argument, the press will greet him at the foot of the courthouse steps to record his views on the case. Davenport holds the senator's gaze. They could be back in the hearing room with the coroner's transcript on the table between them, Nyquist's expression at once bleak and predatory.

Davenport remembers something Keane said to him as they sipped Irish whiskey in chambers. *Working for the Cardinal I had the opportunity to attend inquests all up and down New England.* What effort would it require for Keane's friends in the church to obtain a sealed coroner's report from one of the faithful in the county clerk's office? But what reason would Keane have to do so, and why would he share the transcript with Nyquist? To taunt me, Davenport decides. To distract me. To control me.

Keane and Bauman have abandoned any pretense of conducting their debate through Gormley, and Davenport breaks into the exchange. "Can you tell us, Mr. Gormley, if your state would accept a distinction between physical and mental pain in drawing the line on assisted suicide?"

Cippolone whispers to Davenport, "Madeleine." Davenport looks to where Madeleine sits and sees that she is frowning. Their eyes meet, and she shakes her head almost imperceptibly.

Gormley's eyes question Keane before he says, "The State of Pennsylvania draws no such line, Your Honor. As I said, the law's prohibition of assisted suicide is categorical. It is across the board—"

"Even if it is proposed by the patient's attending physician, counsellor?" The question is from the Chief who, once again and inexplicably, seems concerned with the place of physicians in end-of-life decisions.

Keane doesn't let Gormley answer. "What kind of morality would approve of a professional, a doctor, preying on the weakness of an infirm individual so that he consents to an act that would be unacceptable to any thinking, clear-minded person?"

Gormley can do no more than nod agreement, and it occurs to Davenport that the battle between Keane and the Chief concerns not when or how Randy Clark dies, but rather which of them is to control the court. The two in fact vote on the same side far more often than not, but the Chief will wheedle, manipulate, and compromise in order to win the large majorities that he believes the court's credibility requires, while Keane will write concurring opinions that refuse to compromise.

With Keane's help, Gormley has revived and actually beams as he waits out a question from Carl Shell. "Suppose, Mr. Gormley, that a patient refuses treatment. Is his physician required to honor that request and decline to treat him?"

Gormley consults a card. "Yes, Your Honor, that is the law in Pennsylvania."

On the evidence of Gormley's self-confidence, the index card doesn't warn him that Shell has started down a path from which, given the attorney general's limited aptitude for legal argument, he cannot possibly extricate himself.

Shell says, "This patient can even require his doctor to take him off life support, can't he?" A former governor of Iowa, Shell is as curiously truncated as his name, which Davenport speculates has been carved out from some Eastern European tongue-twister. Davenport chatted with him at Madeleine's welcome party, and not once during the conversation would Shell look directly at him. The words flowed like a politician's, but his thoughts were elsewhere. The averted eyes, the absented attention; some essential part of the man seemed to be missing, as if he were an amputee.

"That's right, Your Honor. We have a statute in Pennsylvania that specifically says withholding life-sustaining treatment at a patient's direction shall not be considered assistance to a suicide."

"So," Shell says, "you have this one law in Pennsylvania that says it is legal for a doctor to honor his patient's request to remove him from life support, but you also have this other law that says it is illegal for this very same doctor to honor the very same patient's request to administer a lethal dose to him, even though the result in both situations is the same: the patient dies."

"Well yes, Your Honor, but the difference is that the removal of life support is an act of omission, while the other is an act of commission."

Gormley is wrong—both circumstances require an affirmative act of the physician—and Davenport wonders if the Pennsylvania attorney general even hears what he is saying. Shell says, "I'm not sure that I see the difference."

Gormley sorts frantically through his index cards and jabs one in Shell's direction. "Well I would think, Your Honor, that it is all the difference in the world, the difference between taking something from somebody and giving something to him—"

Keane's voice pummels the air. "Isn't the relevant distinction, Mr. Attorney General, that when a patient refuses life-sustaining medical treatment, he dies from the underlying fatal condition—"

"That's exactly right, Your Honor," Gormley nods vigorously. "When—"

"Whereas if the patient ingests a lethal medication prescribed by a physician, it is the medication that kills him. In the first case, it is God's will at work, in the second, it is the physician's."

Keane was never the schoolyard bully. No, he was the frail ten-year-old the bully regularly battered, and now, seventy years later, he is practicing his revenge. The most fearsome adversary on the court, he has so intimidated everyone—even the Chief—that Davenport understands that he will not be able to build bridges himself between the other justices without first crushing Keane.

Before Gormley can continue or Keane can come to his rescue, Davenport says, "What about terminal sedation, Mr. Gormley? As I understand it from their amicus brief in this case—and I am sure you will correct me if I'm wrong—the American Medical Association allows physicians to administer sufficient doses of a painkiller to protect terminally ill patients such as Mr. Clark from excruciating pain. Does Pennsylvania permit its physicians to follow this protocol?"

"Yes, we do, Your Honor."

"Will Pennsylvania allow such an extreme dose even if it is clear to the physician that administering the dose will hasten the patient's death?"

"Definitely, Your Honor. The people of Pennsylvania don't want anyone to suffer—"

"How then, Mr. Gormley, do you square your state's position allowing terminal sedation with the distinction that Justice Keane drew just a few moments ago, between God's will and the physician's will, a distinction with which you said you agreed?"

For the second time this morning, Cippolone whispers to Davenport, "Madeleine."

"I'm not sure what you mean, Your Honor."

Davenport looks over to Madeleine's place, but her head is down and she is writing.

"In my example, Mr. Gormley—the example of terminal sedation that you said your state approves for medical practice—it is the painkiller that is the cause of death, isn't it, and not the underlying disease? Because of the painkiller, the patient's death occurs sooner rather than later." Madeleine passes a folded note to Alex Palfrey, sitting next to her. After glancing at it, unopened, Palfrey passes it to the Chief.

Davenport says, "Can you explain to the court how a physician accelerating death by administering a requested, extreme dose of a painkiller—which your state allows—how this is any different from Mr. Clark asking his physician to hasten his death by administering a similarly excessive dose to him?"

"Well the difference, Your Honor, is that in your first example of terminal sedation, the doctor intends only to eliminate pain, even though the effect may be to hasten death. In the second case, the present case, the doctor's intention is to cause death."

"And eliminate pain."

Madeleine's note rests at the base of the Chief's microphone, but he appears not to see it.

"Well, of course, that too, Your Honor. But we draw the line at the primary purpose of the extreme dose, its primary intention." For the first time in his argument, Gormley seems satisfied with his answer.

Shell says, "That sounds like a pretty fine line to me—"

"How does a prosecutor in your state know which of these two physicians to prosecute?" Now that he has captured the rhythm, Davenport is not ready to cede it. "How does he know what the doctor's intention was? Does he ask the doctor, 'Was your intention, when you administered that dose, to relieve pain, or was it to cause death?' Does he put the doctor on the rack and turn the screw until he confesses the truth?" For God's sake, Davenport thinks, the physician himself doesn't know if he intends to ease pain or to cause death. "I don't think the line you're trying to draw between committing and not committing a crime is a thin one, Mr. Gormley. I think it's invisible."

Keane looks over at Davenport, eyes crinkling at the corners, and there is no mistaking his pleasure in what he is about to say. "Mr. Attorney General, in the course of their administration of criminal justice, how many times would you say prosecutors and juries in your state find it necessary to draw lines more difficult than the one that Justice Davenport describes?"

Gormley returns the justice's smile. "Dozens of times, Your Honor. That's what law practice is all about, isn't it? Drawing lines."

"I'm glad to hear that there are still good lawyers in your fine state and lines for them to draw."

"We hope you will come visit us in the capital, Your Honor." Catching himself, Gormley says, "And of course the other justices too."

Davenport considers the impact of the exchange on the other justices. If the new justice is so reckless that he questions the line that separates criminal from innocent intent, is he also wrong to suggest that it is possible to obliterate the distinction between mental and physical suffering? He knows that it was Keane's introduction of that distinction that first derailed his careful plan to build a factual bridge uniting the court in this case. Now his resentment is not only against Keane, but the others as well. The despair he felt in the robing room returns.

Before Davenport can correct the record, the red light switches on and the Chief says, "Thank you, Mr. Gormley. Your time has expired."

The justices rise, and the Chief notices the folded scrap of paper at his place. Without opening the note, he hands it to Davenport as they exit through the curtains. Shell joins Davenport on the walk back to chambers, and then Gilbert Park. Davenport crumples the note and, when they pass a waste receptacle, tosses it in, even though he knows that Madeleine is no more than two or three steps behind and cannot help but see.

· · · · · · · · · · · · · · · · · · · ·

Anne's voice over the intercom informs Davenport that the president is on the line.

"Mr. President."

The voice Davenport has known for more than half his life says, "Welcome to the least dangerous branch." Locke presumably intends the allusion to Alexander Hamilton's description of the judiciary to be ironic, but the two men have not spoken since before Davenport's confirmation, and the words accomplish what that event did not: they seal forever the fact that Davenport's former life is over and that, among other changes, his relationship to Locke has forever altered. "How did your first argument as a justice go?"

"I'm grateful for your interest, Mr. President, but—"

Locke has guessed at the rest because he says, "It's a comfort knowing that, whatever comes before the court, I can trust you to do the right thing, Richard. I don't have to worry that you'll turn your back on me like Souter did to the first Bush. The way Earl Warren surprised Eisenhower."

Davenport doesn't respond to the implicit demand for fealty. If Bush and Eisenhower were surprised by how their appointments turned out, it was only because they didn't have the grip on their nominees that Locke believes he has on him.

The president says, "I have one or two more appointments to the court if I can manage to get myself re-elected. The Chief Justice has been telling bar groups he wants to spend more time hunting and fishing. And now, Bernie Keane getting a bad diagnosis. Lymphoma."

The oncologist and the whiskey in a teacup.

"I'm looking to my legacy, Richard. I figure you've got thirty years ahead of you, maybe forty if you marry someone sensible this time. That's enough to turn the court around the way Earl Warren did. These 5–4 decisions are hell with the voters. If nine justices can't agree on the most fundamental issues, why should the public?"

"Really Mr. President, this call is inappropriate—"

"Just one thing, Richard."

"Of course." Davenport says. "Discretion." The word has come to define their shared secret and to mark the boundary between them. Neither of them has spoken of the incident to anyone—or even to the other—since it happened twenty-six years ago. Although they have not discussed it, the crime—for that is what it was—still throbs like a membrane between them. After it happened, the closeness that he and Locke once shared never revived, not even when Davenport worked as his counsel in the governor's office. On the principle that a ruler should keep his friends close and his enemies closer, it occurs to Davenport to wonder into which category Locke places him.

"Discretion. Exactly!" The president's laugh as he hangs up is guarded.

6

Drinking coffee at her kitchen table with Leonard and Mike Bossio, Gloria recognizes the embarrassed look Mike gets when he's holding something back. He already told them they lost their appeal, so Gloria can guess that now he's going to tell them he can't bring their case to the Supreme Court, which is fine with her if it takes the pressure off Denny giving his consent to the transplant. "If you have something else on your mind, Mike, let's hear it. I have to get to work."

Mike was in real estate sales when he was in law school, which is how Leonard knows him. Along with the transplant case, he's Junior's lawyer on his drug and alcohol charges. Leonard always builds Mike up, bragging how he can win any kind of case, but Mike never impressed Gloria as much more than a nice guy pretending to be a lawyer.

Mike's pudgy finger pushes the half-empty mug to the side. "I could file for a rehearing, but the court was 3–0 against us, so I'm thinking it'll be faster to go right to the Supreme Court."

Leonard tilts back in his chair and sets his eyebrows low, like he's thinking hard about their next step, but Gloria is sure he doesn't know what's coming, that although the case is on its way to Washington, Mike's not the lawyer who is going to take it there. It's warm in the kitchen, but only Mike is perspiring. He says, "I can't take this up to the Supreme Court by myself."

Leonard's chair snaps upright. His anger is up. "What about Junior?"

"I'm not talking about the drug case. I'm still on top of that."

"I mean Junior's future," Leonard says. "The transplant."

Gloria says, "Junior already has a future. He just has to do what his doctor tells him to do and use that machine every night."

Leonard shoots her one of his hard looks and Mike says, "I lined up someone to help me with the appeal. Actually someone to take over the case. A specialist. There's no cost to you." Mike stops to see if Leonard understands before continuing on about the new lawyer he found for them, Christine Corbett.

Gloria hears the words, but their meaning flies by her. She wants to say, "Forget the appeal," but that will just set Leonard off, so the next best thing is for Mike to take the appeal by himself. With his track record so far, he's sure to lose, and that will give her time to think and Denny time to speak. She says, "I want you to handle it, Mike. I never told you to stop billing us."

Mike stares down at the coffee cup. "It's not the fees. I just don't have the resources to do the research."

Leonard says, "I thought you already did the research."

"This is the Supreme Court, Len. It's different. You need a feel for the justices. How they think." He straightens in his chair. "Christine has an organization that will pay her fees. They're called Family Choice. They'll cover the whole thing. All expenses. Soup to nuts. My name would still be on the papers, but hers would be first. She'll do all the heavy lifting. Argue the case."

"Christine?" Leonard says, "A woman?"

"Christine has lots of Supreme Court experience. She's sure she can get the court to hear the appeal."

"Why wouldn't they hear it?"

"It's not automatic like the last time. For every hundred appeals, the Supreme Court maybe hears one."

Gloria is certain Mike didn't know that before. The woman lawyer told him.

"Putting her name on the papers increases our chances. She'll make it an emergency appeal. She argued a case there last week."

Leonard asks how she did and Mike says, "She went up against the attorney general of Pennsylvania."

Leonard says, "I meant, did she win or lose?"

"The decision won't come down for months."

"What does Christine say about our chances?"

Christine, Gloria thinks. Like they're buddies. Now that Leonard's over the problem of having a woman lawyer, he's a big-time player again. But this is moving too fast for her. She doesn't want an emergency appeal. She needs to hear from Denny.

"Christine says our chances are good. She called me yesterday, right after she heard we lost. She's sure we have a lock on at least five justices. All we need to win."

Gloria doesn't believe that the new lawyer told him this. It's just Mike getting ahead of himself, as usual. "If the case is all locked up, why does it matter who our lawyer is?"

"Because, you don't want to take any chances," Mike says.

"I still want you to handle the case."

"You already heard him, Gloria. This is outside Mike's expertise."

Gloria can't think of a week in the last twenty-one years when she didn't ask herself why she married Leonard. She had been popular in high school and got good grades, but she never had a real date, not even for the senior prom. She went to Erie Community College and by the time she graduated, all her girlfriends were married or engaged. She never really thought about being married, just having children, so when Leonard, who she sort of dated on and off in college asked, she said yes. She wanted daughters, but after the problem with Denny, they silently agreed not to push their luck, and now with the situation with Junior, she's glad they didn't. She asks herself if twenty-one years ago she knew how things would turn out, she would have started a family.

"This new lawyer won't be working for us," Gloria says. "She'll take her orders from whoever's paying her bills." Gloria's going to be late for work, but she can't leave these two to themselves. She braces herself for Leonard's reaction. "What if we decide to drop the appeal and she doesn't want to?"

Leonard says, "Why would we drop the appeal?" He gives her that wise-guy look of his that says he knows exactly what she's thinking, but for some reason he doesn't explode.

"Because maybe Denny doesn't want the operation. When you give up an organ, you don't get it back."

"How can he not want to do this for his brother?"

Mike says, "I promise you, Gloria, you and Len will be in charge. Christine will explain it to you. You have to sign off on the change of counsel anyway. Anything the two of you tell her to do, she'll do. She has to. No matter who's paying her bills, you and Len are her clients and her ethical obligation is to you."

Leonard puts on his deep, serious businessman's voice and says to Mike, "But you would still be involved in the case, am I right?"

"Absolutely," Mike says. "I need to keep Christine filled in on the family issues."

Gloria thinks they could be one of those old-time comedy teams, the comic and the straight man, except she doesn't know which would be which. She says, "What family issues?"

Mike and Leonard look at each other. They have talked about this before. Leonard says, "The issue that you're not a hundred percent behind this lawsuit. That you want to drop the appeal. That you don't want Christine, who can actually win the case."

"I need Denny to tell me he wants to do this."

"And how's he going to do that, Gloria? In a letter? In sign language? Your son doesn't talk."

"You don't know that. You're never there. Denny talks."

"What, once?"

Before Gloria can answer, a voice behind her says, "Three times. He talked to me three times."

Gloria turns. It's Junior in a T-shirt and pajama bottoms, pouring coffee at the counter behind her. She doesn't know how long he's been there, in full sight of Leonard and Mike, and she's furious at them for making her take Denny's side against Junior when he is right there, listening.

"And what did he tell you?"

"That he wants to go home," Junior says.

"Just like that?"

"No, just a couple of words. 'Home. Go home.' Like that."

Mike says, "Christine thinks she can get some amici lined up. Friends of the court who will support us."

As if that makes a difference, Gloria thinks. She hears Mike's words, but she's not really listening. She looks at the clock above the stove, the red plastic owl her mother gave her for her wedding, and even though she sets it ten minutes fast, it reminds her she's going to be very late for work. Every corner of her life feels bent. When she was younger, she had no problem connecting with people, but now with all these turned-down corners, she feels cut off. In this kitchen that she wallpapered herself, she feels like a stranger. If only she had the time and strength to straighten out the corners, she could get all this settled. If only she knew what Denny wanted.

Gloria hears Leonard telling Mike the ridiculous story the doctor told them. "Don't say it, Leonard."

Leonard says, "My wife's favorite son is why Junior's sick in the first place."

Gloria's fist flies up, striking Leonard under the chin. The chair he's rocking back and forth flips over, him with it. It occurs to her that this is only the second time in her life that she has struck a member of her family, and both times in the same week. But it wasn't fair for Leonard to say that. It was hurtful. What the doctor told them is that it's rare, but sometimes with twins, there's a condition at birth that one twin damages the kidneys of the other. At birth. As if Denny had any choice in the matter.

Mike, the moron, struggles to hold himself back from laughing at the sight of Leonard on the floor, being helped up by Junior. To Gloria, the three of them are like a football huddle. They throw off that dark, meaty smell men get when they gang up like this.

Upright, Leonard's face is redder than before, and he clasps his hands as if for prayer. "We're a family, Gloria." The blow had an effect on Leonard, because he is putting on his real estate salesman peacemaker act. Still, Gloria hears the impatience in his voice. "Our job is to help each other. Denny giving his kidney to Junior is going to help Junior a lot more than it's going to hurt Denny. It's not going to hurt Denny at all."

Gloria feels sick. It's not the second cup of coffee with no food under it, but the thought of Denny being operated on, not knowing what's happening to him. It's Leonard's words, help Junior more than it hurts Denny—how can you compare the two!—that make her feel this way. They're not even his own words. They're Mike's words. It's what Mike told the judges on the appeals court, and thank God, they didn't listen to him. You don't measure one precious life against another like that, even if Leonard thinks Denny's life is less valuable than Junior's.

Junior says, "Do you really think I'd do anything to hurt my kid brother? I love him more than anybody."

Junior calls Denny his kid brother even though Denny was born only fifteen minutes after him. Gloria knows that Junior would in fact be heartbroken if something happened to Denny, and that he is as torn as she is about the transplant.

Junior says, "What happens if we lose at the Supreme Court?"

"We won't lose," Mike says. "Christine promised—"

"But what if your lady lawyer is wrong, and we lose? We can take Denny to another state, right? One that's not as fucked up as New York. Have the operation there."

"Definitely," Mike says, "we—"

"We have to wait," Gloria says. "Denny is staying right where he is."

Junior says, "What, and leave me hooked up to that damn machine?"

"We'll find another donor if we have to."

"Not a live one," Leonard says. "Not a perfect match. For Pete's sake, Gloria. You were standing right there when the doctor told us. Denny gives Junior the best chance that the transplant will work. And he said Junior can't be on that machine forever. The first time he gets an infection, it's all over."

The machine is in Junior's bedroom, and he just has to use it at night. All he needs is to be careful and he won't get infected. It infuriates Gloria how Leonard can pick and choose what he wants to know. He can drink beer and hunt with Junior like the boy is perfectly healthy, but then he makes it Gloria's job to take him to his doctor's appointments. She is tired of arguing. "Well, he's going to have to wait some more." To Mike, she says, "How long before the Supreme Court hears the case?"

"I told you, we don't even know if they'll take the appeal."

"But how long before they let us know one way or the other?"

"Christine says three weeks, maybe even two."

Gloria hears in his voice how he loves saying that name. Christine. "And after that? If they take the case?"

"Maybe a month."

Junior says, "You said the other case, the one last week, is going to take more time than that." Her son has been listening longer than Gloria thought. It reminds her how attentive Junior can be when he wants something.

"Like I told your parents, Junior, this would be an emergency appeal."

A month, Gloria thinks. If she can hold them off that long, she can come up with some other way to fix this. Maybe in a month's time Denny will be able to tell her what he wants. "Nobody's taking Denny anywhere."

"Junior doesn't have that kind of time," Leonard says.

Gloria says, "You're not listening. We're talking about a month. Until Junior said we should move Denny to another state, you weren't even thinking about that. But now it has to be tomorrow. It would take you that long to find a new doctor." She says *you* so he understands whose responsibility this is going to be, if it happens.

Mike says, "And you'll sign the papers transferring the case to Christine?"

Gloria nods.

Leonard says, "And after that, if we lose in the Supreme Court, we'll move him to another state."

Him, not *Denny*. "We'll talk about it then," Gloria says. "I'm not making a decision now, and I'm not going to let you bully me into making one." She looks up at Junior. "And if you're serious about getting on with your life, the smartest thing you can do is to start cleaning up your act. Stay away from your friends down at Day's Park. Come home at a reasonable hour. I can promise you, when I get around to deciding what we're going to do with Denny, I'll be thinking hard if you're worthy of his sacrifice. I'm also—"

"For God's sake, Mom, that's crazy. Anyone will tell you—"

"And get rid of that shirt. Don't ask me which one. You know which one."

"I'll send it to Goodwill."

Gloria knows he's kidding her and almost smiles. "You'll do no such thing. You'll put it in a paper bag, and I'll dispose of it."

Junior nods and Gloria thinks that was too easy. He'll just get another shirt. And, between him and his father, they'll come up with some way to get Denny out of the state without her knowing. She looks at the clock. She really has to get to work.

7

Davenport is talking with his clerks about the pending vote in the assisted suicide case when a familiar face several tables away distracts him. Certain as he is that the man doesn't belong in the court cafeteria before the building opens to the public, he cannot place him anywhere else. Davenport turns back to the clerks. He knows what his vote will be and, even after his failed performance at the argument, he believes that he can draw more than four other justices to his position.

The two clerks could not be more different. Jack Silverman has the easy manner of an athlete—as an undergraduate he played basketball at Duke—and is in neatly pressed chinos and a plaid shirt. Harold Williams's mismatched jacket and trousers could have been purchased at a second-hand shop. The unfashionably wide tie has a petroleum sheen, and a shirt button has popped at his mid-section. A white pocket square embroidered in an elaborate script with initials not his own peeks from the outside breast pocket of his sports coat.

Jack's suggestion for how to bring the other justices to Davenport's position is analytically crisp and smart, just what Davenport would expect from a young lawyer who earned straight As at the University of Virginia Law School before clerking for a federal appeals judge and then joining the litigation department at Davenport's firm. Davenport could have thought of it himself, and the suggestion is for that reason a disappointment. It is Harold, who grew up in a trailer park and for four years rode a bus to classes at East Tennessee State University, who gives the justice what he needs. "Listen closest to the Chief, but also listen to Palfrey. And stay clear of Keane. We have a saying back home: you don't want to get into a pissing contest with a skunk."

The clerk's disloyalty to his former justice surprises Davenport. "What about the line he drew between physical and mental suffering?"

"That's just one of Justice Keane's tricks. He was trying to throw you off balance."

The young clerk is too polite to say that Keane had succeeded in doing so, just as he was too modest at his interview with Davenport months earlier to mention that he was the first student in the history of Columbia Law School to win the trifecta there—first in his class, editor-in-chief of the law review, and author of the best brief and oral argument in the school's moot court competition.

When the justice and his clerks get up to leave, the stranger at the other table rises too, and now Davenport can place him. He is Oren Nyquist's aide from the confirmation hearings, the pink-cheeked handler of documents. The man's manner as he approaches them, cardboard cup in hand, is casual, almost proprietary, as if he is the host and they the visitors here. The laminated government identification card that hangs from the lanyard around his neck would ordinarily not be enough to get him past the security station at this early hour, so perhaps he is a regular visitor after all. The card bears his photograph and name. Marvin Hillis.

"A minute of your time, Justice Davenport?"

Even before the justice nods for the two clerks to leave, Hillis takes a seat at the table they have just vacated, unconcerned that Davenport shows no inclination to join him. His cup is empty and inside is a teabag, pinched and crushed. He has been waiting for some time. "The senator is very pleased that you're throwing out lifelines in the assisted suicide case." This is not the discreet whisper Hillis used with his boss at the confirmation hearings, and several heads turn in their direction from neighboring tables. "He just needs to be sure that you're throwing them from the right side of the river."

Davenport wants to leave, but worries about what the man will say, and how loudly, if he walks away. He takes the chair opposite and, with the hope that Hillis will follow his example, drops his voice to a murmur. "I don't know what you're talking about."

"We were at the argument on Tuesday. I listened to the tapes later." He has lowered his voice, but it could rise in an instant. "If someone knows what he's looking for, it's easy enough to connect the dots."

This close, Davenport sees that what looked from across the hearing room like an athlete's healthy flush, is in fact the raw complexion of a farm worker who has spent too many harsh winters in the open. Also, Hillis is older than he thought, and in his eyes is just enough of a zealot's rage to warn the justice to be careful. "This conversation is totally inappropriate, Mr. Hillis. Now, if you'll excuse me—"

Hillis rests his hand on the justice's. The pads of his fingers are callused, and again Davenport thinks of a hard life spent outdoors, but the aide's smile is easy. He could be a talk show host in command of his guest.

"You know, the senator was terribly hurt when you refused to meet with him before your confirmation hearings."

Bennett told Davenport that it was Nyquist, not he, who had rejected the offer of a meeting, and Davenport wonders which of the two is lying.

"I would hate for you to disappoint him again. He really hopes you will use this opportunity to forge a compromise."

Davenport hears the threat at once. Tuesday's argument is not all that Nyquist's aide has studied; he read the transcript of the coroner's inquest too. Davenport leans in to be sure the aide doesn't miss a whispered word. "Tell the senator that I know he's bluffing. Tell him that if he makes the transcript public, it's going to ruin him, not me."

Hillis draws back, as if from a blow. "I don't know what you mean. The last thing we want is to injure you." Even on the defensive, Hillis is staunchly earnest. "Senator Nyquist believes that it is part of his responsibility as a member of the Judiciary Committee to ensure that the public continues to place its trust in the federal judiciary."

"The court order that sealed the transcript gave only four people access to it. There's no way your boss could get it without committing a felony."

"If you need to know, we obtained it through entirely lawful means."

"How? Who gave it to you?" In fact, Davenport already knows. The instant he saw the gray transcript in the senator's hand, he knew which of the four numbered copies of the sealed record it was. The stories he had told Bennett and himself—a bribed secretary, Bernie Keane calling in old favors from the Cardinal—were just that: stories to protect himself from the truth.

Hillis says, "You should be proud that your daughter is so civic-minded. She handed it to the senator herself in his office in the Dirksen Building."

Surrounded by people consuming their morning coffee and pastry, the conversation is insane. Davenport lowers his voice further. "Did she talk to him?"

Hillis shrugs. "I'm sure they talked, but I'd only be guessing about what. Why don't you ask her yourself?"

Of course Hillis knows that Nola is estranged from her father. Why else would she hand over the transcript to the senator? "If you've read the transcript, you know there's nothing in it to embarrass me. Also, there's nothing my daughter could have said." Davenport wishes he could believe this. With his daughter whispering family secrets into his ear, even a blind man could read between the lines of the coroner's report. "The senator will ruin himself if he brings this out in public."

"He thinks you have more to lose."

"I don't have constituents to answer to."

"Of course you do. You have eight other justices. Unless you're planning to be a lone wolf, and we don't think that's why you came to the court."

"What does he want?"

"The senator wants only to preserve your authority. This is what I've been trying to explain to you." The clenched jaw is exaggerated; this is an act. "If this information gets out, it will destroy your standing on the court." Hillis nods in the direction of the cafeteria line. "What influence do you think you'll have with Justice Cardona if she knew about this?"

Davenport half turns. Madeleine is paying the cashier. At her side in his wheelchair, Phil holds a paper bag, probably pastries for the staff. Davenport prays that in the crowded room they don't see him.

"You can tell the senator he's nuts." In truth Davenport doesn't know if his words are anything more than bravado. He looks around. Their voices have fallen low and no one can hear. "I'm not giving him my vote."

"You have to believe me, Justice Davenport, the senator would never ask for such a thing. You don't understand him if you think he would."

"Then why is he so interested in my influence?"

"For the same reason you are. To have a united court. No more of these 5–4 decisions."

The tip of Hillis's nose has turned beet red. A drinker. How was it that, for all the gallons of gin she consumed, Olivia managed to retain that unflawed porcelain mask? Genes, he decides, all the way back to her ancestors who took their cocktails on the aft deck of the Mayflower. "United around who? Bernie Keane?"

"Justice Keane has been a great disappointment to the senator," Hillis says. "This is what I'm trying to explain to you. This is why the senator is so sorry you wouldn't meet with him before your hearings. Dissenters have no power to achieve social good. Bridge builders have power. Senator Nyquist believes you have the credibility and the skill to bring the court's liberal and conservative wings together." The aide's expression is prayerful. "He had hoped Chief Justice Bricknell could do it, but he can't. He doesn't have your substance."

Or, Davenport thinks, the baggage of a faithless daughter and an unhappy wife. Nyquist is blackmailing him to vote with the Chief Justice and the conservatives, not only in the assisted suicide case, but in every future case that matters to the senator and his constituents. Davenport's legal career has exposed him to political deals and financial maneuvers that, if made public, would fill the front pages, and decades ago he lost any innocence he may once have possessed. But still he feels defiled. Everything around him seems unclean, and were he to touch the cafeteria table, he expects that it would be greasy with soot. He stands, and this time he doesn't wait for Hillis. "You can tell the senator that he's going after the wrong man."

· · · · · · · · · · · · · · · · · · · ·

After a take-out lunch in the justices' dining room, punctuated by stalled conversations and tense silences, the justices move to the first-floor conference room, the single place where tradition allows no one other than the justices, not even the clerks, to enter. Apart from the American flag on a stand in the corner, it could be the boardroom of a small and venerable private bank. Like those in the courtroom, the leather chairs around the conference table are high-backed. Two easy chairs and a coffee table face a modest fireplace, and there is an antique clock on the mantel beneath the oil portrait of Chief Justice John Marshall. For Davenport, still thinking about the encounter with Marvin Hillis, corruption muddies every corner of the room—from the tired burgundy drapes to the gaudy chandelier.

The ritual round-the-table handshakes are cursory. Bernie Keane's hand, when it grasps Davenport's, is dry and almost fragile, like the bones of a small bird. The Chief's plump, hearty grip, always warm, is today moist, and Davenport wonders why this should be. When they have taken their seats, the Chief coughs to clear his throat. "Are we ready to proceed with *Clark v. Pennsylvania?*" Protocol requires the Chief not only to state his views first, but also in a sentence or two to frame the question for the court's decision, a prerogative that, by setting the terms of debate, some observers believe can affect the outcome of the case.

This afternoon though, the Chief is in a discursive mood. "As we are all aware, there is a great deal of interest in this case among the press and the public. There is also a troubling divisiveness. The clerks have chosen up sides and talk about little else. I honestly don't know where we are going to be by the end of our discussion." Perspiration glazes the Chief's forehead, belying the offhand manner. "It is sometimes said that every time a new justice joins us, we effectively become a new court. So now with Justice Davenport's arrival"—he declines to look at Davenport; it is as if he is speaking of someone absent—"perhaps we will find a way to escape the divisions that have so hobbled politically charged cases like this one, involving end of life."

An alarm sounds in Davenport's mind and he wonders if anyone else caught the Chief's borrowing of Christine Corbett's phrase—end of life—instead of the more traditional "assisted suicide."

"In particular," the Chief says, I don't think we should consider ourselves bound hand and foot by our precedents in the area."

The effect around the table is electric. Color leaves Bernie Keane's face and, in a reflex, he grabs the arms of his chair as if preparing to escape, then frees a hand to massage his chest above his heart. Park's right foot, just inches from Davenport's own, dances a rapid tattoo. Everyone had expected the Chief to vote with Keane, Palfrey, and Park to uphold the assisted suicide ban. Even more startling is his suggestion that the justices abandon precedents a half-century old. Of the others taking in the Chief's bombshell, Madeleine's demeanor is the coolest.

"In reviewing our earlier cases with fresh eyes," the Chief says, "we should bear in mind that no present member of the court was sitting when these precedents were decided." If the Chief is concerned that this is heresy, a direct attack on the myth that the court is greater than the nine individuals who at a given moment occupy its bench, his flat, uninflected tone gives no clue. "Perhaps," he says, his eyes settling on Davenport for the first time, "we can find in the trial record of this case some fact that we can all agree distinguishes it from our precedents." His eyes sharpen, as if he is about to say something more, but he changes his mind and turns to his left. "Justice Bauman?"

Just as Bauman, the most senior justice, will offer his views first, Davenport, as the most junior, will speak last. But it is not too early for him to begin weighing and sifting the remarks of the others to locate some fact in the trial record that all will agree should let Randy Clark die in peace. The Chief has asked for as much, and although Davenport remembers Harold's injunction to listen to Palfrey as well, for the first time, he considers the possibility that he can make this not-very-bright man his ally.

Under the heavy eyebrows, Bauman's eyes are joyful slits. Like most liberal lawyers of his generation, the former law professor divides the world into absolutes. If you don't violently disagree with me, it must be because you agree. And if you agree, logic dictates that your support not be some pale, lukewarm endorsement, but robust and unabashed. Where in the Chief's eccentric opening Davenport sees the possibility for the disruption of existing alliances, Bauman sees the triumph for progressivism that has escaped him for too many bleak years on the court. "I am delighted by the Chief's bold invitation to revisit our precedents. I thought the state's responses at oral argument were, frankly, an embarrassment." In his exuberance, Bauman overlooks that the replies belonged as much to Bernie Keane as to Pennsylvania's attorney general. "I vote to overturn the Pennsylvania statute, and look forward to an opinion for the court that does so in the most sweeping terms."

Keane rises to speak, buttoning his suit jacket as he does. "I haven't a clue what our Chief is talking about, that we are not bound by this court's precedents." Keane has left the chainsaw in the tool shed this afternoon, and his voice barely rises above a whisper. He positions himself at the long table so that his back is to the Chief and his gaze sweeps the bookshelves filled with volumes of the collected opinions of the court. "Since the Chief has chosen to open this Pandora's jar, I would remind you that there is an entire body of constitutional jurisprudence built on the same principles that underlie these precedents, including our decisions restricting the availability of abortions on demand." He turns and looks directly at the Chief. "You don't get to pick and choose. If we undermine the authority of our assisted suicide precedents, it is inevitable that we will undermine the principles behind these other decisions as well. The very foundations of our constitutional jurisprudence will collapse."

Keane is finished, but remains standing, narrow chest thrust out, as if inviting brickbats from the others. By reputation, he is the rare justice who will dash off his opinions on the run, and Davenport guesses that he has just drafted the first paragraph of his dissent in *Clark v. Pennsylvania.*

Keane's performance confirms that while the courtroom belongs to him, the conference belongs to the Chief. The Chief nods at Alex Palfrey, who is next in seniority. On the bench, the justices' black robes—all but the Chief's with its gold chevrons—are a great leveler, and Palfrey, an unembarrassed dandy, thrives off the bench. Today, under his three-piece suit of an expensive-looking tweed, he wears a carnival barker's striped shirt and a paisley bow tie. With his antique brogues tilted up on the conference table where the inlaid green leather abuts the dark oak, he could be Hollywood's idea of an Ivy League law professor, or an upscale clothing salesman.

"I am of course intrigued by the Chief's suggestion that we not treat the relevant precedents on assisted suicide as written in stone. But if we are ultimately to give our earlier decisions some"—Palfrey debates the next word as carefully as he selected his bow tie this morning—"some factual particularity, then I believe we should be unusually careful in doing so. Consequently, while I'm going to cast my vote to uphold the Pennsylvania statute, if someone can identify a fact in the trial record that would make it unconstitutional to apply this statute in these circumstances, I will be prepared to reconsider my vote."

While Palfrey recites which facts from the *Clark* trial record he might find congenial, and which not, Davenport tries to imagine what Nola was thinking when, transcript in hand, she traveled to Washington to meet with Nyquist. Did she really believe that sabotaging her father's nomination would protect the country from having a monster on the Supreme Court? Had she taken even a moment to consider the impact of Nyquist's release of this information on her own life? The story would be all over the news of the spoiled heiress who betrayed her father; of the last in the bloodline of a storied New England family who committed an act of political patricide. This kind of infamy never dies. Decades from now, it will be the lead in her obituary.

"Thank you, Alex. Your observations are noted," the Chief says. "Carl?"

"I agree with the Chief," Shell says, his eyes on the fireplace portrait of Marshall. "This is the perfect time to take a second look at our precedents. I don't know how many people in this country were in favor of assisted suicide when we decided those cases, but there's a Gallup poll last year that 81% of Americans think doctors should be free to terminate a patient's life." Shell's gaze travels around the room, but not once does it settle on a fellow justice. "Two years ago, a Harris poll put the number at 78%. It's clear what the trend is, and I don't think we win respect for this court among the American public by opposing majorities like that." Shell has overstated the poll numbers, which appeared in one of the amicus briefs, but no one corrects him.

It is Madeleine's turn. From her career on the Second Circuit, and now on the Supreme Court, it is safe to speculate that, like Bauman and Shell, she will vote to overturn the Pennsylvania statute for she devoutly believes in a woman's constitutional right to choose in the case of abortion and will for that reason oppose any law that shrinks individual choice. But Davenport has not talked with her since the dark looks and passed note at Tuesday's argument, and knows nothing of her strategy in today's case.

"I think Christine made a good point—that Mr. Clark is still alive, unlike the earlier cases where the patients had died before their cases got here. I wish the briefs had focused more on the point. The argument, too—"

The Chief interrupts. "You're not suggesting we put the case down for reargument, are you, Justice Cardona?"

Madeleine shakes her head, but before she can speak, the Chief says, "The case would be moot by then."

Davenport cannot help himself. "You mean it will be moot because Mr. Clark will be dead."

The Chief gives him a curious look, and Davenport doesn't know if it is for what he just said or for the breach of an unwritten protocol under which only the Chief may speak out of turn.

Madeleine says, "There's no need for new briefs or new arguments. I think we can work through this in chambers in the context of writing our opinion."

Davenport now sees Madeleine's strategy. She will vote to overturn the lower court decision but, as proposed by the Chief, only on the narrowest terms, and her words are a warning to Bauman. As senior justice among the presumptive majority, it will be Bauman's privilege to choose who writes the court's opinion. Madeleine is letting him know that if he insists on writing the opinion himself, in the sweeping terms that are his hallmark, she may defect to the other side, giving the Chief a majority and forcing Bauman into a possibly lonely dissent. But why would she not want the court's opinion to be a bold proclamation staking out the primacy of individual choice?

Donna Cippolone has been a roughly idling engine, waiting her turn to speak. Of all the justices at the table, she alone has made use of the white legal pad at her place, inscribing a dense train of tiny overlapping rectangles, deploying her felt-tip pen as a wood carver might a chisel. "I am prepared to vote with Madeleine." The words rush out, and when Madeleine glances at her, Cippolone takes a breath before continuing. "But like Madeleine and Alex and you, Chief, I think there's a lot of work that needs to be done before I can sign on to an opinion."

The Chief quickly intercepts the suggestion that he will join a liberal majority. "There will be plenty of time for the clerks to parse the cases, if that's the route we decide to follow. That's what we hire them for, and I'm sure they'll do a fine job."

Cippolone starts to speak, has second thoughts, and gestures with a hand toward Gilbert Park. Court watchers call Park Bernie Keane's Asian twin, the only justice since McWhorter's death whose views will occasionally veer to the right of Keane's. Today Park informs the conference in two short sentences that he will vote with Keane and join any opinion that Keane writes.

The picture in Davenport's mind of Nola's meeting with Nyquist is vivid, but wordless. What could his daughter have told the senator if, as he believes, he had always shielded her from his angry exchanges with Olivia? Unless she lied to Nyquist about her parents' relationship, what could she have told him that would indict her father? Either she lied then, or Nyquist's aide is lying now.

The Chief waits, his smile communicating nothing. "Justice Davenport?"

Davenport's mind races, but unlike Cippolone he is in no hurry to speak. He has been searching not only in the Chief's words and Palfrey's, but in those of the other justices, even Shell and Park, for points at which pressure can be applied to force them onto a patch of shared ground. He knows where he wants the court to finish—with a decision that allows assisted suicide and draws no line between mental and physical pain— but in his career as a trial lawyer he negotiated too many settlements and plea bargains to make the mistake now of starting closer to the terms of the final compromise than is absolutely necessary. Better to take an extreme position, like the ideologues Keane and Bauman, and use that as leverage to secure the compromise he desires. Davenport says, "As presently disposed, I will vote with Justice Bauman to overturn our precedents in the area and to do so in the strongest terms possible."

Bauman is pleased and, to Davenport's surprise, Madeleine nods approval. Keane shoots him a grin and a wink to let him know that he understands what the new justice is doing. The Chief's expression is blank, a poker player's. He is too shrewd not to understand that, if he wants a compromise, the next step is for him to approach Davenport. "Well, this is fine," the Chief says. "Why don't I draft an opinion for the court and circulate it for comments."

Again, the Chief's words throw the conference into confusion. It is an ironclad rule that the chief justice can assign the writing of the court's opinion, including to himself, only in cases in which he votes with the majority. There are differences around the table, but there is no doubt that five of the justices—Bauman, Shell, Cippolone, Madeleine, and Davenport—will vote to overturn the Pennsylvania statute, and that the Chief plainly stated that he would depart from the precedents and strike down the statute only if someone persuaded him that there was a distinguishing fact to the contrary. And he has said nothing to indicate that anyone has done so.

Keane asks if the Chief has changed his position.

The Chief says, "No, not necessarily. I'll just take a hand at the opinion and we'll see what comes out in the writing."

Before Keane or Palfrey or Park can object, Madeleine says, "I agree. Let's see what the Chief comes up with."

Cippolone says, "Whoever's writing the opinion, let's get it done sooner rather than later. We have at least five votes for Mr. Clark, and it would be tragic to force this unfortunate man to live any longer than he has to."

. . . .

At home in Harbour Square, between reading the briefs and memos for tomorrow's arguments, Davenport leaves messages on Nola's cellphone and on the answering machine in her Columbia apartment, but she returns none of them. What does his daughter know about the circumstances of her mother's death that she could want to share with a United States senator? Everything is already there, in the report of the coroner's inquest. On the 8:10 p.m. Hy-Line ferry, the "Grey Lady," a forty-five-year-old woman slipped overboard into a roiling sea. Her blood alcohol was at a level that on land would convict her of drunk driving three times over. But was it an accident? Or, in light of her emotional state as testified to by her psychiatrist, and her history of suicide attempts as evidenced by her medical records, did she take her own life? Why was this long-time summer resident of 'Sconset out on a ferry's aft deck in seas described by the state's expert meteorologist as treacherous? How close to his wife's side was her husband? Why did he not save her? Beyond this, Davenport asks himself, what does his daughter know of her parents' life together?

More than once in the months after their wedding, Olivia told Davenport that, by marrying her, he had saved her life. When he asked what she meant, she would just laugh and change the subject, but the fact was that in those early years when he was finishing law school and starting in practice, Olivia could go for weeks without drinking herself into oblivion. Over the next several years, she joined a succession of charity boards that were eager for access to her wealth and social connections, and only later were surprised to discover her brilliance and bottomless energy. Each of these commitments ended badly as Olivia discovered her board colleagues' limitations. They were self-centered blockheads and dilettantes, more interested in cocktail gossip than in dirtying their hands in the organization's mission. It was not enough for Olivia to raise funds for the literacy organization on whose board she served; she had to go into the South Bronx herself to teach these people how to read. Why would no other board member of her medical nonprofit follow the now-pregnant Olivia into the Central African bush to hand out medical supplies to victims of the latest catastrophe there? Then Nola arrived, and Olivia abandoned charity boards altogether, promising to devote her time instead to raising her daughter, although to Davenport's eyes it was to resume drinking, but now full time.

Davenport is reviewing a bench memo for tomorrow's second argument when the telephone rings.

"Richard?"

It is a woman's voice that he doesn't recognize.

"I'm a friend of Nola's." The tone is insolent. "She asked me to call you."

The use of his first name startles Davenport, but of course Nola would instruct her friend to do this. "How is she?"

"She doesn't want to talk to you. She wants you to stop filling her voice mail with messages."

It occurs to Davenport that Nola is there in her apartment, stage-managing this dismissal of her father; that she was in the room each time he left a message. Olivia once confessed to him that she herself did this when he would call from a business trip to check in on her. She would sit by the telephone and not pick up, knowing the anxiety this caused him.

"Just tell me how my daughter is!"

"She said you would get emotional. She asked me to tell you that you have no claim on her. She doesn't want you to call again." There is a sharp crack as the receiver slams down.

As an infant, Nola suffered colic, and on nights when the nanny was off and Olivia was helplessly drunk or passed out, it was Davenport who would hold and rock his daughter, pacing through their apartment for what seemed like hours, until the episode passed. Even now, alone in his study, his hand still on the telephone, he can see that angry fist of a face, inconsolable in its pain, and in the clenched muscles of his chest he can still feel his own struggle not to be consumed by the terror that so painfully gripped the bewildered child.

8

Jack wants the court to make a grand statement, but Harold does not. Across from the justice in his rocker, Jack argues that since five justices have now voted to overturn decades of precedent outlawing assisted suicide, Justice Bauman and his Yale clerks should write a bold opinion that condemns statutes like Pennsylvania's in the most sweeping terms. "So what if it's only 5–4? That never stopped the conservatives from writing big opinions when they had a majority."

Harold explains that sometimes a big majority with a narrow opinion is better than a close majority with a broad one. Harold has an offer to join the Harvard law faculty after his clerkship ends, and Davenport thinks that, just as putting the right frame around the most amateurish painting can make it look like a work of art, so surrounding his awkward clerk's bitten-down nails and dated clothes with Harvard Law School's ivy-covered brick will instantly transform Boyce Harold Williams III into a completely plausible, even commanding figure.

Davenport is not above lecturing to Jack. "My first concern is to let this fireman die quickly and peacefully. We can do that with a narrow opinion or a broad one. The advantage of a narrow opinion is that we can probably get three more justices to join it, and that can only increase public respect for the decision. Other than that, we're just talking about ideology, and that's none of my business."

"And if you can't get three others?"

"Then I'll reconsider your point."

Jack nods, but when he follows Harold out of the office, Davenport knows that his clerk is unhappy with him. Fine; join the club.

Edward knocks on the open door and tells Davenport that the Chief is on his way back from Capitol Hill and wants to see him. The messenger has a shoe box in one hand and a sheet torn from a legal pad in the other. He places the shoebox on Davenport's desk. "These are the letters that I picked out from the mail on the *Clark* case."

Davenport realizes that he not only forgot his request of Edward to sort through the overflowing mail bins, but also that he didn't tell his messenger that the *Clark* conference was yesterday. The sheet of paper is dense with words and numbers, and while Davenport reads, Edward uses the poker to rearrange the burning logs in the fireplace. In small, neat handwriting Edward has tallied and divided the thousands of letters into two columns, for and against the Pennsylvania statute, and further subdivided the "For" column into four categories—"Right to Life," "Abortion," "Disabled," "Poor"—each group worried for its own reasons about assisted suicide's devaluation of human life.

Finished with the fireplace, Edward moves to the Second Street window, blocking the gray, wintry light. From the reflection in the glass, Davenport sees that, behind his messenger's back, one hand holds the other by the wrist. "The letters in the shoebox are the ones you want to read, Justice Davenport. They're all from disabled people."

"Why did you pick those?"

"These are the folks who are really going to suffer if you let this fireman take his own life, the ones who always fall through the cracks. Nobody wants disabled people around. You know what the doctor's going to say to someone who's disabled and poor. He's going to say, 'You know, you're a burden on your family. You really want to lift that burden, don't you? How much of a life do you have anyway?' Godless nonsense like that."

"Did you make suggestions like this to Justice McWhorter?"

"Only when it was important. And—"

"And?"

"When I was certain I was right and that he was going to make a mistake."

"Did he follow your advice?"

"As often as not."

Davenport offers the shoe box back to Edward, but keeps the sheet of paper. "Thanks very much for this, Mr. Cunningham. This is good work."

"No, you keep the letters. I know the justices had their conference yesterday but maybe you'll find time to read them. A justice can always change his vote before the final decision."

How does his messenger know how he voted? Davenport remembers asking Edward to separate any personal correspondence from the bins and, when the messenger is at the door, asks him if he found any. Edward says no, and reminds the justice that the Chief wants to see him.

· · · · · · · · · · · · · · · · · · · ·

Rubbing his hands before the blazing fireplace, Bricknell has brought the cold from outdoors into his office. He may believe that casual drop-ins to other justices' offices will cultivate the collegial tone he desires for his court, but he also understands the home field advantage of holding the important meetings in his own. It has been more than a month since Davenport's confirmation and, although this is his first visit to the Chief's chambers, the new justice has competed away from home too often to be intimidated by unfamiliar surroundings.

Bricknell says, "I'm curious about your vote in the assisted suicide case." He continues to knead his hands as if trying to banish some affliction deeper than the cold. "I hope that my little … surprise at the beginning of the conference about the importance of keeping an open mind isn't why you voted to reverse."

"No," Davenport says. "I'd already decided. I thought maybe it was my vote that changed your mind."

The Chief hadn't anticipated this, and his hands fall still. "What makes you think I changed my mind?"

"When you said you would write the majority opinion, I thought that meant you were joining Herb, Madeleine, Carl, Donna, and me."

"Sign on with the five of you?" The Chief affects a laugh and, indicating the upholstered chair next to the fireplace, takes the matching chair across from it for himself. His face is flushed from the heat and there is a fragrance about him of after-shave, tobacco, and wood smoke. "Actually, I was thinking it might be reasonable to expect that you would join me, along with Alex, Gil, and Bernie, and make our own majority. You know, a conference vote isn't written in stone. A justice can change his vote right up until we announce the court's decision."

"So my messenger informs me." Davenport hadn't expected Bricknell to engage on the case so quickly.

"This case is going to be a milestone," the Chief says. "I was hoping we might get a substantial majority behind the opinion. If not all of us, then maybe seven or eight. I'm not asking anyone to be ... disloyal but, as I said, I do think we should be open-minded."

Davenport needs to slow this down, and he looks around the office for a diversion. The trophies, plaques, and photographs, along with the scattered jumble of lamps and end tables, give the place the appearance of a second-hand furniture shop. His host has no idea how much tactical advantage clutter like this cedes to a guest. Davenport waits for Bricknell's eyes to catch up with his, which have come to rest on the opposite wall where a mounted sailfish hangs, its blues, greens, and silvers as garish as neon.

"I didn't know you were a fisherman." Davenport speculates that the Chief is one of those sportsmen who, even as he reels in his catch, is already thinking of the stories he will tell to visitors.

Bricknell says, "That one? Key West. Of course I was a much younger man then. These days I stick mainly to streams. Bass. Some steelhead." With an effort, he gets up from the chair. "For sport, of course. I always throw back my catch."

Davenport rises and follows the Chief past photographs showing him with other robed figures, some of the garments as vividly colored as the sailfish—"The chief justices of all the important African and Asian countries; some from Europe too"—and then pictures of him with United States presidents and senators—"Politicians," he says dismissively. They stop at the far wall, hung with photographs of the Chief posed with his fishing companions. Arms extended, they hold in front of them the part of the day's catch they didn't throw back. Other pictures are of the Chief and some of the same men in hunting garb, rifles under their arms and feathered game scattered at their feet like trash. Each picture receives its own well-buffed anecdote, and at one, the Chief reminisce about members of the group.

"Doc Gordon, over here, is quite a character." He points to a large, bespectacled man in camouflage gear. "I would never hunt without him. Steady as a rock. Heart as big as the great outdoors, but always with impeccable judgment."

The Chief turns away from the pictures, returns to the facing chairs, and sits in one. When Davenport takes the other, Bricknell says, "You know, if I hadn't decided to go into the law, I would have chosen medicine. Physicians are God's gatekeepers, aren't they? Guarding the passage between life and death."

And so, in the Chief's clumsy way, they are back to assisted suicide, and it appears that doctors like the ones who joined Randy Clark's appeal are going to be the pivot of the proposed compromise. The negotiation has begun, and Davenport takes care to keep his tone casual. "There would have to be limits on the physician's range of discretion."

"You mean, no death panels," the Chief says. "Of course not."

"And the physician couldn't initiate the end-of-life decision. The patient would have to request it."

"That may be a problem for Alex. Gil too."

"But you would be willing to talk with them about it." Like Davenport, the Chief apparently assumes that it will be impossible to get Bernie Keane to join a decision accepting assisted suicide on any terms.

"Of course. That's what this little discussion is about, isn't it?"

"And where the patient can't afford his own personal physician?" Davenport is thinking about the lecture from Edward. "Perhaps it would be appropriate to require that a second doctor sign off on the decision, just as a safeguard."

The Chief rises, and Davenport wonders why the modest suggestion would bring their discussion to so abrupt an end, but his host gestures for him to stay where he is and walks to his desk. "Do you know what hunting requires, even more than quick reflexes and a sharp eye?" A handsome mahogany humidor sits on the corner of the desk, and Bricknell lifts the top. "Cigar?" He winks. "Cuban. Cohiba Espléndidos."

When Davenport shakes his head, the Chief extracts for himself a cigar, the length and heft of which Davenport associates with photographs of Winston Churchill. "Patience," the Chief says. "Even more than fishing, hunting requires patience." Back in his chair, he trims and lights the cigar, tossing the detritus into the fire. "A second opinion is an excellent idea. It should make our decision more acceptable to the do-gooders. But where would you draw the line?"

Davenport doesn't understand. "On the number of doctors who have to agree?"

"No, I mean on when a physician can say, yes, administer the fatal dose, and when he can't. There has to be a line."

Davenport worries that, like Keane, the Chief will want to draw the line at physical pain. He remembers the exchange at the end of the Pennsylvania attorney general's oral argument. "I would think that the line Gormley drew would do the trick. If the increased dose is exclusively to ease the patient's pain, it would be acceptable, even if the patient dies. But if the dose is principally intended to cause death, it is unacceptable."

The thick eyelids lower, and again Bricknell pulls on the cigar so that the ember glares as bright as the fire behind him. "That's a rough approximation of what I had in mind." His finger-play with the cigar communicates that he is enjoying this. "So long as the doctor makes his decision solely to alleviate pain, it would be fine with me." The Chief is generous in not reminding Davenport of his own skepticism about the distinction at the argument and his subsequent humiliation by Keane.

In the fireplace a log spits and snaps, setting off a shower of sparks. Davenport knows that in the real world of medical decisions, none of this hair-splitting will make a difference. Doctors in their daily practice don't examine and distinguish among their motives—pain or its relief; life or its end. Only lawyers do. Constitutional law professors will debate the court's line-drawing with their students for years to come, but in fact the distinction will be of consequence neither to the doctor nor to his patient. The distinction is purely cosmetic; it is all for show.

Davenport says, "Will Alex go along?"

"He's the one who suggested it to me."

"And Gil?"

"You mean will Bernie stop his protégé from joining us?" Again, left unspoken is that Keane himself will never let Randy Clark die on his own terms. "He'll certainly try, but don't underestimate Gil. He got to like being in the majority when McWhorter was the swing vote. He got spoiled. I think he'll join us. What can you do with your side—Herb? Madeleine? The others?"

Davenport sees the trap and steps around it. "You're forgetting, Chief, I don't have a side." Although the prospect doesn't trouble him, he hadn't anticipated that the Chief would ask him to recruit the liberals to the compromise and decides that a measure of deference might work to his advantage. "I thought you would talk with them."

Absently, Bricknell extends a hand to the globe that rests in a wooden cradle next to his chair and with long fingers, sends it spinning. "You know, Richard, I'm not ashamed to say that Earl Warren is one of my judicial heroes. After John Marshall, maybe my biggest hero. Not his politics, of course. Warren's social views cast a blight on American law from which we're still recovering. But his technique was impeccable and worthy of study. Have you read the Schwartz biography? You should. He tells the story of how Warren got a unanimous decision in Brown v. Board, even though the court in the 1950s was as divided on segregation as the rest of the country. By some miracle, he orchestrated it so there were no dissents. Not even a single concurring opinion. Complete unanimity. You will understand why in the present circumstances Chief Justice Warren would have asked you to cultivate the other side of the garden." Through the cloud of cigar smoke, he gives his visitor a sly look. "That is, assuming you are comfortable with that side of the garden."

"I don't know if I can get them to agree." The Chief has fought with the court's liberals for years and knows them far better than Davenport, who has only a lawyer's impressionistic sense of their judicial philosophies, and none at all of their unbreachable thresholds.

"Tell them that if they don't sign on, you're going to vote with me and my three to uphold the Pennsylvania statute, and that I'll assign Bernie to write the opinion. That should do the trick."

"I can probably get Herb. Carl too." Davenport is improvising. "I don't know about Madeleine or Donna." Another thought, one he had told himself was off-limits, stops him: Will Nyquist accept the compromise? If Keane won't accept it, why would the senator? But it is too late to turn back. "I think Herb was planning to keep the majority opinion for himself."

"That's his right, but only if I'm not in the majority." The Chief's rumbling baritone is the perfect accompaniment to the glow of the fire, a cosseting blanket against the harsh November afternoon. "If our agreement holds and I'm in the majority, I get to choose who writes the opinion."

They have come a full circle to the Chief's baffling announcement at the end of the conference that he would write the majority opinion in the case.

"So," the Chief says, hands on knees, ready to rise. "It appears that we have an agreement."

From experience, Davenport knows that it is at the end of negotiations, when his opponent believes that all has been settled, that the opportunity arises to win the greatest concessions. "I want the opinion to make clear that in measuring the pain that justifies these decisions, no line can be drawn between physical and mental pain." He owes Olivia this much.

"As long as we don't mention the distinction, it would be implicit, wouldn't it?"

"Then you should have no problem making it explicit."

"Why don't we let the clerks deal with this when they write up their draft—"

"I don't want to leave it to the clerks." No sooner does Davenport say this than he sees his tactical error. This can be left to the clerks, after all. But observing the issue's importance to Davenport, the Chief makes a demand of his own. "Why don't we wait and see how well you do in persuading Madeleine and Donna to sign on."

"Madeleine, yes. But I can't promise Donna." He can't promise Madeleine either, but he'll find a way to get her to join. "But if you want Madeleine, it can't be you who writes the opinion."

"Why would that be a problem?"

"She won't sign on to an opinion written by Alex or Gil either." Davenport hopes that, intent on creating the appearance that he knows his colleagues' inclinations, the Chief won't question whether the new justice in fact knows Madeleine's mind.

"And she wants—you want—me to assign the opinion to her?"

"No," Davenport says. "I want you to give it to me."

The Chief draws on his cigar, but it has gone out. His smile is guarded. "Alex warned me to watch out for you."

. . . .

In the courtyard opposite their adjoining chambers, Madeleine flicks the ash from a cigarette. With her free hand, she pulls her overcoat close against the cold and, when she sees Davenport returning down the corridor, gestures for him to join her. "I know it's a nasty habit, but my staff goes nuts if I smoke in chambers."

"Not to mention that it's against the law." Unless of course you're the Chief Justice of the United States smoking a Cuban cigar. Davenport remembers Madeleine's dark looks from Tuesday's argument and the discarded note. "Did I say something at the *Clark* argument you disagreed with?"

She shrugs off the question. "I wanted to talk to you, but not about *Clark*. Your secretary said you were with the Chief."

Although Herb Bauman is the most senior member of the court's liberal camp, Madeleine is the most influential, and she will be the first justice Davenport approaches with the compromise that he and the Chief have just struck. But he still needs to assess her weak points.

Madeleine says, "I hope the Chief wasn't twisting your arm on *Straubinger*."

Straubinger v. New York has been on and off Davenport's mind since the confirmation hearings. Even when he was Locke's emissary to the New York legislature, fighting passage of the Susie Briscoe Act, he knew that the statute's fate would ultimately be decided in the federal courts, and that its symbolic importance would make an appeal to the Supreme Court inevitable. "The Second Circuit decision came down?"

"Tuesday. They upheld the Act. Christine filed an emergency petition for the family."

Madeleine's protégé is making a name for herself in the culture wars. Now that Davenport knows what Madeleine wants from him, he begins calculating his leverage in getting her to join his compromise in the assisted suicide case. "What's the emergency?"

"The boy has a condition that makes the usual kind of dialysis impossible, and the kind that he's getting has a high risk of infection.

Read Christine's petition. He's going to die if he doesn't get a transplant soon."

"Why would it have to be from his brother?" Davenport knows the answer, but he wants to gauge the depth of her commitment to taking the appeal.

"I told you, read the petition. There are a hundred thousand people in the United States on the waiting list for kidney transplants. Five thousand of them die every year."

Corbett is fortunate. How many Supreme Court advocates get to have their own justice touting their cases? "Your former clerk has her work cut out for her." Davenport remembers Nyquist's graphic description of the statute as targeting people who scavenge spare body parts from the disabled as if they were wrecked cars.

Madeleine says, "We need you for our fourth."

She could be asking him to join her and two others for bridge, and not to complete the quota of justices required to accept an appeal to the court. "Who else do you have?"

"Donna and Herb."

"What about Carl?" Shell had voted with the other three to take the assisted suicide appeal, and, although transplants raises different issues, the two cases have produced the same ideological split. If Madeleine gets her fourth, *Straubinger* will quickly become the most talked about—and polarizing—case on the court's docket this term.

"Carl has a rule on emergency petitions: no emergency, no petition. Death row petitions are an emergency when the warden's a day away from throwing the switch. But the boy isn't infected yet. He's not dying." She drops the cigarette and stubs it out with her shoe.

"And Corbett's real reason for making it an emergency?" His vote to hear the appeal will not commit him to vote with Madeleine when the court ultimately decides the case, but she is going to pay for it.

"Of course I haven't talked with Christine"—Madeleine stares at him hard so that he understands her dealings with her former clerk are at arm's length—"but assisted suicide is still on the front pages, and the *Times* and *Post* editorials are saying we're heartless to let this fireman suffer while we debate whether to let him die with dignity. So it's a fair guess that Christine thinks we're more likely to decide in favor of her transplant client now than six months from now, when everything quiets down."

"She can play whatever strategy she wants. That's no reason for us to buy into it. Let her client stand in line with everyone else. When the time comes, Carl will vote to grant the appeal, and we'll decide the case in plenty of time for this fellow to get his transplant."

"Or not get it." Madeleine says. "I agree with Christine's strategy. I think we're more likely to get a good result now than later."

"I was Locke's counsel when the bill was in front of the New York legislature. I fought to stop them from overriding his veto."

"You're saying you'd recuse yourself?" She retreats into one of her eternal silences. Davenport remembers how spontaneously this happens. You are arguing an appeal before her, and she appears to be listening—like now, she may even ask you a question—and in the next instant, she shuts down. Her eyes remain on his, but her vision has switched inward; she has turned off the lights.

Finally, Madeleine says, "If I remember the transcript of your hearings, you made no representation to the committee that you would recuse yourself if this case came to the court. You simply said you would consider recusal as an option. You don't have a financial interest in the case, and you haven't expressed a legal opinion on its merits."

Davenport has read the ethical rules too. "I have to disqualify myself if my impartiality can reasonably be questioned. Some people will think my work for the governor has compromised me." Does Madeleine see that he is offering to negotiate? That he will give her the fourth signature she wants if she gives him what he wants in return? This close, Davenport is aware of the careful edge of ebony makeup she has penciled in around her dark eyes, and also of her fragrance, some elusive, doubtless very costly, scent. Who, he wonders, is she trying to seduce?

Madeleine says, "We have an obligation not to recuse ourselves. There's no one to replace us if we drop out."

"You don't know that, even if I vote with you now, I won't vote against you later when we decide the case."

"I'll take that risk. What do you want, from me?" When Davenport hesitates, she says, "This is about assisted suicide, isn't it? That's what you and the Chief were talking about. You were making a deal on *Clark*."

"We think we can put together a strong majority. Better than 5–4. Not 9–0, but probably 8–1." He describes the compromise under which the court, with Bernie Keane dissenting, will vote to strike down Pennsylvania's prohibition against assisted suicide, so long as it results from a physician's decision to ameliorate the patient's pain. Davenport doesn't add that as part of the deal, he will write the court's opinion.

Madeleine glares at him. "I couldn't possibly sign on to that! Was this the Chief's idea or yours?"

"It was Alex's, but we think it is a good basis for compromise."

Davenport cannot understand why such an inconsequential distinction as whether death is initiated by the doctor or the patient, or whether it is for the purpose of ending life or relieving pain would trouble a lawyer as smart and experienced as Madeleine.

"Did you think to ask a woman about this? Me? Donna? Your own daughter? We've struggled for a half-a-century to establish a woman's right to choose. We're still fighting to keep the religious right from stealing the gains we made. And then your little men's club has a private meeting and makes a decision that gives them everything they've been asking for."

"There's no connection between this and abortion rights."

"You're being disingenuous, Richard, or you're blind. The next time a right to choose case comes up, the Chief and Alex, Bernie and Gil are going to point to your compromise and say that the only constitutional ground on which a life—an unborn child's life—can be terminated is a doctor's decision that it's necessary to save the life of the mother. That's where the law was fifty years ago, and that's what we're going back to, thanks to you. Back to the Dark Ages."

Not only is Madeleine wrong about this; she knows it. This is an act. Madeleine is negotiating.

"What's sad, Richard, is you didn't need a compromise to make a deal. With Herb, Carl, and Donna, we already had 5–4 to reverse. Herb would have written a strong opinion."

"I'd rather have 8–1 and a narrow opinion."

"And if we don't give it to you?"

"If you and the others don't sign on, I'll join the Chief, Bernie, Alex, and Gil and affirm."

Madeleine may think he's bluffing, but she doesn't yet know him well enough—no one does—to call him on it. "It will just be 5–4 one way rather than the other. I'd still prefer to reverse 8–1."

"And if I join you—"

"And bring Donna, Carl, and Herb with you?"

"Say that I can."

"Then I'll give you your fourth in the transplant case."

The air around them loses some of its charge, and Madeleine says, "I'll have to think about this. It would help if, in addition to supporting the appeal, you agree to vote with us that the boy should get his transplant."

Let's take it one decision at a time," Davenport says.

"Like I said, I'll think about it."

．．．．．．．．．．．．．．．．．．．．

Briefs, telephone calls, and meetings fill the rest of Davenport's day, and when he walks across chambers to get Harold and Jack started on a draft of his opinion in the assisted suicide case, the lights and computers in their office are off. Anne is gone too, even Edward. He switches off the overhead lights in his own office and from the credenza, removes Bernie Keane's bottle of Jameson's, pours two fingers into one of Justice McWhorter's china cups, and takes the rocker. By the light of the single standing lamp, the pool of gold at the bottom of the tea cup could be a sun-dazzled pond, its currents lie that deep.

Davenport considers what he has gained and lost this afternoon. The compromise in the assisted suicide case will postpone a confrontation with Nyquist, but, as the transplant case moves forward, he expects another meeting with Hillis, or with the senator himself. Because he lobbied against the law when it was in the New York legislature, court watchers will predict that he will vote to strike it down when the court reaches the merits of the case. But Nyquist will know, or think that he knows, better. What did Nola tell the senator?

9

In the sliver of light between door and door frame, Nola's eyes meet Davenport's but tell him nothing. He has no plan, and he didn't call ahead because if he had, she would have left. The entry to the Columbia brownstone was unlocked, so he had walked up to the second-floor apartment and knocked. "I'll leave if you want, Nola. But I hope you'll see me."

The crack in the doorway widens, and her face disappears. Davenport says, "This won't take more than five minutes."

The security chain slides in its groove and Nola opens the door another inch. She has Olivia's pale, feverish beauty, but the blank stare that communicates nothing, she inherited from him.

"I won't bother you again. No phone calls. No messages."

She shrugs, but opens the door for him to enter.

With its high ceiling and ornamented molding, the apartment might have been a dining room in the brownstone's earlier life. Tall windows fill the room with light, and there is more than ample space for the two beds, sofa, easy chair, and two desks. Because it has the smallest pile of laundry for him to remove, Davenport takes the easy chair. "This is nice. Are you comfortable here?"

Nola's thick dark hair is pulled back in a neat pony tail. She has a delicate scent of lavender about her, and Davenport recognizes the fragrance of the bath soap that had been Olivia's favorite. "Is this really how you want to use your five minutes?" There is no trace of irony in her tone.

Nola continues to stand, forcing him to look up at her, and Davenport decides that if his daughter needs this to feel that she is in control, he will not object. If she sits, he will take that as a sign of progress.

She sees that his survey of the room has settled on an end table where a bottle of Bombay gin, her mother's brand, is two-thirds empty, and she reads his mind. "My roommate's going through a 1950s phase. She likes a martini before dinner."

The roommate with the insolent voice.

Nola says, "I don't drink." She slips a cellphone from her back pocket and checks the time.

In his fantasies of reunion, Davenport forgets that conversations with Nola have always been stiff, even stilted, and that he envied Olivia's easy rapport with their daughter. "I know you gave the coroner's transcript to Senator Nyquist."

At once her entire bearing relaxes and her relief, now that he knows, is unmistakable.

"And you want to know why."

"No, I just need to know what you said to him."

"Why would it matter? I read the transcript twice. There's nothing that connects you to how Olivia died."

"I need to know if you told Nyquist something about your mother or me. About our relationship."

Nola sets her hands on her hips, one of her mother's poses. The neatly manicured nails, the eyeliner deftly applied. His daughter has absorbed so many of Olivia's ways. "Even if I did, why would it be important?"

"I have an important decision coming up. Nyquist is trying to use the transcript and whatever you told him to get me to vote his way."

"Would you do that? Change your vote?"

"Of course not."

"Then why would it matter what I said to him?"

"I need to know how real he thinks his threats are."

"If he can't control how you vote, I don't see why he even matters."

"Can you sit down? I'm getting a crick in my neck looking up at you."

When Nola takes the edge of the bed behind her, Davenport says, "He wants my seat on the court. He would have Olivia disinterred and autopsied all over again if he thought it would force me to resign."

"That's your business, not mine."

For all of her mother's grown-up attitudes, Nola is still a twenty-year-old and Davenport considers how little she understands about life. "It will become your business very quickly if he gets the district attorney in Barnstable to reopen the inquest and subpoena you to testify to what you told him. Nyquist won't be there in person, but I can promise you he will be dictating every line of the media story of how a young woman, betrayed by her father, had to seek justice from a sympathetic senator."

"Or," Nola says, "how a spoiled heiress betrayed her father."

For the first time with his daughter, Davenport feels hope. "That's exactly my point. There's nothing I can do to control what he says, but I can try to control the damage. And I can't do that without knowing what you told him. I can't walk into this blind."

"Did you push her?" It is more a cry than a question. This is to be Nola's retaliation for confronting her over the transcript. "Did you just stand there on the deck, or did you push her over the rail?"

The coroner's inquest had asked why Davenport didn't do more to save Olivia. But to ask if he pushed her off the rail requires a daughter. And a senator bent on destroying him.

"Is that what you told Nyquist? That I killed your mother?" Davenport looks around the grand room and absorbs it like a sponge, for he believes that he may never be allowed to come here, or to see his daughter, again.

"No, I didn't say that."

"Then, what?"

"I told him what you said to Olivia in the hospital the last time she tried to kill herself. I was in the hallway outside the room, but I heard you."

Davenport had regretted the angry words the instant they were out. *The next time you try to kill yourself, do us all a favor and finish the job.*

Nola says, "You don't trust me, do you? You never have."

Nola is the only living person he knows who would understand why he did what he did. Davenport has no belief in confession's power of redemption, but if it would loosen the grip of his conscience just for a moment, that would be enough. He hasn't told Nola what happened because, having lost her mother, it would mean losing her father, too. But if he has already lost her anyway, what difference would that make?

On the ferry's heaving deck, Olivia was on the rail and Davenport's hands gripped her waist. He was screaming at her to climb down. Suddenly, Olivia thrust forward so that her face was inches from his, her hair streaming like blood. Let go of me! It was impossible to hear her in the tumult, but he had no doubt of the words. "I dare you to let me go!" In one way or another, Olivia had been saying this for as long as Davenport could remember, but this time she did not want him to resist. The strange thing was, after he released her, and her arms lifted from the railing, Olivia didn't fall. The deck rose and plunged, but somehow she remained fixed in place. She leaned in again, grabbing for him, but Davenport had already moved to the side, out of reach. Olivia was still clawing at air when Davenport placed a hand on her shoulder and—he could have been sliding an empty carton along a shelf, it was that easy—he pushed her off the rail and into the sea.

Nola says, "Did you? Push her?" It could be Olivia staring back at him, the likeness is that striking.

"No," Davenport says. "Of course not."

Nola glances at her wrist as if she is wearing a watch. "Your five minutes are up."

"Will I see you again?"

For a long moment, Nola thinks. "I'm putting the 'Sconset house on the market in the spring."

She has inherited these, too, from her father: a talent for brutality and for evading the things that matter most.

10

When Gloria comes down for breakfast, she sees that the keys for the van are missing from the hook by the door and she knows that Junior is gone. She has been expecting something since the morning when, with Junior standing right here in the kitchen, Leonard accused her of sabotaging their case. Junior's license is suspended and she doesn't know where he would go, only that, even if he doesn't hurt someone else, he is going to injure himself.

Leonard sleeps in on Sundays, and Gloria is on her second cup of coffee when he comes into the kitchen, smelling of after shave. Gloria tells him Junior's taken the van and left and, when he says he doesn't believe her, she leads him into the garage where the space next to the big Lincoln is empty except for a fresh oil stain. Leonard is looking at where cases of beer are stacked in the corner behind the Lincoln. "He took a whole case of Genny," he says. "There were four cases there."

Gloria thinks of the stupid things men do when they drink, and says, "Where's his gun?"

"You mean his rifle? Junior doesn't own a gun."

Gloria follows Leonard into the basement, and when he opens the closet door next to the work bench only his own gun is inside—whatever Leonard calls it, it's a gun—dark wood and oiled blue steel, as nasty-looking as a snake. The habit of worrying for her boys has hollowed out a space inside Gloria that no other feeling can fill; there is just terror there, all by itself. When Leonard turns, she can see that he's scared, too.

Gloria says, "I already looked in his bedroom. It's still there. He didn't take it with him." The dialysis unit is only inches bigger than their DVR. Her son would load a case of beer into the van before taking off, but not the machine that keeps him alive.

"How long can he go without it?"

Gloria stuffs down her rage at Leonard's ignorance. They may be hunting buddies, but her husband knows little about the details of his son's illness or its treatment. He's lazy like that, or maybe he just doesn't want to know. "The doctor says he needs to use it every night."

"You know what doctors are like."

"I know what Junior is like. He thinks the rules don't apply to him."

"Did you call his cell?"

"He didn't answer."

"Maybe he went hunting with his friends," Leonard says. "He's not going through a case of Genny all by himself."

"I thought hunting season was over."

"Like you said, when was the last time Junior cared about rules?" Leonard forces a smile, and Gloria senses that it's not just worry. He knows something that he's not telling her. This is why Leonard will never be a success in real estate: he doesn't have the skill to appear sincere when he's lying or holding something back. "Maybe he went to visit his brother."

"With a gun?"

"A rifle."

Gloria says, "We need to call the police."

"No police."

"If he leaves the county, it will violate his bail." The Freedom Home is in Cattaraugus County, the next county over.

Leonard says, "That's why I said no police."

"Maybe he should spend a day or two in jail and learn something about consequences."

They make a deal. For now, she won't call the police, but they have to drive over to Allentown and Day's Park, where Junior hangs out with his buddies. If he's not there, they'll go to the Home and see if Junior is visiting Denny. Gloria thinks maybe she won't fly to Washington tonight after all.

Leonard's Lincoln is seven years old, but it still smells like new from the upholstery spray he buys at AutoZone. According to Leonard, the car you drive counts for everything in the real estate business, but Gloria doesn't think the young couples he shows fix-uppers to over on the East Side would care if he rode them around on the handlebar of a bicycle. Leonard drives down the sides streets—College, Mariner, Park, Irving—and covers the full length of Allen Street, from Main to Day's Park in both directions. At Gloria's insistence, they get out of the car and look in the Tops market, but there is no sign of Junior or any of his friends that Gloria would recognize.

By now Gloria knows they are wasting their time here. Junior has gone to the Home, but not just to visit Denny like Leonard said. This is what Leonard is holding back. Junior has been thinking about this since that morning in the kitchen. He's going to take Denny from the Home and drive him out of the state. Dr. Burroughs may have told Gloria that she's the only family member who can sign Denny out, but Junior's not someone who thinks about asking permission, and the security at the Home never impressed her as being particularly attentive. No, Junior's going to storm in, take Denny and then start driving. He's probably done so already. But of course her son with the high IQ hasn't thought ahead. It's not going to be like the shows on television where you just show up at a hospital and get a transplant.

They are on Route 16 and, the way Leonard adjusts himself in his seat, Gloria thinks he's going to tell her what he's been holding back, but instead he reaches over and massages her neck at the exact place where it feels like a pinched nerve. She hadn't said anything to him, but he must have seen her discomfort from the way she's sitting. When it's just the two of them like this, Leonard can surprise her with his consideration. It's mostly when other people are around, usually men like Mike Bossio or Junior, that he has to show off what a tough guy he is.

Leonard says, "Are we still going to Washington tonight?"

"Let's wait and see what happens with Junior."

"Christine told Mike she's worried about the trial record."

Another man in love with a name. *Christine.* "I don't know what you're talking about. Do you know what you're talking about?"

Leonard says, "Mike wasn't able to get all the facts about Junior and Denny out at the trial. Christine says the Supreme Court won't hear anything that didn't come out at trial."

"Well," Gloria says, "Mike should have done a better job."

"He never thought he had your support."

"What difference would that make?" Gloria starts to turn her head, but the pain in her neck stops her. She wishes Leonard would massage the tender spot again, but she's afraid that if she asks he'll ignore her. "We paid him to win the case, not lose it."

They pass the Pik Ur Punkin lot. Last week when Gloria drove by, the pumpkins that were too small or deformed for the Halloween crowd were scattered all over the lot. The farmer has apparently tried to disk them into the ground, but the soil is frozen hard, so now it looks like a field full of broken orange crockery. Gloria says, "But she still thinks we're going to win? Christine?"

"That's what she said. The new judge makes it 5–4 in our favor."

Gloria thinks about her decision to go to Washington with Leonard and Mike to watch Christine in court tomorrow. Christine said they don't have to be at the court, but Gloria disagrees. She knows how important it will be for the judges to see that Junior has a family behind him, supporting him. But what if, after Junior takes Denny from the Home, Denny has one of his acting-out episodes in the van? Junior won't know what to do. He'll probably crash the van and kill them both.

There are other cars in the Home's parking lot, but no van. A dozen or so cows, all with identical ink-blot markings, graze the frozen ground on the other side of the split rails. Maybe it's the familiar sight of the cows, but something settles inside Gloria.

Leonard says, "If Junior's not here, why don't you sign Denny out for a couple of hours, and we can take him into Arcade to see the Christmas lights." The suggestion startles Gloria, because Leonard will usually do anything to avoid spending time with Denny.

The guard at the front desk tells Gloria he hasn't seen Junior since she was here with him last week. His smile disappears when she tells him she wants to take Denny into Arcade for a couple of hours. "I'm sorry but you can't do that."

The guard could have punched her, the way the air goes right out of her. No one has ever stopped her from taking Denny out for an adventure. "I don't understand." Junior has been here and gone, she thinks, and the guard is covering up. Or something bad has happened to Denny.

"You need to talk to Dr. Burroughs."

Gloria presses the elevator button and when the doors don't immediately open, flies up the stairs to the director's office. Unable to remain still, she paces the small reception area until Dr. Burroughs comes out.

"Gloria! I wasn't expecting you. You usually call." She waits for Gloria to follow her into the office so she can close the door.

"What's wrong with Denny?"

But Dr. Burroughs will not be hurried, and Gloria has to take the chair facing her and decline a glass of water before the superintendent says, "Denny is perfectly fine."

Gloria doesn't believe her. Loyalty to her family stops her from confessing her worry that Junior has taken his brother, so she says, "Where is he?"

"Why, in his regular workroom, I would suppose." Dr. Burroughs aims the television remote control on her desk at the screen above the door and pushes buttons until the room Gloria visited last week comes on. Denny is at his table with what looks like the same tower, only taller.

"Then why did the guard say I can't take him into town? Denny loves the Christmas lights."

"Didn't you get the order? I was sure you already knew. We received a court order Friday that Denny can't be removed from the Home until after your case is over. I thought your lawyer would tell you."

Outside, over the superintendent's shoulder, a tiny gray-brown bird alights on the sill and looks in. Gloria asks herself why, when it could so easily fly south, the bird would remain here, exposed to the harsh reality of winter in western New York. Because it can, she concludes, and in the overheated room, the thought sends a shiver through her. How foolish she has been! Denny is not going to speak, and even if he does, it won't be to say more than one or two words. Denny is not going to tell her that he is willing to subject himself to an operation to give a kidney to his brother. And if she is to be of use to her family, she must accept the reality of the situation. Reality is not just that Denny won't speak, but that he will never light up when he sees her, the way he does with Junior. Reality is that, without a transplant, Junior is going to die.

"When I was here last week, you told me I could take Denny out whenever I wanted."

"I just told you, we didn't get the order until Friday. It's because of your Supreme Court appeal. I'm sure they sent a copy to your lawyer. My secretary has it if you want to see it."

Dr. Ice. The superintendent's perfect face seems a hideous mask. "I don't want to see the order. I want to take Denny as far away from here as I can. Now."

"I expect that's why they issued the order. To stop you. I'm sure you will be able to take Denny as soon as the Supreme Court says you can have the transplant."

"What if they say we can't?"

"I'm sorry, Gloria, but Denny is my patient, not Junior. The court order is to protect him."

"Denny won't ever be able to leave."

"You have to ask your lawyer about that."

"We're going to Washington tonight. Our lawyer is arguing our case tomorrow morning." Gloria feels dumb saying this, for it changes nothing.

"Well that's perfect, then. You'll have your answer very soon."

Gloria says, "You have to make this right."

"Well really, Gloria, I know you're upset, but—"

"No," Gloria says, "I want you to put a tree and Christmas lights in Denny's bedroom. The lights have to be colored and flash on and off."

"I don't know if the regulations allow lights like that in patient rooms. But we can try to find a small tree. Denny can put on paper decorations if he likes."

"Not a small tree, a big one. If you don't, I'm going to call Channel 7 and tell them how you run this place."

"A big tree, then."

· · · · · · · · · · · · · · · · · · ·

In the Lincoln, Gloria snaps the seat belt into the buckle. "We have to win tomorrow."

"Well, hallelujah!" Leonard starts up the engine. "Welcome to the team."

"It's the only way we can get Denny out of here." Gloria tells Leonard what Dr. Burroughs said about the court order.

"I warned you about that bitch," he says.

"It's not her," Gloria says, even though she blames the superintendent. "It's the court. Mike should have told us they would do that."

This throws Leonard into one of his funks, and Gloria shifts in her seat so she can look out the side window.

Leonard keeps his eyes hard on the blacktop. "I think Junior took the van to Washington."

"What do you mean 'think'? Did he call when I was inside?"

"He told me last night. You know how Junior talks. You never know if he's kidding."

So this is what Leonard has been holding back. "If he wanted to go to the court, he could have come down on the plane with us."

"He didn't say anything about going to court."

"Then why would he go to Washington?"

"He's going to talk with the judge. The new one. He wants to explain the situation to him."

Gloria has only just started to get comfortable with the idea of the transplant, and now Junior, stinking of beer and waving a gun, is going to ruin it. "We have to stop him before he gets there."

"Come on, Gloria. How is he even going to find this guy?"

"On the Internet. Junior can find anything on the Internet. Anyone can. We have to call the police and stop him."

"And say what? That our nineteen-year-old son is on his way to Washington, driving on a suspended license to talk to a Supreme Court judge? Oh, and by the way, he's drunk and he's carrying a rifle and ammunition."

Gloria isn't thinking about the gun or the beer. Or the judge. She is thinking Junior needs to get to a hospital soon. She says, "Do you know if he got rid of that shirt of his?"

11

"Sunday is for family, wouldn't you agree, Richard?" When Keane shows Davenport into his home, the double doorway diminishes the slight figure. "As I recall, you still have family. A daughter, I believe."

Still, Davenport thinks. "In New York. She's a student at Columbia."

Keane leads his guest from the front hall through the dining room. The table is set and the flower arrangement Davenport ordered is the centerpiece, its mild perfume mixing with old-house smells of ancient wallpaper and stale trapped air. Kitchen noises come from the other side of a swinging door. "My oldest, Beth, is visiting from Seattle." Keane stops for a moment, as if he is trying to remember something, and tilts his head in the direction of a room behind them. "Husband trouble, I suppose. My youngest is coming, but late if he's true to form. Kevin. With his girlfriend." He pushes the swinging door open an inch or two and the fragrance of roasting meat escapes. "Mary! Our guest is here."

Since Davenport's phone call with the president, he has heard nothing of Keane's lymphoma, and the justice's vigor and good color this afternoon give no sign of illness. The door swings open and Mary Keane comes into the dining room. Davenport met her once before, at the party Madeleine gave to welcome him to the court. She is easily twenty years younger than her husband and, if she stood erect, would be an imposing figure, large-framed and almost a head taller than him. Her posture sags though, and the way she clasps her hands in front of her, drawing her shoulders inward, gives the impression of someone trying to disappear. Still, she is a handsome woman. Her smile is warm and amusement plays in the lovely eyes.

"Thank you for the beautiful flowers, Justice Davenport." She nods past him toward the arrangement. "They are just what the room needs." At Madeleine's party, she had seemed diffident, but here in her own house, Mary Keane's voice is decisive, even resonant. "Now if you and the Justice will excuse me, I'll just finish up with dinner."

Keane leads Davenport back through the front hall into a living room dense with dark surfaces, tufted leather and an abundance of drapery, all the while offering a well-practiced history of the house, which rambles over more than an acre and is a jumble of rooms—"The boys had to share bedrooms before Beth went off to college"—added over the centuries to a cottage built in the eighteenth century. "We moved here when I came on the court. By then, all the construction was finished. Here's the parlor."

Olivia would have dismissed "parlor" as lace-curtain Irish and called the windowed rectangle a sunroom. The furniture is oversized, mostly white-painted wicker with brightly colored pillows, and Davenport imagines that this is the one public room where Mary Keane had her way. Keane's daughter, Beth, puts down her wine glass and rises from a cushioned chair to greet them. She is an attractive woman with an open, friendly face and, though built like her mother, her back is straighter, her shoulders level, the result, perhaps, of her relative youth, or of living a continent away from her father.

"If you'd like a cocktail, Richard, I'm sure Beth can get you one, but there will be wine with dinner, to which"—he turns to his daughter—"we shall sit down precisely at 2:00, whether your brother arrives on time or not."

Davenport declines a drink and asks Beth about life in Seattle where he spent five weeks in trial several years ago. The conversation is easy, except for interruptions from Keane, his voice dampened from the harsh chainsaw of the courtroom, but still insistent, even petulant. "I can't understand how an American city can be so obsessed with coffee. A beverage, for heaven's sake!" And a few minutes later, "I don't know how you stand all that rain. Why you choose to live there and not here, I'll never understand."

"It's where my family is, Dad. John's work."

"That's not much of a reason."

Through the small-paned windows that make up three of the room's walls, the trees are bare and the brown grass is frostbitten. Davenport admires the frugal elegance of the grounds. While Beth twists her wedding band and talks about day care, Keane hums with impatience, and finally interrupts her mid-sentence. "It's five to two. We should join your mother in the dining room."

Davenport's days in Washington begin before six and rarely end before midnight and, despite the exhilaration of a new job, fatigue now tracks his every step. On the way into the dining room, dizziness overtakes him and he stumbles. Pale colors swirl, a bitter taste touches his tongue, and he senses that he is about to black out. His reflexes are intact, though, and he grabs the back of a chair for support. After a moment, he straightens and as his head clears, continues walking. All of this must have happened in an instant, for neither Keane nor Beth, who are walking ahead of him, appears to have noticed.

Not since Davenport was a first-year law firm associate has the burden of work so consumed him. This is why, other than his required presence at Madeleine's welcome party, he has declined all invitations but Keane's. He has no illusion that the camaraderie of a Sunday dinner will win Keane over to his side, but he does have business to transact here. He completed his opinion for the assisted suicide case two weeks ago and, after suggesting some small changes, the other seven justices accepted it as the opinion of the court. Keane, however, has yet to distribute his dissenting opinion and, until he does, the Chief cannot release the court's decision and free Randy Clark from his impossible existence.

Salad is already plated, and wine fills the goblets at five places, though not Keane's, where there is water instead. A roast leg of lamb, beautifully browned and fragrant with rosemary is on a platter at the head of the table. Mary Keane is a careful and knowledgeable cook. The serving dishes, which look like heirlooms, are heaped with oven-crisped potatoes and green beans frenched and tossed with slivered almonds.

When he was in the room earlier, Davenport hadn't noticed the sideboard against the far wall. Black, ugly, and obdurate, with hammered metal plating at the corners, it is a massive piece, completely out of scale with the other furniture in the house, and he imagines it as the trophy of a contest of wills between husband and wife. Davenport's parents had such a contested object in their living room—not a sideboard, but a coffee table, a free form glass surface resting atop a sprawling maple abstraction of driftwood with easy, asymmetrical curves. It was the only piece of its kind in a house otherwise decorated with staid, traditional furniture, and in Davenport's mind, it came to embody the impermeable core of the silence that divided his parents, the emblem of one's triumph and the other's never-forgiven defeat.

Keane indicates his guest's chair, next to Mary, but makes no comment on the two empty chairs, and when he sits, it is a signal for the others to do so. He takes a sip of water. "My doctors have denied me alcohol. They say it interferes with my medication." The teacups of Irish whiskey are apparently to be his secret with Davenport. Quiet falls over the table and casually, almost as an afterthought it seems, Keane offers grace. "Bless us, O Lord, and these Thy gifts which we are about to receive from Thy bounty, through Christ our Lord. Amen." Davenport doesn't know why, but he expected something more from the lawyer who spent his career putting out fires for the Catholic Church.

Mary says, "The Justice always likes a roast on Sundays," and Davenport wonders what she calls Keane in private. "Bernie" seems too familiar for the old world formality he detects between them.

Salad is finished and Keane is carving the roast when a cold draft of air sweeps in from the front hall.

"Ah, the prodigal son returns to the father's feast." Keane's manner is light, but the same edge as when he questioned Beth about living in Seattle coarsens his tone. "Kevin is a second-year law student at Georgetown. The first of my sons who thinks he can compete in the same arena as his father." No one objects that the observation implicitly excludes Keane's daughters from the field.

"I'm sorry," Kevin says. "I slept late and then I had to go into Maryland to pick up Natalie." Unlike his father's oak grip, the son's hand is soft, fleshy. Kevin is easily Davenport's height, but thicker and broader, and it occurs to Davenport that, if they stood up straight, Keane's children, like his wife, would tower over him. Davenport once had a client, a Norwegian banker, who was easily 6'7". Standing next to him had the effect on Davenport that he supposes Keane's family has on him: he felt diminished.

To Kevin's girlfriend Keane says, "And don't you go making excuses for him, Natalie. My son hasn't got you pregnant, I hope? I read a piece in the *Post* that half the unwed mothers today are under thirty. Lots of them college-educated girls, like you."

Natalie smiles the question away. She is no more than twenty, pretty and with the same fair complexion as Mary Keane's and eyes almost as fine. She hasn't yet lost all her baby fat, and is the only person in the room who isn't taller than the Justice.

"Natalie's half Irish, half Italian," Keane says to his guest. "It's your mother who's Irish, isn't it?" He doesn't wait for an answer. "A dangerous combination. Too much for my son, anyway." Keane doesn't let the patter interrupt his carving, although Mary and Beth exchange glances. Kevin's arrival may have tautened the bow, but Davenport suspects that it was strung long ago.

"I hope Kevin's not telling you he has too much work to take you to a movie. I don't know what it's like for undergraduates, but from what I hear about the law school, Kevin's professors aren't overtaxing their students. Not like when I was working my way through B.C."

"The only reason you weren't overworked is that you didn't have to fight your way through the constitutional law opinions of Justice Bernard Keane." Kevin's voice is tight, uneven, and his smile when he looks around the table for approval is over-wide.

"I'm sure Kevin is doing just fine," Mary says. Tension strains her voice too.

Keane looks mildly astonished that he has sliced half the roast, and he sets down the knife. "And what pearls of wisdom does your constitutional law professor offer about our current docket?"

The attitude around the table has changed. Before Kevin's arrival, the conversation had been animated—everyone with an opinion on the relative merits of private and public schools for Beth's ten-year-old son. But now it has turned into a performance with Keane at the center. Mary Keane looks apprehensive, and she sits more erect than before. Beth resumes twisting her wedding band. Kevin glances at Natalie and, from the position of his arm, Davenport guesses that she has taken his hand.

Kevin says, "Professor Weintraub? According to her—"

"Ah, yes," Keane says, "Weintraub." There is amazement in his voice at how it has come to pass that a woman named Weintraub should be teaching constitutional law at America's oldest Jesuit university.

"She thinks that Justice Davenport"—he nods across the table politely—"is the wild card. She says everyone's waiting to see what questions he asks tomorrow in the transplant case." Keane winks at Davenport so that the others can see. "And how does Professor Weintraub think Justice Davenport should vote? Or is she going to leave that up to him?"

The duel is one-sided and is to be exclusively between father and son. Davenport sees where it is going and has no wish to be pulled in, but he is interested to see where Keane marks the line between family and the justices' strictures of confidentiality.

Kevin says, "He should vote to strike down the New York law and let the parents decide whether to go through with the transplant."

"On what ground?"

"On the ground that the statute violates family dignity and autonomy."

"I'm sure your professor couldn't have said that."

"How would you even—"

Keane says, "I want to know on what *constitutional* grounds your *constitutional law* professor would have Justice Davenport overturn the statute." The smile is mocking, but it is impossible for Davenport to gauge from the reactions around the table how much of this is joking and how much is malice.

Davenport wants to warn Kevin away from this, just as Madeleine and Harold warned him, for surely experience has taught the youth not to engage his father on the slippery terrain of doctrine. Kevin avoids his glance. "You want government to stay out of people's affairs, except when it doesn't fit your own warped morality. Then you're happy to let some bureaucrat tell a family they can't get a transplant to save their son's life."

This is not a lawyer's argument. Davenport can think of no light remark to derail it, and to engage the conflict on its own terms would only deepen the struggle between father and son. From the fact that neither mother nor sister has taken Kevin's part, Davenport gathers that this is a family ritual, as solid and unmovable as the hideous black sideboard.

"Let's examine your premise," Keane says. "Say that, God forbid, your sister needs an immediate transplant and you're the only match available—"

Kevin looks over at Beth. "I'd give it to her, without question."

"But let's say, like the poor boy in this case tomorrow, you are incapable of giving consent. Who should decide in that case? An impartial state official following guidelines set down by a committee of thoughtful medical and religious people? Or your parents? Remember, there's going to be a risk to your life—not only from the transplant operation, but also if you later need that kidney yourself. The same disease that Beth has may some day affect you."

"I'd want you and Mom to decide," Kevin says, and then, as an aside, "except maybe not you."

Keane hears the remark, but plunges past it. "You would do so even if your parents weighed against you and your health the fact that Beth has a husband and three children, and that you are single, with no family that is depending on you?"

Beth's smile is tricky, an older sister's. "Suppose they just like me more than they like you?"

Kevin ignores the remark. "I'd still take the family over the state."

"Because?"

"Because," Kevin says, "I could be confident that you cared about us. A government employee wouldn't care."

"That's precisely my point," Keane says. "Love, caring, and affection are fine if they're divisible and if you are their beneficiary. But an organ is not divisible, and let's say you're not the object of affection. Really, Kevin, love and affection are the last things you want in a situation like this. You want a dispassionate appraisal of costs and benefits."

Keane could be on the bench or in the justices' conference room, centering all attention on himself, with the striking difference that his passion today—blood courses through it—makes those others seem a gaudy performance.

"Weighing costs and benefits is heartless," Kevin says.

"Which is the very reason it's right." A rosebud smile purses Keane's delicate features. He says to Natalie, "I can't imagine what a girl as smart and pretty as you sees in someone as ignorant as my son."

Natalie releases her lower lip from under her teeth, where it had been since the start of Keane's cross-examination. "I think he's pretty smart," she says, and looks to Mary and Beth for approval, but their eyes are on their plates, as they have been for minutes now.

Keane's hand rests on the carving knife. "Your head's in the clouds, boy. Do you ever talk to real people? Talk to Harold Williams who clerked for me last year. He'll tell you what the world is like. Talk to Edward Cunningham, Justice Davenport's messenger. He has more common sense in his little finger than you have in your whole body."

Kevin is flushed and out of breath. No wonder he was late to dinner. What finally brought him here, Davenport suspects, was not love or appetite, but the dream that, just once, he might win.

"I never thought I'd come to regret using my influence to get you into Georgetown," Keane says. "Agree to let them use my name on their Board of Visitors. Help them with their fundraising."

The confusion in Kevin's eyes tells Davenport that the boy didn't know this. This is new territory for father and son.

"You don't really think you got into Georgetown on your own merits, do you? Did Kevin tell you that, Natalie? Just ask any of his classmates what their law boards were. Their undergraduate averages. Kevin didn't even come close."

"You're, you're—" Breathlessness strangles the boy's voice. What Davenport has missed in the combat so far is the battering's full impact on Kevin, and only at his father's last remark does he see the tears welling in the boy's eyes, the shiver in his jaw. "You're a heartless old man. Go ahead and die, for all I care."

"Don't you ever talk to me like that!" Keane's has risen, and now his face too is red, and his hand actually grasps the handle of the carving knife. "You think you're bigger than your father? Well I don't think so. I can always cut you down to size."

Davenport looks at Mary Keane. What mother in these circumstances would not come to her son's defense? If he wants to measure the toll that Keane's selfishness has exacted from his family, it would not be in Kevin's tears, but in Mary's silence.

Kevin starts to speak, but cannot continue. With hands that have become fists, he pushes himself clear of the table and, sobbing, flees the room.

Even in his anger, Keane is alert to the emotions at the table, and when Natalie moves her chair back he says, "Leave him be," and to Davenport, "Kevin's the most emotional of my boys. He gets upset too easily. But I promise you, he'll get over it." He returns to Natalie. "Now, tell me what you're doing in school, what courses you're taking. Who your favorite teachers are."

Gradually and unevenly, conversation resumes. They learn about Natalie's courses—she is a junior at Georgetown and plans to be a school teacher—and return to the question of public or private school for Beth's son. Mary Keane offers her views and skillfully moves the conversation along, so that, against Davenport's reservations, he joins in too. Second helpings of lamb, potatoes, and vegetables are passed, and a warm Indian pudding capped with a scoop of vanilla ice cream is served for dessert. Above the eating and the friendly chatter, Bernie Keane presides, once again McLean, Virginia's favorite and most endearing paterfamilias.

After dessert, just the two of them in the parlor with their coffee, Davenport studies Keane for a sign of humanity, even if only of his mortality. The old justice has taken a chair next to the windowed wall and the afternoon's dying light rakes the small, fine features. The battle with Kevin has depleted him, or maybe it is just the hour, but he seems fragile, and the papery skin creates an illusion of translucence; Davenport imagines that he can see the fine bones at work beneath it. Keane cocks his head as if preparing to spar. "You think I should pick on someone my own size." If the diminutive justice intends irony, he gives no indication.

"How you talk to your son is none of my business."

"But you are here for a reason. I understand you've turned down all the other justices' invitations to dinner."

"My opinion in the assisted suicide case has been ready for release since before Thanksgiving."

Keane's coffee cup rattles in its saucer, and he sets it down. His mouth forms the same grim fighter's smile as when he was pummeling Kevin at dinner. "I'm sure you know that it is the privilege of each justice to take as much time as he thinks necessary to come to a decision and, if he wants to file separately, to prepare his opinion for publication."

"The court can't hand down its decision until every opinion is ready to be released. You're making it impossible for an eight-member majority to announce its vote."

"That's my right, just as it will be yours when the time comes."

The cruelty of the man's self-regard staggers Davenport. "And you will use a court rule to keep this fireman alive even though every other justice on the court would let him choose to die."

"Perhaps you have failed to consider the most obvious explanation for my delay. That I haven't yet decided how I'm going to vote."

Davenport doesn't believe him. "Your little speech at the conference sounded conclusive to me."

"At the time, I didn't have your compromise in front of me. That's an interesting idea, letting the doctor decide if the treatment is to alleviate pain or cause death. As I recall, you didn't think much of it at oral argument. But now that you've reconsidered, maybe I should too."

"I didn't think your position left any room for compromise."

"People greatly exaggerate the influence of ideology on the justices' votes." Keane leans forward, hands on knees. "How comfortable are you with your own motives for wanting to allow assisted suicide?"

Once again, the gray transcript. The Cardinal's emissary, scuttling up and down the New England coast collecting rumors to feed to Nyquist.

Keane says, "It would surprise you, but secrets can be more consequential than ideology in influencing our colleagues' votes. Did you know that Carl Shell has an out-of-wedlock daughter from the time he spent in the service in Munich? That Gil Park fantasizes that his life is a motion picture in which he is not only the leading man, but the director? Every justice has at least one secret. Your friend Madeleine has several. It's surprising how much you can learn just by listening, particularly after a tumbler of whiskey or two."

Or a teacup, Davenport thinks. He hears and instantly rejects the implicit invitation to disclose his own secret. "And you? Your secret?"

"That's why you came to dinner, isn't it? To poke and prod for secrets."

"Isn't that why you invited me? To find out mine?"

"Before, in the dining room, what was the real reason you didn't come to Kevin's rescue?"

"I told you. I don't think it's my place to meddle in family matters."

"And that's why on the ferry, you didn't rescue your wife?"

The question is so offhand, and the golden late afternoon light so enchanting, that Davenport fails for a moment to take in its ferocity.

"I'm sorry. That was a terribly rude thing for me to ask." The charming leprechaun winks at him. "Do you know how you're going to vote in tomorrow's case?"

"I haven't finished reading the briefs or Harold's bench memo."

"Well, you may find that it's a harder case than Kevin's knee-jerk law professor thinks it is. Harder than some of our colleagues will find it too. And it's an emergency appeal, so the Chief's going to want a quick vote."

"Why would I find it harder than others?"

"Because you care about facts."

"What's special about the *Straubinger* facts?"

"What's special is that there are so few of them. It's the thinnest record I've seen in years. The family's lawyer deserves to be disbarred." Keane rises to indicate the conversation is over and takes Davenport's elbow to lead him out of the room. "Tomorrow's argument is going to be quite a spectacle."

Mary Keane joins them at the door. Keane says, "We enjoyed the opportunity to get to know you better. Please give our regards to your daughter. I am sure she will be very proud of her father."

Davenport weighs if the remark is cruel or merely negligent. If Keane had watched the confirmation hearings, he surely would have seen that the family chair was empty. He glances at Mary and, only after he says to her husband, "Just as I am sure Kevin is proud of you," does he realize that Keane said Nola will be proud, not that she already is.

12

Even before Davenport left chambers on Friday, the line for *Straubinger v. New York* had begun to form outside the court building. When he returned this morning, Jack, who worked through the weekend, told him that newcomers continued arriving on Saturday and Sunday, many with backpacks and sleeping bags. The signs pitched like tent poles around the encampment leave no doubt as to what these people shaking sleep and cold from their bones believe. THE BODY IS SACRED. PEOPLE ARE NOT SPARE PARTS. This is Oren Nyquist's clan. Seats in the courtroom's public section will accommodate only a small number, but this is not why these people are here. Like bees at a hive, they surround the television news crews on the sidewalk in front of the court and make themselves as much a part of the story as the Straubinger twins.

Precisely at 10:00 a.m., the Chief calls the morning's single case. "Number 15-1160. *Straubinger v. New York*. Ms. Corbett?"

For today's argument, the Supreme Court lawyer has arranged an elegant emerald-green scarf around her shoulders, and her posture as she positions herself at the lectern is regal. She says, "I have reserved five minutes for rebuttal, Mr. Chief Justice."

It is unusual for an advocate to announce her intentions for rebuttal in advance, and Corbett hadn't set aside rebuttal time when she argued the assisted suicide case. Davenport speculates on what ambush she anticipates from her adversary or from one of the justices that she would do so now, and on what signal she is attempting to send to them. If Bernie Keane debates pending cases with his son, what conversations does Madeleine's former clerk have with her mentor?

"The case for petitioners, Mr. and Mrs. Leonard Straubinger, is simple and straightforward. They want the State of New York to let them raise their twin boys in the same loving and supportive manner as they have for the past two decades. Nothing that the Straubingers propose to do will injure either of the boys, or anyone in the community, or indeed anyone in the entire State of New York. They want you to declare New York's Susie Briscoe Act unconstitutional so that they can arrange for the transplant of a kidney from one son to the other and so that they can go about the care of their two boys in the manner they consider best."

The Straubingers' case is of course neither simple nor straightforward, for every judge who has heard the case so far—the trial judge and the three appellate judges on the Second Circuit—has ruled against them. But the Supreme Court rarely pays much deference to lower courts in constitutional cases and, tactically, Corbett is right to start afresh.

"What does the US Constitution have to say about this, counselor?" Bauman's question is a softball, embarrassing in its innocence, and Davenport wonders if the senior justice is capable of more.

"The family's decision, Justice Bauman, is perfectly aligned with constitutional decisions of this court going back almost a century and holding that parents have a constitutional right to raise their children as they see fit. This court has reaffirmed that principle, that it is the parents, not the state, that have primary responsibility for directing the care of children, in virtually every decade since."

Keane's racketing chain saw starts up abruptly, without cough or sputter. "I understand the constitutional principle, counselor, but how do we know that these particular parents, the Straubingers, are in fact acting in the best interest of these particular children? What evidence is there of that in the record?"

"Well, Justice Keane, there is a well-established presumption that parents will act in the best interests of their child—"

"Leaving aside whether there is such a presumption, or whether it is well-established, or whether it has anything to do with the United States Constitution, what evidence is there in the record that it applies to this case?" Keane cocks his head so that the corner of an eye catches Davenport.

Before Corbett can answer, Madeleine says, "I think Justice Keane is asking if there is any testimony in the record from a qualified physician that this decision of the parents was in fact in the best interests of both boys."

Madeleine knows there is no physician testimony on this in the trial record. But why would she want to magnify this flaw in Corbett's case?

"There is expert testimony in the record, Justice Cardona, that a patient's best chance to benefit from a transplant is from a living relative. Apart from a lower chance of rejection—the very first kidney transplant, in 1954, was from one identical twin to another—patients tend to get sicker over time. In Leonard, Jr.'s case, because of the nature of the dialysis he is required to use, that risk is a clear and present danger. For him, even the waiting list is no solution."

"You haven't answered Justice Cardona's question." It is Palfrey, hawk-like, leaning over the bench. Today's bowtie of yellow and red paisley perches like a butterfly above the collar of his robe. "Is there in the record even one medical opinion that this transplant is in the best interest of the two children, both the sick boy, and his brother?"

"There is a 1969 Kentucky decision, Justice Palfrey, that allowed a mother to arrange for a kidney to be removed from one son, Jerry, who was incompetent and institutionalized, for transplantation in her other son, Tommy, who was dying of kidney disease. The trial court found that the operation would be beneficial not only to Tommy, but to Jerry as well, because Jerry depended greatly upon Tommy, emotionally and psychologically, so that Jerry's loss of his brother would more severely jeopardize his well-being than the removal of a kidney."

"I was asking about evidence from the record in this case, counselor, not some other case." Palfrey's exasperation is for show. He knows, as do the other justices, that Corbett is attempting sleight of hand, using the record of a 1969 Kentucky case to make up for the absence from the present record of testimony from psychiatrists and psychologists to prove the mutual dependence of the Straubinger twins.

"Yes, Justice Palfrey, but—"

"Presumably," Madeleine says, "the Straubingers consulted with physicians and other professionals at the time they tried to arrange this transplant procedure."

"Yes, Justice Cardona, I am confident they did."

Corbett appears puzzled by Madeleine's persistence on the subject of doctors, but Davenport now sees what his colleague is doing. What Madeleine knows, but Corbett does not, is that the court has already decided in the assisted suicide case that families can make life and death decisions only if a physician is involved. Had the court released its assisted suicide decision before Corbett took the appeal in the present case, she could have asked that the case be sent back to the trial court so that the record could be supplemented by testimony addressed to the court's newly announced rule. But because Keane hasn't yet filed his dissent, Corbett doesn't know. This is why Keane has delayed filing his opinion in *Clark*, and not, as Davenport thought, solely to prolong the fireman's agony. As soon as Keane filed his opinion, the court clerk would release the decision, and Corbett would learn of the court's new requirement in life-and-death cases.

Cippolone says, "Which child's welfare are we to consider, Ms. Corbett, the one with the kidney, or the one who needs it?"

Corbett turns away from the bench and toward the packed court room, and for a moment Davenport believes she will do the unthinkable and address the crowd. But she does something even more extraordinary. With an outstretched hand, she gestures to a woman and man on the far aisle. The two nod in acknowledgment. The woman is middle-aged, angular, and quick-eyed, and Davenport imagines that, at home in her kitchen, curlers and a mug of morning coffee would complete the portrait. The man, who sits close enough to suggest that they are husband and wife, is lumpish and dull-looking. The Straubingers. This is a stagey move, the kind of drama a flamboyant lawyer might indulge at trial. Few lawyers would dare to do this on appeal, and certainly not in the Supreme Court. Without a trial record to lean on, Corbett is doing her best to put a human face on her cause.

Corbett turns back to the bench. "In this case, Justice Cippolone, we are talking about Denny Straubinger, the child who wants to donate a kidney to his brother. His parents"—she raises her open hand and, without turning, gestures behind her in the direction of the couple— "the two people who best know their son and his desires, have made a judgment that Denny will benefit, not suffer, from his twin brother's survival."

While Corbett speaks, Davenport studies the Straubingers. He guesses that the bulky man whispering to the husband is their feckless trial lawyer, but where is the sick son? Surely Corbett would want to include the suffering victim in her dramatic tableau. Unless there was something in the youth's appearance that would put the justices off. Or unless the boy himself had decided to have no part of this. Davenport thinks, Our faithless children!

Davenport looks for his adversary, but neither Nyquist nor his aide is in the packed courtroom today. Could the senator's information be so good that he knew the Straubingers would be here? It is one thing to make an appearance when your opponents are Supreme Court justices and safely distant on the bench, quite another when they are a suffering family and you are sitting in their midst.

Corbett knows that her time is running out, but the boldness of her performance has given her command of the courtroom and she challenges anyone to interrupt her. "What stronger record could there be of the care and pain that went into this parental decision than the unwavering commitment of these two parents, both working people, through all of the unimaginable stress of the trial and appeals in this case, to do the best for their two sons? Of course there is some risk of harm to Denny. Obviously his parents understand that. And, even if Denny is incapable of understanding this completely, they are nonetheless satisfied that any possible risk of harm to him is more than outweighed by the benefit of having his brother alive and at his side."

"But does one brother have a duty to save another?"

"Do you mean a legal duty, Justice Keane?"

"Legal. Moral. It's really the same, or should be."

"Well, there's the biblical injunction about being your brother's keeper."

"The Book of Genesis said only that Cain shouldn't have killed Abel, not that he had a duty to donate an organ to him."

And that's why, on the ferry, you didn't rescue your wife? Where is Keane going with this? Davenport glances down the bench, but Madeleine offers no sign of warning. On the lectern, the white, five-minute warning light flashes on. Davenport leans into his microphone and is about to speak when the Chief says, "Thank you, Ms. Corbett. If you are saving five minutes for rebuttal, your time is up. Mr. Winick?"

The room sighs, as if everyone has been holding their breath for Corbett's answer to Keane's question. Although Davenport blames Keane for holding back the court's release of its assisted suicide decision, and thus blinding Corbett to the legal rule that will in fact govern her case, he accepts that the fault also lies with him, for if he had voted with Madeleine and the other three, and not struck his compromise with the Chief, there would have been no new legal rule to hijack her case.

In engaging Neil Winick to brief and argue New York's case, the state's attorney general has avoided the mistake that the Pennsylvania attorney general made in appointing himself to argue the assisted suicide case. Though he may lack Christine Corbett's magnetism, Winick has a reputation for thorough preparation. Still, he is not without surprises, and a gasp erupts from the public section when the lawyer rises from his chair and lurches forward, thrusting himself head-first in the direction of the lectern.

A childhood disease has so twisted Winick's slender frame that the impression as he stands before the bench is that some invisible bully has thrust a knee into his lower spine while wrenching an arm upwards behind his back. The anguish that fills his narrow features—this could be a face from Rodin's Gates of Hell—makes it all the more astonishing that the lawyer's words, when he speaks, are as even and well-shaped as an actor's would be. "Mr. Chief Justice, and may it please the court. Counsel for petitioners would have you believe that the dispute before this court is between her clients on the one side and the State of New York on the other; between caring parents and a government that would meddle in their affairs."

Winick pauses, not to catch his breath, but to create an effect. "However, there is a third party in this case, indeed the most important party, yet one whom counsel for petitioners would have this court ignore: Denny Straubinger, just as surely a viable, feeling human being as anyone in this courtroom, even if deprived by autism spectrum disorder of the ability to decide for himself, or at least to express for himself, whether to subject his body to the hazards of surgery in order to give up an organ to his brother."

When Tony Locke was New York governor and Davenport was his counsel, Davenport regularly fought turf battles with New York's attorney general, Eric Klosterman, each trying to preserve and expand the prerogatives of their respective offices. One such battle involved the Susie Briscoe Act itself, when Davenport took the administration's lead in the legislative battle and Klosterman tried to usurp it for himself. At the time, Davenport thought that Klosterman secretly favored the law, which is why he didn't trust him to lobby for its defeat. Competent as Neil Winick is to defend the law, Davenport sees as nothing less than cynical Klosterman's choice of this physically compromised lawyer to invoke the interests of the challenged Denny Straubinger.

Herb Bauman again asserts the privilege of the court's most senior justice to speak first. "That's a fine thought counselor, and well-phrased, but you would agree, wouldn't you, that it is in the nature of minors and other incompetents that they don't know their own best interests? Isn't that why this court has consistently deferred to the individuals closest to the child—the parents—to represent the child's best interests?"

"That may be true in principle, Justice Bauman. But the petitioners in this case, Denny Straubinger's parents, had the opportunity to build a record at trial that reflected the circumstances of Denny's life, his hopes and fears as well as his relationship with his brother, but they manifestly failed to do so. This court is not free to roam at large outside the four corners of the record. So, because we—you and the other justices—have no facts from which to discern even the faintest picture of what Denny's best interests are—"

"Doesn't that argue too much, counselor?" It is Cippolone. "The state also came up short on the facts. It proffered no evidence that the Straubingers are negligent or abusive parents, or indeed that they are anything but loving parents who care deeply about the welfare of their son, Denny."

"Yes, Justice Cippolone, but the burden is on the parents to demonstrate that they have at heart only the best interests of their incompetent child—this child, Denny Straubinger. When all we have is an empty record from which no inferences can be drawn one way or another, we can only presume that, where the welfare of two children is involved, even—or perhaps especially—the most devoted parents will be torn between them."

In asking only for a modest ruling that the trial record doesn't support the relief sought, Winick and his client have wisely decided not to seek a grand declaration of principle. But the meagerness of the record makes it inevitable that the court's two camps will make principle their battleground.

Davenport now sees the guile through which the Chief has entrapped him. If Davenport is right, the papers for the emergency appeal in *Straubinger* were in the Chief's desk drawer even as the two of them were negotiating their compromise in the assisted suicide case. At the very moment the Chief so graciously agreed to let Davenport write the opinion in the case, he knew that a case was coming before the court in which the importance of a physician's opinion would be even more conclusive than it was in the assisted suicide case. By granting his request to write the opinion, the Chief has forever silenced the junior justice from questioning its result. The Chief knew how much Davenport wanted his first opinion for the court to have a majority greater than 5–4, and he let the new justice stumble—no, run—into his trap.

Davenport hears the volleys between Winick and the other justices, but only in the background. His thoughts are elsewhere. He imagines what Olivia, who traveled to East Harlem to teach adults to read, and to the African bush to deliver medical supplies, would say if she were here now. "Words," she would say, "nothing but words," just as she dismissed the earnest chatter of their friends over cocktails or dinner. "Where is the passion? The human connection?" He thinks of the Olivia he married, and feels closer to her than to any of his colleagues. He knows where he needs to take the debate if he is to repair the wreckage created by his over-hasty embrace of the Chief's compromise. Where Keane was going earlier. He says, "What about the duty of rescue?"

The Chief makes a throat-clearing noise, and Davenport realizes that he has interrupted an exchange between Winick and Carl Shell. Shell nods for him to continue, and Davenport says, "I'm interested in legal duty, Mr. Winick, not moral duty. Does New York law impose a duty on one person to come to the aid of another person in peril? If so, that should help us to understand not only if Denny Straubinger has a duty to save this brother, but also, if he does, whether that duty makes a physician's opinion on the subject unnecessary."

Winick practices law in the District of Columbia, not New York, and duty of rescue was addressed neither in the briefs of the parties nor those of the amici. Nothing has prepared the lawyer for this detour in the closing minutes of his argument. "I certainly see the connection you are drawing, Justice Davenport, and while I recall from my law school days that there is no common law duty of one person to rescue another, I must confess that I don't know whether New York follows the common law rule, or has created exceptions to it, or has overridden it by statute. But I would—"

Keane cuts him off. "But your memory is the same as mine as to the general common law rule, is it not? The state cannot compel a person to give up even a shred of his liberty in order to save another person, no matter how small the cost to him, or how great the benefit to the other would be. So if there is nothing in the trial record to reflect this boy's intention to rescue his brother by handing over one of his vital organs, the rule in the face of his silence must be the common law rule, that he cannot be forced to rescue his brother."

The red lamp on the lectern flashes on. "The general rule, yes, Justice Keane. I would be glad to file a supplemental brief on the point if the court wishes."

"Thank you," the Chief says, "but there will be no need for that. And your time is up, counsel. Ms. Corbett, I believe you reserved five minutes."

All impatient courtesy, Corbett waits at the lectern while Winick slowly maneuvers back into his chair. Davenport wonders if, in her half-hour away from the lectern, she has made sense of Madeleine's attempt to signal that her best strategy will be to ask the court for a remand to the trial court in order to supplement the record with a medical opinion.

"Thank you, Mr. Chief Justice. I would like to pick up on Justice Davenport's line of questioning, about duty of rescue. I believe the law on this subject amply illustrates the fundamental place of family obligations in the constitutional scheme."

It would have been better for Corbett to remain silent, Davenport thinks. Although he raised the question of rescue, he genuinely doesn't know where it will lead, only that it is the single right question to control resolution of the case. Smart as she is, he doesn't believe that Corbett knows where it will lead either, and unwittingly she may be sabotaging her clients' case.

"While Mr. Winick's memory from his law school days is correct, that the common law imposes no duty on one individual to rescue another, apparently he has forgotten that there are exceptions to the general rule, most notably in the case of family members—"

"An exception for parent and child?" Keane has rejoined his question.

"I believe in some states between parent and child, Justice Keane. That's the germinal exception. A parent is under a duty to rescue her child if the child is in peril."

"And vice-versa?"

"Yes, Justice Keane. I believe vice-versa."

"But this case isn't about parent and child." Keane's eyes are on Davenport as he speaks, and hold the same condescension as they did in his parlor yesterday when he explained why he was withholding his opinion in the assisted suicide case. "This case is about one brother being forced to save another. What does the common law have to say about that?"

"I would have to research the law on that, Justice Keane, but the principle would certainly appear to be the same, based on familial duty." As Davenport feared, the undertow of Keane's question has drawn Corbett into waters in which she cannot possibly stay afloat. The lawyer's shoulders drop. She has lost the skirmish. "Like counsel for respondent, we would be glad to file a supplemental brief."

The Chief says, "There will be no need for that, counsel. And, also, you are out of—"

"Hold on just a minute." Keane's voice pitches high, and his eyes remain on Davenport. "These exceptions to the rule on rescue that you allude to, counselor. Do they extend to the relationship between a husband and wife? Must a husband rescue his wife if she is in peril?"

"I believe so, Justice Keane, but I would have to check."

Progress is an illusion. For all of his struggle, Davenport has not moved an inch from his place on the wildly rising and falling deck of the Hy-Line ferry from Nantucket Harbor to Hyannis.

Again, the red lamp flashes. Corbett's five minutes are up.

"Ms. Corbett," Davenport says, "I am less interested in Justice Keane's abstract question, whether there is a duty to rescue than I am in the question, when. When must the duty of rescue be exercised? And of what does the duty consist?"

"To answer that, Justice Davenport—"

"Thank you, counsel," the Chief says. His color is high and he does nothing to hide his annoyance with Davenport. "Your time has expired. The case is submitted."

13

Gloria promised herself when she got married that she would keep no secrets from Leonard, and it is a source of pride that her few lapses, like today's, have been small. They are in the waiting area by the US Airways gates at National Airport—Mike took the 3:40 flight back to Buffalo, and she and Leonard stayed—and are talking about anything but Junior. Like Junior's condition, Leonard thinks that if they don't talk about where their son is, nothing bad will happen to him, and Gloria knows better than to challenge him. They wait because they know that if Junior turns up in Washington and gets into some kind of trouble, they need to be here.

Leonard is rambling on about the Supreme Court. Gloria caught pieces of what the lawyers and judges were saying in the courtroom, but she didn't really follow them. It was like the time at college that she went to a student performance of *Merchant of Venice*. She knew the play was in English but, with all the odd words and the postures and accents of the actors, the play could have been in a foreign language.

Leonard says, "I think Christine did a pretty good job."

Gloria says, "I don't like that she didn't talk about the boys. She talked about those twins in Kentucky, but not Denny and Junior."

"I already told you," Leonard says. "She explained it to us. Mike wasn't able to get all the facts about Junior and Denny into the trial, and Supreme Court judges won't listen to anything that didn't come out at the trial."

Gloria doesn't need Leonard to remind her that until last week she had been at best half-hearted about the case. She wonders what secrets Leonard keeps from her. Nothing to do with other women, she is sure of that. Mostly, his feelings, she suspects. Secretly, Gloria has called Junior's cell number a half-dozen times, and the last time the recording said his mailbox was full. She believes that Leonard has been calling too.

Leonard says, "That was really something, wasn't it, when Christine turned and looked at us. I thought she was going to ask us to stand up so she could introduce us."

"I really wasn't paying attention." She is tired of hearing about Christine.

"At lunch she told me and Mike she'd never done anything like that before. Never seen anyone else do it either." He glances over, but doesn't see that Gloria is not impressed. "Christine still thinks the new judge is going to vote for us. Mike too."

"I'm glad it's not up to that little white-haired one."

"You mean the cutie-pie with that fake Irish accent? I promise you, if we lose, it's because of him."

"How old do you think he is?"

"Cutie-pie?"

"No," Gloria says, "the new judge."

"I don't know. Fifty. Fifty-five? Why?"

Gloria says, "He's younger than that, but he has sad eyes, like he's older. He was the only one up there without a wedding band."

"I liked the Spanish-looking one."

"You would. She hardly said anything."

"Maybe her mind's on lover boy. Your boyfriend with the sad eyes."

"You're being silly."

"She didn't take her eyes off him once."

More like Leonard couldn't take his eyes off her, Gloria thinks.

"Do you think he's banging her?"

When Leonard gets like this, Gloria knows the only thing to do is ignore him. Sometimes she imagines that Junior is her child and Denny is Leonard's; that Junior inherited his quickness from her, and Denny his cinder-block dullness from Leonard. After a while she says, "I'm going to write to him."

"Who? Lover boy? You should talk to Mike first."

"Mike doesn't know anything about the Supreme Court."

"Then Christine."

"No, I'm going to write to him."

"What can you write that would make a difference?"

"I'll think of something. A mother's point of view." Gloria is already organizing the letter in her mind, putting her ideas into words.

The last flight is at 10:59, and at 10:00, Gloria says to Leonard, "You go home. If Junior heads back, you can be there to help him."

"What about you?"

"I'll go back to the hotel. I'm sure they have a room." Gloria skipped lunch and hasn't had dinner. She doesn't spend much time in airports, but the food never looks like anything you'd really want to eat, so she'll get something close to the hotel. "That way we'll have both bases covered."

Leonard says, "He's gone without the machine before. When we went hunting last year."

"But not more than one night. And he's sicker now. Dr. Hershberger said even one day is a stretch."

"When did you talk to Hershberger?"

"When you were having lunch." Gloria had said she was going for a walk, but had used the time first to talk to Junior's specialist, and then, breaking her promise to Leonard, she called the New York and Maryland State Police. Neither desk officer she spoke to seemed as interested in locating Junior as she expected them to be, even after she told them he was under age and driving with a case of beer in the back of the van. She didn't tell them about the gun or that he was going to Washington to talk to a Supreme Court judge. All she wants is for them to stop him and get him to a hospital. Maybe she's watched too many episodes of *Law & Order*, but Gloria is afraid they'll turn this into one of those manhunts that never ends well.

Gloria has thought about the possibility of Junior dying for as long as she can remember, but it has never seemed this real to her. A picture snaps into her mind of the van stalled on a rural dead-end under a bare tree and a gray sky and Junior slumped over the steering wheel. "I know you're scared," she says to Leonard. "So am I."

14

The disapproval in Anne's voice over the intercom is conspicuous. "The president wants to talk to you."

Davenport picks up the phone and a voice less struck by the occasion says, "Please hold for the president."

"Mr. Justice."

"Mr. President."

"Congratulations on your opinion in the assisted suicide case. That was a brilliant compromise, bringing Bernie Keane along like that. 9–0 is an impressive debut. A beautifully crafted opinion, too." This last is Bennett Jaffe's appraisal, not Locke's, for the president is a man impatient with lawyers and their work, and has not read the opinion. Keane had filed his vote at the start of court business today, and at 10:30 in the morning, a copy of the opinion was on Davenport's desk. One-third of the way down the first page, below the case name and docket number, was a single line:

Davenport, J., delivered the opinion of the unanimous Court.

Davenport doesn't try to convince himself that his plea to the justice after Sunday dinner had any impact. Bernie Keane had delayed his vote for no other reason than to hide the court's newly announced rule from Christine Corbett, crippling her argument in the transplant case. But that doesn't explain his decision to vote with the majority. After his passionate plea at the conference, why had he not filed one of his customary dissents?

Locke says, "This transplant case looks like it's going to need your magic wand."

Washington is a city of few subtleties, and Davenport can guess the real reason for the president's call. "What's on your mind, Mr. President?"

"The public interest, Richard. Balance. Two steps forward, one back. You just wrote an important opinion, a milestone. But we don't want to go too far, too fast. Those people camping out on your steps have lots of support. And it's not just the Tea Party crazies. Our polls show Democrats all across the country moving to the right."

The crowd outside the courthouse waiting for the court to decide *Straubinger* has in fact dwindled to a hardy few, but their placards, wilting and streaked from the weather, leave no doubt about the fervor behind their vigil. "You called to lobby me."

"I'd never do that. I just thought you might be interested in the views of an old friend."

"I haven't decided—"

"Good. That means—"

"No, it means, I won't reach a decision until I've had the chance to consider the facts and the law." And, Davenport thinks, to examine every corner of any proposed compromise for treachery of the sort practiced by Keane and the Chief. He is not going to repeat his mistake.

"Bennett says your opinion in the assisted suicide case doesn't leave you much breathing room for your vote in a case like this. Maybe no room at all. He thinks there's no way you can vote against the New York transplant statute and still honor what you wrote in your opinion."

"You want me to vote in favor of the same law you vetoed when you were governor."

"I did a lot of things as governor that I'd never do as president. Fighting that bill cost me a good deal of political capital. If you'd done a better job of killing it in the legislature, I wouldn't have had to veto it, and we wouldn't have this damn case today. That boy would have a new kidney by now."

"You vetoed the bill because you thought that was the right thing to do. How can you turn around today and say it's a good law?"

"You're missing my point, Richard. That law's not my responsibility any more. It's yours, and you don't even have to say it's a good law. All you have to say is that it's not unconstitutional. It's not going to help me get re-elected if the voters think my first appointment to the Supreme Court belongs to the radical left."

Davenport thinks of Anne's disapproving tone on the intercom. "There's a doctrine called separation of powers."

"This is the American public, Richard. Do you think they care about the fine points of constitutional law?"

"An independent judiciary isn't a fine point, and I wasn't talking about the public. I was talking about you. You shouldn't have called."

"If I'd lost the election, do you know who would be sitting in your seat right now? Oren Nyquist. And if I lose next November, you can be sure he'll be the Republican's number one choice for the next open seat. Your next colleague. No nominee is easier to get confirmed than a sitting US senator."

"You mean they'll be glad to have him out of the Senate."

"Not everyone values loyalty as deeply as we do."

From their days at Harvard, Locke knows the shortest route to his vulnerability, and it dismays but doesn't surprise Davenport that decades later Locke still believes that his college swim team partner will not cross him.

Locke's ancestors had arrived in America almost as many generations ago as Olivia's and, like Olivia, his youth was defined by private schools, debutante balls and ski vacations in Switzerland. For the twenty-year-old Davenport, a product of the middle class and the Midwest, the friendship which began in their junior year opened the door to a world that he had only vaguely imagined. The mystique wore thin by senior year, but by then Locke had introduced him to Olivia, and the two couples—Davenport and Olivia, Locke and his girlfriend Caroline—had become inseparable.

One afternoon that year, on a gray winter day not unlike today, Davenport had gone to Locke's rooms at Adams House to pick him up for swim practice. From the groan of bed springs and muffled gasps as he approached his friend's bedroom door, Davenport assumed that Locke was with Caroline, and turned to leave. He was on his way out of the suite when the cries from behind the door—by now he realized they were not Caroline's—grew louder and more urgent. "No! No! Stop! No!" Locke must have guessed that he was there because over the clamor he called out. "Come on in, Richard! Get yourself a piece of this!"

The bedroom door was unlocked and, even now in his chambers, gripping the telephone receiver with Locke at the other end, Davenport feels in the tips of his fingers the apprehension he felt as he turned the doorknob. He remembers every detail of the scene: the drawn curtains, the single lamp illuminating paperback titles of Melville and Henry James, the squash racket propped against the bookcase. On the wall was a framed print of the Monitor and the Merrimack at war. The bed cover, thrown back, had twisted into the top sheet and two figures writhed on the bed—Locke, muscled and tanned on top, and beneath him the girl, pale legs and arms flailing helplessly. The girl's skirt—it was green and red plaid—was up around her waist, and her cries had become a whimper. For an instant, Davenport caught a glimpse of a small white face, eyes wide and filled with terror, but it was the knife that Locke held at the girl's slender neck—a small, dull-edged boy scout knife they used to pop bottle caps—that made the sordid scene incomprehensible.

Physically, Davenport was more than Locke's equal, and what he did next was a reflex. He pulled Locke off the girl and threw him against the wall, pinning him there. When Locke's hands rose in defense, Davenport threw a fist in his stomach, and when he doubled over struck him across the jaw so that when Davenport finally released him, Locke crumpled to the floor, too broken even to cover himself.

When Davenport looked around, the girl was at the foot of the bed, in shock, adjusting her clothes. "I'm sorry," was all he could think to say to her. He turned back to Locke, still incredulous at what his friend had done. Incredulous, but also not, for he believes that he knew this about Locke from their very first meeting; that assault on a helpless girl—rape—was only one of the unspeakable acts of which his new friend was capable. "I'm sorry," he said again, but when he turned, the girl was gone.

He didn't call the police or report the crime to the Harvard authorities. Sometimes Davenport thinks that if he is ever to truly understand himself, loyalty will be the key that opens the door. He doesn't remember if in the beginning he expected Locke to return his constancy, but, if he ever had such expectations, they evaporated years ago. Locke, however, still counts on Davenport's loyalty as his due, dispensing or withholding rewards at will—he knew but didn't care that Davenport wanted to be attorney general more than he wanted to be a Supreme Court justice—and demanding tribute, just as he is now. When Davenport saw Locke at swim practice the next day, no more than an exchange of embarrassed shrugs passed between them before they resumed their regular routine.

Unexpectedly, Davenport's remorse over the incident has grown, not receded, with time. Nola is today no older than Locke's victim was then, and since her entry into the world of dating and young men, the immorality of Locke's violence and Davenport's complicity has tormented him. Nola puts on a show of tough sophistication, but her helplessness is frightening. Times change; boys do not; evil does not. Davenport has never asked if Locke feels the same anxiousness for the two teenage daughters of his second marriage, or if he has deceived himself into thinking that a Secret Service detail can protect them from young men like themselves. He says, "I was thinking about what happened that afternoon in your room at Ames House."

"Is that still bothering you? The girl was just a townie."

Davenport hadn't thought whether the girl was from Harvard or one of the local colleges or, as Locke put it, a townie, and sufficiently taken in by the good looks, wealth and charisma of this Harvard man to go to his room with him. In his own way, hadn't Locke so seduced Davenport himself?

"It was just horse play," the voice on the phone says. "College hi-jinks."

"It was rape, Tony. What I saw was a college athlete assaulting a helpless girl. Holding a knife to her throat."

"It was a boy scout knife, for God's sake. It was nothing."

Davenport would have liked Locke's response to surprise him. He would have wanted to expect repentance, a willingness to acknowledge his wrongdoing. But he has no expectations. There is a shriveled, depraved part of the man's soul that will never grow beyond that of a schoolyard bully's. "There is no excuse for what you did."

Locke says, "You know, Richard, there's another reason you will want to vote for this transplant law."

Davenport hasn't been listening as closely to Locke as he should, but if he knows his old teammate, the reason the president is about to give him to vote to uphold the Susie Briscoe Act is the real one.

"It's very important to Bernie Keane that the court reach the right result in this case."

"Why would I care what Keane wants? Why would you care?"

"He knows he's dying. He thinks if the court can get this case right, it will be the last piece in the puzzle for the court's retreat on abortion."

This had been Madeleine's warning when Davenport described to her his compromise in the assisted suicide case, that by requiring a doctor's opinion for life and death decisions, the court would be laying the foundation for a future decision requiring a woman seeking an abortion to get a doctor to swear that the abortion is necessary to save her life. And now he thinks he sees why Keane had made the decision unanimous: to set the court's new path in stone.

But if this was so, why had Madeleine joined the compromise, and brought three other justices with her? All that Davenport had given Madeleine in return was his vote to take the *Straubinger* appeal, hardly a fair exchange for the cause that had defined her legal career.

Davenport says to the president, "There's only the most abstract connection between this case and abortion." The fact that, along with dozens of other pieces of possible testimony, a doctor's opinion is missing from the *Straubinger* trial record doesn't mean that one is required. "The assisted suicide case is not going to be a precedent."

"That's what Bennett said. But I don't care if it's a precedent or if Cardinal McGowan drove his Mercedes down from Boston and whispered this into Keane's ear himself. What matters is that Keane thinks he's right—"

"Which matters to you because—"

"—because Keane said that if I can persuade you to vote with him and the Chief Justice, Palfrey, and Park, he won't wait until after the election to retire. He'll submit his resignation in June, at the end of the term. Win or lose, I get to appoint the next justice."

"You're telling me he's giving you a free seat because he thinks *Straubinger* can lock up the court's next vote on abortion."

"Exactly."

"He's way too smart for that. He'll find a way to double-cross you."

"For all I know, he'll be dead by November, in which case I'll get the appointment anyway. There's something here for both of us."

"Who knows about this?"

"No one. Just me, Bennett, and now you."

"Not the Chief?"

"Especially not Bricknell."

Again, Davenport is not concentrating on the conversation as closely as he should. A part of him is still at the doorway to Locke's Adams House bedroom. He can see Locke's face as clearly now as he did then, a face not much changed over the years, one that, as it rose over his victim thrashing about, grew full with triumph, rage and glee; the face truly of a sadist and madman.

"So, are you on board?"

Davenport wonders what part of him is missing, that he can know all this and yet remain so rigidly bound to his one-time friend. He tests the bond as he might a hitch knot. "How important is this to you?"

"For us. Vote for the transplant statute and no Republican president will ever get to appoint Oren Nyquist to Bernie Keane's seat."

Davenport tries to focus, but can't.

Locke says, "Do you know what Bennett told me when we discussed your nomination? He said any time you appoint a Supreme Court justice you make enemies of all the people you didn't nominate and an ingrate of the one you did."

"I haven't made up my mind."

"You know, Richard, people are raising questions about what happened on that ferry."

If loyalty fails, try blackmail. For the first time, Davenport observes how fearful the presidency has made Locke. "This is why Bennett got Nyquist to bury the coroner's report at my confirmation hearing. So there wouldn't be a scandal about your nominee. It didn't matter to you that Nyquist would try to use it against me now."

Locke's silence tells Davenport more than anything the president could possibly say. Locke knows the senator is trying to blackmail him. Davenport says, "I'm not worried about the coroner's report, but it's inspiring to watch the three branches of government work so closely together."

"I don't know what you mean."

"You, Nyquist, Keane." Davenport doesn't know whether to be pleased or dismayed at his new aptitude for unscrambling Washington's small conspiracies. "Of course Keane offered to resign. You promised him that when he does, you'll give his seat to Oren Nyquist. He won't have to wait for the election. A Democrat will appoint Nyquist. You."

The silence at the other end of the line resumes, and then there is a click and the line goes dead.

15

Madeleine makes a quick survey of the office, not hiding her dismay that Davenport has put nothing up on the walls since her first visit. Maybe because he knew her before he came to Washington, Davenport expected a closer relationship to develop with Madeleine, but it has not. Still, despite her patronizing attitude, he feels more comfortable with her than he does with the other justices. And just as Davenport expects the Chief to lobby him to vote with the conservatives to uphold New York's transplant law, he accepts as inevitable that Madeleine will try to persuade him to vote with her, Herb, Carl, and Donna to overturn it.

"How are you going to vote in *Straubinger*?"

Davenport says, "I haven't decided."

"Good. Because you can't vote with us. Not after your opinion in *Clark*. There's not a shred of physician testimony in the trial record. You have to vote with the Chief and the others."

Beyond the Second Street window it is another gray and bitter day and the pedestrians' collars are up, their heads down. A jet's white trail, sharply etched across the pale sky, gives the impression of severing the universe in two. Why would Madeleine want him to vote with the conservatives? For him to do so would put her in the minority and, if Bernie Keane is right, the decision will seal the court's retreat on its abortion decisions. "Why would you want me to vote with Keane?"

"You have no choice."

"If there's a problem with my *Clark* opinion, you have it, too. You signed onto it."

"But I didn't write it. The court watchers need only one scapegoat, and you're going to be it. They're going to be all over you. One day you say a doctor's opinion is needed in life and death cases like this, and the next day you say it's not."

"The press is background noise. It doesn't mean anything."

"It does if they start digging into your wife's death. They'll paint you as a hypocrite. You sign an opinion that says one family member has a duty to rescue another but, when it comes to your own wife, you do nothing to save her."

"You can't believe that."

"It doesn't matter what I believe. This is the press."

No, Madeleine, he thinks; this is you. "The court's opinion doesn't have to say anything about duty of rescue."

"Whatever the majority says, you can be sure Keane will write about it in his opinion. Why else do you think he raised it at argument? He's put you in a corner where you have no choice but to vote with him."

"I've had Harold do some research—"

"I warned you about Harold—"

"The law on rescue is more complicated than Corbett said. Or Winick."

"You really need to ease up on yourself, Richard. You don't have to fight every issue that comes to the court. You wouldn't know it to talk to him, but, Phil beats himself up every day over his accident. What he could have done differently. That he's ruined my life as well as his own."

Madeleine has drawn so near that Davenport is aware of the fragrance of her morning tea, something flowery and doubtless rare. If he just leaned forward, his lips would touch hers. He says, "I don't know what you mean."

"From what I read in the news, in a storm like that, no matter how good a swimmer you are, you never could have saved her. Don't punish yourself like this."

Madeleine is wrong, of course. Olivia did not have to die, at least not in the waters off Nantucket Island. "You don't really believe I would let Keane control my vote, do you?"

"I think you should stop torturing yourself over this idea of rescue." Madeleine steps back. "In my experience, Richard, the more you think about a case, the harder it is to decide."

"And you make cases easier by not thinking about them. You let your ideology decide them for you."

"That's what I'm trying to tell you. You have no ideological commitments. You're free to vote with the Chief or with me. I'm suggesting that, for our own good, you vote with the Chief on this one. Bernie will make a big thing about rescue at the conference. Maybe Alex too. But only because they think it's the way to force you to vote with them."

"I suppose we'll just have to wait and see."

. . . .

Because this is an emergency appeal, the conference is off the regular calendar. The Chief has spared his colleagues their ritual lunch, and no handshakes are exchanged. Yesterday's announcement of the court's decision in the assisted suicide case seems to have lifted a dark encumbrance, for the tone in the conference room is light, and even Bernie Keane, chatting with Donna Cippolone, is in good spirits. Where the cuff on Gilbert Park's trousers has come undone, Davenport notices that someone has crudely repaired it with an office stapler.

There is also an energy in the room, as of an idling engine, and the Chief takes his seat and starts even before the others take theirs. "We have just one case on our agenda," he says. "Number 15-1160, *Straubinger v. New York*. The record below leaves much to be desired, but the case has been well-briefed and well-argued and, as it is an emergency appeal, I believe we would do well to dispose of it in short order." His pace signals that, unlike his odd introduction of the assisted suicide case, today's framing of the issue for decision will be brisk. "On one side is the Constitution's protection of parental decisions respecting the welfare of their children. On the other side is due process for those who cannot speak for themselves." He turns to his right, "Herb?"

Jarred by the telegraphic brevity of the Chief's introduction, Bauman takes a moment to recover. "Well, yes... yes..." The senior justice fumbles with the papers in front of him, probably a clerk's bench memo. "Well, as you say, Chief, I suppose I'd be happier if we had a more complete record. But, even if we did, what do we ever know, really, when parents make decisions about their children?" Caterpillar eyebrows navigate an inquiring glance around the table and a schoolboy's innocence spreads across Bauman's features. "It's just a harmless operation, for heaven's sake! It's not like they want to terminate a pregnancy. My vote is to strike down the statute."

The vote is no surprise, and the Chief makes a notation on the pad in front of him. "Bernie?"

Keane rises, evidently his custom at conference. His eyes travel the same circuit as Bauman's, but he stops for the briefest moment to lock eyes with each justice. "The starting point for me," Keane says, "is the question that I raised at argument. Does one person have a legal duty to rescue another? Unless—"

"That's not on the table, Bernie." The Chief is not going to let rescue derail the conference. "If you want to address the constitutional issues, that's fine. Otherwise, all we need is a simple Yay or Nay on the New York statute."

"Then I'll have to pass," Keane says.

"This isn't poker, Bernie. You know we don't pass." The Chief's color is up and he glances at Davenport, a warning.

Keane says, "Like it or not, Chief, as we go around the table, that's what we're going to be talking about. Whether the state can impose on one individual a duty to rescue another."

"Well, be that as it may—"

Keane ignores him. "The reason we can't decide this case without talking about rescue is that, without it, we don't know whether this young man has a legal obligation to save his brother. If he doesn't, then his parents have no constitutionally protected right to hand him over to the surgeons."

Bauman leans in to the table. "Well, if we're going to look at the issue in terms of rescue—"

"Let's go in order, Herb," the Chief says. "And we're not going to talk about rescue."

Davenport observes how profoundly Bricknell despises Keane. If Davenport still doesn't see how Keane's ambush of the Chief's constitutional agenda will further his own plan to discredit the court's abortion decisions, it is impossible not to admire his political genius. The court's conservatives and liberals alike may disavow Keane's extreme positions, but his views irresistibly draw both sides in his direction. No Supreme Court worthy of a nation's faith can harbor a lunatic and, if only to make Keane appear less mad, the others will move closer to him.

Keane says, "Just so everyone understands what's at stake here, my reading of the case law is that one brother has no legal duty to rescue another, which means that these parents have no right to arrange for a transplant. But I'd like to hear from our colleagues if they've come to a different conclusion."

"Alex?" The Chief is glad to move the spotlight off Keane.

"I'm voting to uphold the statute and its application for the reason we gave in our assisted suicide opinion. There's no medical testimony in the record to prove that the benefit to this sick boy outweighs the risk of harm to his brother. As Justice Davenport wrote so eloquently and for a unanimous court, life and death measures require a medical opinion."

Even before Madeleine's warning, Davenport had been anticipating the inevitable consequence of his blunder and, now that Palfrey has raised it, his grand compromise in the assisted suicide case is about to consume its first victim.

"I also support the New York statute because I oppose the creation of a market for human organs, and I hope the opinion will reflect that. No bazaars for body parts."

"Thank you, Alex." The Chief is relieved at the discussion's move away from rescue. "Carl, do you—"

"Just a minute, Chief." Gilbert Park places his hands flat on the surface of the table, as if to steady himself. "I'll vote with Alex to support the statute because, as he said, there's no medical testimony, but I won't sign on to his objections to a market for human organs—"

"It's not the market I object to—"

"Well, I think it's perfectly fine to have such a market."

"So long as the rich get first dibs." It is Donna who has been trying to restrain herself. The Chief says to Park, "I'm putting you down with Alex and me to affirm." He turns to Shell, who would have been next in order, but Keane interrupts. "I don't see why we would need to talk about medical testimony in this case. I'm sure that whoever writes the majority opinion can manage to do so without talking about our assisted suicide decision."

The Chief studies the back of his hands, a quarterback no longer in command of his team. Davenport thinks he understands Keane's insistence that they talk about rescue, but if the assisted suicide decision was an element of his strategy to rein in the court's abortion jurisprudence, why would he drop it now? Whatever his motives, has Keane so cowed the others that they would drop a hard-won compromise in order not to displease him? Davenport is even farther from understanding the court than he was on his first day here.

"That's completely unacceptable." Alex Palfrey is not intimidated. "I only joined the assisted suicide opinion because of its requirement of medical testimony—"

"And you got that requirement, even though some of us were unhappy about it," Donna says. "What Bernie is saying—and I agree with him—is that we don't have to make it the centerpiece of this case. We don't have to mention it at all."

Davenport now sees what the two are doing. Keane believes that, with the requirement of physician testimony off the table, Davenport will feel free to join his side on the ground that there is no legal duty to rescue. Cippolone thinks that removing physician testimony as the hurdle will make it possible for Davenport to join her and the liberals on the ground that the rules on rescue should not apply.

"None of this would have to appear in an opinion," Keane says. "Still, it's sad that, thanks to the knucklehead who tried the case for the family, we don't have a clue as to the facts."

Palfrey is plainly unhappy. "Whatever gets written in the majority opinion, I'm going to write my own opinion to remind people that two days ago we agreed unanimously that there has to be physician testimony in life and death cases."

The Chief says, "Carl?"

Shell looks around the table. "I think framing the issue in terms of rescue could be very helpful."

The Chief closes his eyes and throws up his hands in mock dismay, but fury boils behind the comic gesture.

Shell's long fingers massage his bald head as carefully as if he is fondling a newborn. "Of course Bernie is right, that there's no legal duty of rescue, but he's wrong to stop there. This is one of those areas where the law is miles behind public attitudes. I had one of my clerks research this. There's a Pew Poll that most Americans will jump at the chance to rescue even a complete stranger. And if a stranger, why not a brother?" Ever the politician, Shell would have public pollsters take over the court's business if he could.

The Chief places another mark on the sheet in front of him, "I'm putting Carl down with Herb to overturn the New York statute."

Madeleine is next in order, but before the Chief can call on her, Cippolone says, "You should be aware, Bernie, that your American rule against rescue is no more than another reflection of the male bias in American law favoring individual autonomy over more compassionate behavior."

"Mea culpa," Keane says, with the amiability of a victor accepting surrender. "Mea maxima culpa."

Apart from Davenport, the Chief is the only one at the table who doesn't smile. Bernie Keane has entirely preempted his framing of the issue and drawn the liberals, if not to Keane's side, then to the terms he has set for debate.

"Carl's right," Cippolone says. "Do you have any idea how far from the rest of the world we are on duty of rescue? Did you know that, outside of England and Ireland, there's not a country in Europe that doesn't impose a legal duty of rescue? Germany, France, Holland, all of them make it a duty. What does that tell you about the shortcomings of the American rule on rescue?"

"If you remember," Keane says, "your oath was to uphold the American constitution, not the Dutch constitution."

"Or any other socialist system," Park says. "Not a single one of your countries respects an individual's personal liberty."

The exchange appears to amuse Cippolone, and she nods when the Chief asks if he should put her down with Herb and Carl.

"Madeleine?"

Madeleine has not only been silent, but still. Earlier, she had pushed her chair several inches away from her neighbors on either side, Park and Palfrey, and at an angle to the conference table. Davenport recalls her performance as the circuit court judge who, at the very end of an argument repeatedly interrupted by her two fellow judges, asked him the single question that cut to the heart of his position.

"Rescue isn't always that simple," Madeleine says. "What if it puts this hero you all believe in at serious risk?"

Cippolone says, "I read the Kentucky case that Christine cited. The doctors testified that the operative risk to a kidney donor is no more than 0.05 percent, and that the long-term risk is no more than 0.07 percent. And those numbers are from almost fifty years ago. The danger has to be even smaller today. I'd say these parents are doing the right thing for both their sons in asking for the transplant."

"But what do you know about the sons?" Madeleine's question pares like a scalpel. "The fact that one of their sons will die if he doesn't get a new organ tells us nothing about what kind of person he is or if he deserves this—"

"You can't mean that!" Cippolone is half out of her chair.

"Of course she can," Keane says. "No one in our politically correct culture wants to talk about it, but that's one of the reasons we don't burden individuals with a duty of rescue. Some people just don't deserve the expenditure associated with rescue."

Madeleine looks directly at Davenport. "And what if the victim doesn't want to be rescued?"

Keane smacks the table top with astonishing vigor. "In which case," he says, "we're back where we started all this. With assisted suicide."

Just where, Davenport thinks, Keane wants him to be. Madeleine was right. Keane had engineered this from the beginning. A woman with a history of two suicide attempts sits on the rail of a ferry over a dangerous sea and dares her companion to push her off to her certain death. Should the companion comply, or should he pull her in from her peril? Confronted with a life so tortured, of what does rescue consist? That night on the ferry, was Davenport saving Olivia or was he saving himself? But no one at this table, except perhaps Keane, would understand the complexity of what he had done. If he doesn't join Keane, he will look like a hypocrite.

"I must confess that I'm completely baffled," the Chief says. "Madeleine, I honestly don't know where you stand on this. Do you want me to put you down with Alex, Gilbert, and me, or with Herb, Carl, and Donna?"

"Oh," Madeleine says, "you can put me down with Herb, Carl and Donna." Her voice is now light, even coquettish. "I was just thinking out loud."

"Fine," the Chief says. "Presumably Bernie will join Alex, Gilbert and me when he gets around to voting. So that makes it 4–4." He turns to Davenport. "Richard?"

"I haven't decided."

"I already reminded Bernie that it's not acceptable practice to pass."

"I didn't say I was passing. I said I'm undecided."

The Chief says, "In a moment I'm going to put Bernie's feet to the fire and get him to cast his vote. You're next."

"This was a grand discussion," Keane says, cranking up his some-time brogue. "I certainly heard much that was persuasive on both sides of our... debate. I expect I'll file my own opinion, but I support the statute and you can put me down for a vote to affirm. "

Madeleine says, "I don't see why Richard shouldn't recuse himself. He was deeply involved with the statute when it was in the New York Legislature. That's enough of a reason for him to recuse himself now."

When she was lobbying him to join her, Bauman and Cippolone to take the *Straubinger* appeal, Madeleine had rebutted his every argument for recusal, and Davenport doesn't understand why she would change her position now. If he recuses himself and the court divides 4–4, the effect will be to leave the New York law standing, a victory—though far from a complete one—for the Chief, Keane, Palfrey, and Park, and a loss for Madeleine and the other liberals.

The Chief says, "This is an emergency appeal, Richard. You voted to bring it here. People are waiting on us." He turns to Madeleine. "Do we have any idea how pressing the situation with this boy is?"

"Only what's in the papers they filed, Chief." She resents the suggestion that she has private access to the facts through her former clerk.

Palfrey says, "So it's an emergency, but not really an emergency."

"That depends on your point of view," Cippolone says.

Davenport says, "I am not recusing myself, and I am not passing."

"And rescue," Keane says. "Do you have any thoughts to share in our little seminar on rescue?"

According to Harold's research, exceptions riddle the American rule on rescue, particularly in the case of one family member's duties to another. But there was something in what Shell said just now that Davenport thinks he might use to steer his colleagues toward a unanimous decision. For some reason, he imagines Olivia as a child. "Say a small girl is at the deep end of a swimming pool, helpless, bobbing and sinking, just seconds from drowning. An Olympic swimmer in his prime is watching from six feet away, and it would require little effort and no risk for him to rescue the girl. Would you say he's under a duty to rescue her?"

"A legal duty? No," Keane says. "He could walk away and let the girl drown. That's what I've been trying to explain, that—"

"Forget about the law for just a minute. Instead of asking what the law would let the Olympic swimmer do, look at what in fact the swimmer would do. Unless he's entirely depraved, he would dive into the pool and save the girl, wouldn't he?"

"Of course he would," Palfrey says. "But—"

"So would most people," Davenport says. "Dive right into the pool and save the girl. So would this autistic Straubinger boy, if he were capable of responding to real-life situations. We're talking about life here, not some legal rule book."

"As I recall," Palfrey says, "you testified at your confirmation hearing that your philosophy as a justice would be to strictly follow the facts and the law. There are no facts in this case. And now you're saying you want us to ignore the law."

"But not the Constitution," Davenport says. "When we apply the Constitution, why don't we assume that people will behave the way normal people actually do, and not as legal rules let them behave? They'd save the girl. If the rule book assumes the worst of people, isn't it the point of the Constitution to assume the best?"

"We're talking about transplants, not swimming accidents," Palfrey says.

"Well, instead of requiring these parents to prove that one of their sons would be willing to donate his kidney to the other, why don't we require the State of New York to prove that he would not be willing?"

The Chief lifts his pen. "Does this mean you want me to put you down with Herb, Carl, Madeleine, and Donna?"

Maybe a unanimous decision, Davenport thinks, but not one that will extricate him from the corner into which Keane has maneuvered him. "No, it's just an idea, but I think we should all consider it seriously."

The Chief studies him, and Davenport guesses that, like the others, the Chief believes that the newest justice is squeezing as much advantage as he can from holding the swing vote. He doesn't care what they think. He says, "The Straubingers are just going to have to wait for an answer."

"How long?" Cippolone asks.

"I can't say. For as long as it takes me to get comfortable with a decision."

"You can't do that. You—"

The Chief leans into the table. "Of course he can, Donna—"

"No," Palfrey says. "You're in or you're out. This isn't a debate."

The Chief puts up a hand. "This is fine," he says, pleased at last to have the conference under control.

"Take your time, Richard, and keep me informed of your thinking."

"Of course, Chief."

And with that, the emergency conference on *Straubinger v. New York* adjourns.

16

Anne's voice on the intercom announces the arrival of "Justice Bricknell" in chambers, and seconds later the Chief drops heavily into the chair across from Davenport. His snow-white hair is as usual carefully brushed back, but a single dislocated tendril at either side of his brow gives him a rakish aspect. "I'd be grateful if you had a word with your secretary about proper decorum, Richard."

Anne had dropped "Chief" from his title once too often. "But that's not why you came to see me."

"Do you know she accosted me yesterday getting out of my car? And for no other reason than to introduce me to her husband! Big fellow, a New York City policeman. My driver actually went for his weapon. Really, I wish you would talk to her." The Chief's frown when he sinks back into the chair leaves no question that the new justice is as much the source of his ire as the new justice's secretary. "I need to have your vote by tomorrow morning."

As Davenport suspected, this morning's casual acceptance of his indecision was only Bricknell's way of demonstrating that he was in control. "You'll be the first to know."

"Can you imagine what our docket would look like if we took this long to agonize over every decision?"

"Not many of them are this hard."

"All you have to do is read the briefs. That's the beauty of the adversary system, isn't it? Let the two sides exhaust all the relevant arguments, and then you pick one. You decide the case in front of you, and then forget about it and go on to the next one. I find that my first instinct is usually the right one."

"You mean your knee-jerk."

"Do I have a framework for reaching decisions? Of course I do. Maybe if you're a lower court judge you don't need one, but if you're a Supreme Court justice, you're not doing your job if you don't have a well thought-out philosophy to guide you."

"I follow the facts."

"And when, like this case, there are no facts?" The Chief looks over at the volumes of Kant, Hume and Rawls that Edward collected for Davenport from the Library of Congress yesterday, and piled on the coffee table. He picks the Kant treatise off the top, riffles through it, and returns it to the pile. "You're not going to find your answer there."

He knows Bricknell is right. At 2:00 this morning, when Davenport finally left chambers, he had found that the abstractions of philosophy were no more instructive than when he was an undergraduate taking an introductory course on the subject. But what else did he have?

The Chief says, "I'd like to propose a compromise in this case."

"Like you did in the assisted suicide case?"

"You think I sandbagged you, don't you?

"You're the only one who knew the Straubingers had filed an appeal. It was in your desk drawer when we were negotiating the compromise."

"If you remember," the Chief says, "it was you who insisted on writing the opinion. I offered to give it to Madeleine. Or to write it myself. No, my friend, the assisted suicide opinion was entirely your own doing." The Chief again picks up the volume of Kant, just to have something to do with his hands, and as he leans forward the sour smell of stale cigar smoke rises from his fine navy suit. "We're not going to get to 9–0 in this case, but we can do better than 5–4 if you just drop Bernie's crazy idea about rescue and follow what you wrote in your *Clark* opinion, that a doctor's testimony is required in cases like this, and since we have no such testimony in the record we have no choice but to affirm."

"We can't do that to the family. After all they've been through—the trial court, the court of appeals, now here—they're entitled to a clear statement from us about why they won or lost. And not some procedural detail about the trial record not being complete."

"You're wrong. What they deserve is a prompt decision."

"What, that we're affirming the court below, and they won't get their transplant, because their lawyer did a lousy job?"

"At least they'll know where they stand." The man is like one of those punching dummies that, no matter how hard you strike, always pops back. "There's also the public to think about. Did you see last week's *Times* poll? Our approval rating's dropped to 44%. That's lower than your president. Just three points better than Congress."

Davenport thinks of the unabridged dictionary that lifts the Chief above the others, the gold chevrons on his sleeves. "Some people would tell you that marble is greatly overrated."

To Davenport's surprise, the Chief picks up the allusion at once. "What faith would the public have in our court if we dispensed justice from a nine-by-twelve nook with plasterboard walls and linoleum floors, like some welfare office?"

"I think that would depend on the quality of the law and of the judge dispensing it."

"Don't tell me I misjudged you, Richard." Bricknell pats a breast pocket for a cigar, thinks better of it, and says, "From the success of our effort together on the assisted suicide case, I thought you'd be willing to try again here. I'd be glad to give you the opinion. We can announce our decision tomorrow, and you might want to say a few words from bench, but you can take all the time you need to write the opinion. I'm sure none of your colleagues will be expecting a grand statement of principle. We can leave that for another day."

"What you're missing, Chief, is that until I find that principle, I don't know how I'm going to vote."

"That's why I'm proposing that we compromise."

"How can I compromise if I don't know where I'm starting from?"

Bricknell fixes Davenport with a stupid grin. "We have our quarrels as all families do. But we also have enough sense to look out for each other. I'm confident that with you on board in this case, some of the others will follow, maybe all of them, like the last time." He rises to leave, but stops to look around and with a vague gesture takes in the entire office. "You could use some pictures here. You know, family photos. Warm up the place."

The Chief has heard nothing he said. He came into the office with but one thought, to walk out with Davenport's vote, and he has let himself hear nothing that would upset that expectation. Like the letters in the mail bins, the new justice is just an obstacle to be removed from his path forward. "No, Chief, as I said, I'm undecided."

"We can't wait forever, Richard. I need your vote by 9:00 tomorrow morning. This is an emergency appeal. People will think—"

"I'll let you know when I've made up my mind."

"I wouldn't wait too long."

"Or," Davenport says, "vote against you?"

"Be careful, Richard. This is a dangerous game you're playing."

"That's the difference between us, Chief. I don't see it as a game."

· · · · · · · · · · · · · · · · · · · ·

Few men wear three piece suits these days, and none better than Davenport's messenger. Today's navy pinstripe looks like it was made for him. "Mr. Clark died an hour ago," Edward says. "The fireman. I thought you would want to know. It was on the CNN website."

Although Randy Clark's peaceful death was the aim of the lawsuit and the object of Davenport's compromise, the news takes him by surprise, and saddens him. How easy it had been for the accumulated drama of the fireman's case and the thousands of spilled words to obscure that it was about one man's life and death.

Inside the manila folder that Edward hands the justice is a stack of letters, some typed, others handwritten. A week ago Davenport had forgotten his request of Edward to sort through the bins of mail about Randy Clark's case, and it now appears that, unbidden, Edward has done the same for the *Straubinger* case. "Not as many people wrote as they did in Mr. Clark's case, but most of them support the New York law. They're still worried about these death panels. If you're poor and someone with money wants your organs, you're not going to be safe anywhere near a hospital."

Davenport hands the folder back to Edward. "I'm sure you selected them carefully, Mr. Cunningham. But at this point letters aren't going to help."

Edward's features drop. The age freckles beneath his eyes seem to darken, punctuating his disappointment. "I thought you'd find something here, Justice Davenport. Just tell me what you're looking for, and I can try to find it."

It occurs to Davenport that, of all the people he has met at the court, including the other eight justices, none seems to belong to this place more than his messenger. "Have you ever been in a situation where, whatever you do, you're afraid it's going to be wrong?"

Edward turns and, after a long moment says, "More often than I care to remember."

"How do you decide what to do?"

"I pray on it."

Olivia's atheism had rubbed off on Davenport early in their marriage, and he realizes how desperate he must be that he would ask Edward a question to which he already knew the answer. "And when you pray, what kind of answer do you get?"

"Usually?" Edward's smile is tentative. "That I should do nothing."

"That's the answer to your prayer? To do nothing?"

"One time at our church—this was several years ago—the plate was being passed, and I saw one of our oldest members sitting in front of me, a deacon, drop a single bill into the plate and then, like it was a five-dollar bill he put there, take four singles out. I didn't want to believe it, but when the plate got to me, there were no five dollar bills in it, only ones. So I thought, should I tell this fellow that I'd seen what he did? Should I tell the preacher? Or should I just keep quiet, even if that made me an accomplice in his theft?"

"So you did nothing."

"Well, I prayed, so that was something. Some time later another member told me this fellow had been out of work for almost a year, but that he had just got a new position. I tried not to watch what he put in the plate after that, but there were times when he was right in front of me, so I couldn't help seeing. Sure enough, week after week, he was putting several bills into the plate and not taking any out."

"I don't think I have the luxury of doing nothing."

"Well, you may just surprise yourself, Justice Davenport." He tucks the manila folder under his arm. "Will you be needing anything else?"

"No, thank you, Mr. Cunningham. You have been very helpful."

Bricknell has been busy, dispatching first Palfrey, then Park to lobby him. Palfrey wanted to talk about his own family's social connections to Olivia's, Park to explain how he is not Bernie Keane's ideological twin. The two succeeded only in stealing time from Davenport's progress through the pile of books on his coffee table. At 6:00 p.m., Edward came in to leave a brown and gold overnight envelope on his desk, and a few minutes later Davenport heard the staff depart. When he looks up, Keane is at the open door. "Another emissary from the Chief?"

"Hardly."

Keane gestures for Davenport to stay where he is, and proceeds on a brief tour of the room, inspecting book shelves, looking behind the desk, running a familiar hand over the fireplace mantel, humming to himself as he advances around the office that formerly belonged to his oldest friend on the court. As with Edward, his presence makes Davenport feel like a trespasser. A full minute passes before he realizes that Keane is not revisiting the past, but is looking for something.

Keane's fingertips slide past the brown and gold envelope. "You wouldn't still have a drop of that Jameson's, would you?"

Davenport remembers the water-filled wine glass at the Sunday dinner table. "Are you sure?"

Keane nods, smiling. "At some point in the process of dying you get to be your own physician."

Davenport removes the tea set from the credenza and pours a dollop of whiskey into the justice's cup and another into his own. Keane takes the upholstered chair across from the rocker, and when Davenport sits, the fatigue that has dogged him for weeks suddenly drains him. If he were to attempt to rise, he believes he could not. He says, "The Chief seems to think that if I join him, we can do better than 5–4. Maybe even 7–2."

"The Chief is a case of arrested development, all these fantasies he has. The decision is going to be 5–4."

"Are you also going to predict in which direction?"

"Well, I suppose a cup of Jameson's isn't my only reason for being here. The Chief thinks you're playing politics, but I got the impression at conference that this case genuinely troubles you."

"Madeleine and the Chief think there's no connection between the law on rescue and constitutional law."

"Alex, too." Keane remembers his drink and takes a deep sip. But that's the grand thing about our job, Richard. Five of us can give a constitutional dimension to any subject we want and, short of a constitutional amendment, there's no majority in Congress or in the entire country that can overrule us. The law professors can second-guess us, but that's about it."

"But you don't think there's a duty of rescue."

"Between parent and child, I think there's a duty." He studies Davenport over the rim of the teacup. "And between husband and wife. But otherwise, no."

"Not for a man going to the death chamber because the court clerk was confused about a filing date?"

Keane shrugs. "Why should we treat a boy's rescue of his brother differently than rescue of a stranger?"

"What about the Good Samaritan?"

A red coin blossoms on each cheek. "You mean do I take the Gospels literally like Oren Nyquist and his crowd? Of course not." He sips at the teacup again, but finds it empty. "Your friend the senator seems to think you pushed your late wife off the railing."

If Keane is right, Davenport has not underestimated Nyquist. The senator is going to use the coroner's transcript and his conversation with Nola to paint him as a murderer, and not as a husband who merely stood by as his wife jumped to her death. "And what do you think?"

"I don't know, and I don't care to know, what happened between you and your wife on that ferry. But I take a more generous view of human nature, and if I had to guess, I'd say you simply declined to rescue her. I'm sure that as an accomplished swimmer you at some point considered diving into the water and saving her, but if you vote against this New York law on the ground that there is a duty, legal or moral, for one family member to rescue another—a brother rescuing a brother, a husband rescuing a wife—Senator Nyquist is going to get the public very interested in your behavior, and what some might consider your hypocrisy."

"But not you."

"Blackmail is the most cowardly crime there is."

The whiskey, which seems to have invigorated Keane, has only deep-ened Davenport's fatigue. When his visitor glances at the bottle on the side table, Davenport fills the justice's empty cup to a quarter-inch from the brim.

"Whoa, Nelly!" Keane cries.

At this moment, Davenport doesn't care if his guest takes the whole thing down in a gulp and drops dead on the carpet. He could be Randy Clark's physician handing his patient the fatal dose. "You didn't answer my question about the difference between family and a stranger."

Keane glances at the pile of books on the coffee table. "The mistake your philosophers make with rescue is that they always look at the hero and not the victim. They never ask if the victim truly wishes to be rescued."

"You mean what Madeleine said at the conference."

"It's truly sad. Madeleine has the makings of a fine justice. Womens' rights is one of the great issues of our time, and she's the court's leading voice, but then she goes off and sabotages herself, backpedaling and voting for the Chief's compromises. I don't know why she does that."

It intrigues Davenport that Keane should think well of women's rights and that he would criticize Madeleine only for falling short in their pursuit. "You signed onto the compromise, too."

"But I had a principled reason for doing so.'

"Principle or strategy?"

Keane's expression turns hard. "So he told you. That can be a dan-gerous habit, you know, a sitting justice talking with the president." Keane takes a delicate sip from the still-full cup. "Your friend didn't do you any favors when he nominated you to the court."

The whiskey may explain Keane's candor, but for the first time since arriving at the court, Davenport hears an invitation to be frank. "I'm beginning to think that myself."

"I knew you were in trouble when Kevin and I watched your hear-ings. Kevin saw it, too."

"What's that?"

"Your little speech about following the facts and the law and not going anywhere near something as volatile as justice. Law and facts can take you only so far—"

"And that's your problem with me?"

"No that's your problem with you. The other justices let their ideologies and politics decide their cases for them, but you're not the kind of person who can do that."

"So what's left?"

"What are you looking for in these philosophy books of yours?"

"A just result," Davenport says. Keane has trapped him. "Justice."

"That's what it has always come down to for the few serious people who have sat on this court."

"So you didn't come here to get me to vote with you."

"I would never do that." Keane is absolutely sober. "You can ask anyone here. Don't let the Chief rush you. Don't vote until you are confident it is on the side of justice. Do that, and as I told you when you came to my home for dinner, your daughter will be proud of you."

"I remember being curious that you put it that way."

"Also curious about my little exchange with Kevin."

"Appalled would be more accurate."

Keane laughs. "Kevin sometimes forgets that he's not as naturally gifted as my other boys, and he needs to be reminded that if he's going to compete with the best lawyers in town when he starts practice he's going to have to work harder than the others."

"That was more than a reminder."

"Kevin's stubborn, and sometimes he needs a two-by-four across the head. I don't have much tread left on me, and I'm not going to be there to help him along."

"And you think that by humiliating—"

"Humbling, Richard, not humiliating. I'm sure you would do the same for your own daughter if it came to that."

"How do you know that competing with the best is what Kevin wants?"

"It doesn't matter what Kevin wants. I only care about what he needs."

"How do you even know that?"

"I could ask what you knew of your poor wife's needs. We know because I'm Kevin's father, and you were her husband. Who would know better? We're alike that way. We care for our families more than anything else in life."

"And if you had to choose between Kevin and the court?"

Again Keane glances at the stack of books on the coffee table. "Is that what's holding up your vote—your obligation to your daughter?"

When Davenport doesn't answer, Keane says, "Of course I would choose Kevin, or any member of my family, over the court. One is about love. The other is just duty." Keane must see Davenport's skepticism because he says, "But that's not an excuse to be stupid about it. The trick is to keep them far enough apart that you don't have to choose."

After Keane leaves, Davenport lifts the brown and gold express envelope from his desk, but instantly puts it down when he sees the name on the return address.

17

J ustice Keane died last night." The voice of the Chief's secretary over
Davenport's cellphone cleaves the early morning like a scythe. "He
lay down for a nap before dinner and woke up two hours later with
chest pains. He wouldn't let Mary call an ambulance, but finally she
drove him to an emergency room in McLean. The Chief wants you in
the justices' conference room at 10:30."

Davenport got the call coming out of the "Y," and he is at a traf-
fic light on his way to the court before he truly takes in the fact of
the justice's death. He hadn't expected Keane to die so suddenly. He
thought he would retire from the court and then fade into his disease;
that his eventual passing would be no more than a footnote to the day
on which it occurred. Fragments of their short history together crowd
in: the bottle of fine Irish whiskey welcoming the new justice to Magh
Meall; Keane posturing at the *Clark* conference and stirring the pot
in *Straubinger* with his errant digression into the law of rescue; his
mocking expression from across the bench to let Davenport know that
a solitary dissent can control more territory than Davenport could ever
hope to command with a majority; their meeting yesterday evening and
the consolations of philosophy. Davenport realizes that he may have
been the last justice to see him.

The depth of Davenport's grief surprises him. He would have expected
to feel relief at the passing of this vain man whose arrogant self-confidence had brought misery to the lives of others: the dying fireman; the
death row inmate, his papers misfiled by a hapless clerk; his own son;
Davenport himself. But he can only mourn Bernie Keane. Even as he
imagines Mary, Kevin and the rest of the justice's family straightening

their shoulders and standing tall, he knows that he will miss him. It is not only the depth of his sorrow that Davenport failed to anticipate, but its containment. Unlike Olivia's death, which overflows every bank of his life, Keane's absence feels more like a well—dark and deep, maybe even bottomless, but discrete. It is a straight shot, 100 proof.

Not until he turns onto 2nd Street and the Supreme Court building comes into view does Davenport start to calculate the impact of Keane's death on the votes of the other justices in the *Straubinger* case, and on his own.

. . . .

When Davenport comes into the room, Palfrey and Park are standing at one end of the conference table and the Chief, Bauman, Shell, and Cippolone are at the other. Madeleine is studying the portrait of John Marshall over the fireplace that she must by now have committed to memory. Davenport remembers the Chief saying that every time a new justice arrives, a new court is formed, and wonders if the same occurs when one dies. The fixity of the scene suggests to Davenport that the Chief had instructed his colleagues to arrive earlier, probably at 10:00, to discuss the tardy junior justice who has yet to cast his vote in one of the term's most important decisions.

The Chief clears his throat. "Well, I suppose we should get started."

Madeleine joins the others around the table, but no one moves to sit. The Chief sees the dilemma at the same moment Davenport does. "Alex, you are now our second most senior associate justice, so you should take Justice Keane's chair and everyone else should take the next one in order." When no one moves, the Chief glances at Palfrey, and a silent message passes between them. "Well, just for today, in Bernie's memory, why don't we keep his seat vacant."

That frees the others to take their regular places, and when they are settled, the Chief clasps his hands and lowers his head, as if in prayer. "Out of respect for Justice Keane's memory, the court is officially closed to business today and the flag is at half-staff. For ourselves, let us share a moment of silence to remember our colleague and friend."

The interval lasts for no more than thirty fidgety seconds of legs crossing and the backs of hands being examined. Davenport wonders at the impatience of his colleagues, and suspects that it is the implicit intimacy of the moment that so discomforts them. Bricknell's glance circles the table once before he breaks the silence. "Now let's get down to the business of *Straubinger*."

That's it. There will of course be a memorial service and inflated eulogies from the Chief and Palfrey, and probably one from Bauman for political balance. But apart from the momentary awkwardness over the late justice's empty chair, on the day that Bernie Keane died, this is the sum of his absence for the people with whom he spent the most important years of his professional life. There are no signs of grief or, indeed, of any emotion and if Davenport had to characterize the demeanor around the table he would describe it in terms of the marble that lines the court's public areas. Even Gilbert Park is impassive, and it occurs to Davenport that, although the two were the court's only Catholics, Keane and Park may not have been friends at all.

The Chief says, "I have informed the press office that we will release our order in this case at the start of business tomorrow." He pulls the legal pad in front of him closer, as if to read from it, but it is blank. "Procedurally, as I see the situation, we can take either of two actions. One is to announce our decision on the merits. Right now, the vote stands at three in favor of affirming the decision below—Justices Palfrey, Park and myself—and four for reversal—Justices Bauman, Cardona, Shell and Cippolone." He looks at Davenport. "On the assumption that our late colleague is ready to vote—"

Nervous laughter from the others stops him.

"You mean Justice Davenport," Carl Shell says. "Not our late colleague."

"Of course," the Chief says. "An unfortunate choice of words. I should say our delinquent colleague. If we can have your vote today, Richard, we can either reverse 5–3 or divide 4–4. But make no mistake. If we don't have your vote, the press office will release the 4–3 decision tomorrow morning and you can explain to the public why you failed in your duty as an associate justice."

"Alternatively," Bricknell says, "we can put the case down for reargument after the president appoints and the Senate confirms a new associate justice for Justice Keane's seat. That way, we would have a full court considering the issue. You will recall"—the Chief glances at Palfrey—"we did that in two cases after Justice McWhorter died."

Several times while the Chief was speaking, Gilbert Park gestured as if to interrupt, but then abruptly pulled back. Now he leans in again. "If you remember, Chief, we only did that because Justice McWhorter didn't participate in the conferences in those cases before he died, so we didn't have his vote. Justice Keane not only participated in the *Straubinger* conference; he cast his vote."

When the Chief shakes his head, Davenport notices a patch of gray stubble on his cheek. He hadn't gone back to sleep after receiving the midnight phone call from Mary Keane. "I hope you aren't saying, Gilbert, that we should count the vote of a justice who is no longer with us."

"I don't see why not."

"The 'why not' is that a justice can change his vote at any time before the court announces its decision."

Park clasps his hand firmly in front of him and his voice is tight. "Does anyone here believe that Justice Keane would have changed his vote between yesterday and today?"

Donna Cippolone says, "There's never a guarantee that a justice won't change her vote. Even the most predictable justice."

"That's purely hypothetical," Park says.

"No," Donna says, "we've all seen justices change position before. Bernie did it himself in the assisted suicide case."

"Well, surely," Park says, "if Justice Keane knew—"

"Gil makes a good point," Madeleine says. "Bernie changed his position in *Clark* only because, thanks to the compromise that Richard worked out with the Chief, he and the rest of us were voting on a different question. No one's changed the question in the case."

"We simply can't do that." Bauman appears stunned by Madeleine's support for counting Keane's vote. Davenport hadn't previously made the connection that Madeleine was enrolled at Yale when Bauman was on the faculty there. What must it feel like to have your former student not only sit on the same court as you but, as Madeleine has, usurp control of the bloc in which you vote?

"Of course, Herb is right," the Chief says. "We can't do what Gilbert proposes. There's no precedent for it." The Chief has unscrewed his fountain pen and is making check marks on the blank lines of his legal pad, just to have something to do. "No vote counts until the court announces its decision and"—he looks at Davenport—"we have not yet announced our decision."

Palfrey's bowtie this morning is a condolent deep purple and his brogues are crossed on the edge of the conference table so that the soles face Davenport at the other end. "I entirely agree with you, Chief. We can't count Bernie's vote. But there's another way we can honor it. Whatever other justices have done in the past, and for whatever reasons, we do know that Bernie, God bless him, would not have changed his vote in this case."

Madeleine sees where Palfrey is going, and nods. "An interesting idea—"

Whatever proposition Madeleine discerns has eluded Davenport, and evidently the Chief, too. Had she and Palfrey talked about this? The idea is absurd.

"What are you proposing?" The Chief's check marks have filled one column on the page, and he starts on another.

"I'm merely suggesting that if Justice Davenport is having a difficult time deciding on which side to come off the fence he's been sitting on, he might do the institutionally appropriate thing and cast his vote as Bernie would have. He could be Bernie's proxy."

The politics behind the suggestion are transparent. Like Park, Palfrey fears that the president will nominate a liberal to take Keane's seat so that, if they put the case down for reargument before the full court, there will be five votes to strike down the New York law, however Davenport votes. In this of course Park and Palfrey are wrong, for Davenport knows from his last conversation with Tony Locke that the president will extract from his new Supreme Court nominee a pledge to vote with the conservatives to uphold the New York law. Or the president will simply nominate Oren Nyquist.

The Chief dismisses Palfrey's suggestion as he did Park's. "Richard has taken some time to make up his mind, but I'm sure he has no desire to be anyone's proxy." He puts down his pen. "I think we're ready to vote on whether to decide this case on the merits now, or to put it down for reargument."

Carl Shell says, "If we care at all about the public's approval, I think it would be a mistake to rule on an important case like this without a full complement of justices." This has more to do with politics than with Shell's pathological regard for public opinion. Like Palfrey and Park, Shell mistakenly believes that a new justice will guarantee a liberal majority.

"A full complement has already voted," Palfrey says. "Or at least it will have done so once Justice Davenport casts his vote. The only difference is that one of those votes—Justice Keane's—will not be recorded. Also, if you're truly concerned with the court's image, you might want to remember that this is as an emergency appeal. This boy could be dead by the time a new justice is confirmed and the case is reargued."

"No deader than he'll be if Justice Davenport votes with you and we have a 4–4 tie." Cippolone says.

"Let's have a show of hands," the Chief says. "How many to put *Straubinger* down for reargument?"

Bauman and Shell raise their hands. The Chief looks at Cippolone. "Donna?"

Davenport thinks that she knows something; that the president is in political trouble and plans to nominate a conservative as his next justice. But she only shrugs and, eyes on Madeleine, says, "I'm with Herb and Carl."

"How many opposed?"

Palfrey and Park raise their hands and, after a long moment, Madeleine joins them. Unlike Donna, she has evidently divined Locke's plans for his next appointment and believes that it would be better to have the vote right now. Again disappointed by his former student, Bauman shakes his head.

"Including my vote," the Chief says, "that makes it 4–3 to decide the case now. How do you vote, Richard?"

What would happen, Davenport thinks, if he joined Donna, Carl and Herb to make the vote for reargument 4–4? He decides not to find out, and follows Madeleine's political calculation instead. "I think we should vote on the case now."

"Excellent." The Chief beams. "So all we need is your vote on the merits, Richard, and we can announce our decision."

Coming into the conference room, Davenport was certain of his vote. But now he distrusts the Chief's simple arithmetic. What if something other than an insider's knowledge about the president's next nomination explains Madeleine's vote to decide the case today and her support for Park's suggestion that they count Keane's vote? There was Donna's reminder, too, that even the most predictable justices have changed their votes in the past, and then her hesitation over deciding the case now. In the justices' maneuvering, and with Keane gone, Davenport sees the possibility for engineering a unanimous vote.

"Richard?"

"You said you plan to announce the decision tomorrow morning?"

"At 10:00."

"Give me until Friday—"

"That's impossible—"

"Why? It's just one more day. What difference could it make? I'll get my decision to you Thursday night before 6:00."

"You can't do that!" Palfrey swings his feet off the table and half rises. "This is disgraceful behavior. I have never—"

"Alex is right, Richard." It is the Chief. "We have to reach closure on this."

"You will have closure, Chief—"

"We already have closure," Madeleine says.

All at the table turn, and it is clear where her protégé, Christine, learned her regal bearing. Madeleine is silent for an unbearable few seconds, and when she speaks again the tone is almost offhand. "I vote with the Chief, Alex and Gilbert to affirm the decision below." As if there could be any misunderstanding, she says, "I am changing my vote. So we now have 4–3 to affirm, 5–3 if Richard joins us. If he doesn't join us, the vote will be 4–4, which still leaves the decision below standing."

The reaction around the table is muted. Bauman is shaking his head again, but Cippolone is still. Shell, as usual, makes eye contact with no one. The Chief, Palfrey, and Park give no sign of pleasure at their victory. Davenport has the impression that Madeleine has done this before, and suspects that Donna's remark about the most predictable justices changing their votes had been directed at her.

The Chief looks at Davenport. Until this moment, Bricknell had failed to consider the most obvious reason for Davenport's delay; that he thinks he can forge a unanimous vote. "You want to talk to us before you vote. See how comfortable you are with our draft opinion." The Chief can be magnanimous, for the worst his side can now do is a 4–4 vote.

Davenport says, "I'll want to look at Herb's opinion, too."

"We can do that," Donna says. "Herb wrote a draft, but Carl and I contributed some of the language."

"Well then, I don't believe there's any problem with doing that," the Chief says. "So long as we have your vote by 6:00 p.m. Thursday." He looks around the table. "Does anyone have—"

"I do," Palfrey says. "Justice Davenport wants to hijack our opinion. He wants to dilute it to the point where it can incorporate Herb's views and Carl's and hers." He points at Donna, as if he's forgotten her name. "You're going to try to turn this into an 8–0 opinion—"

"I can imagine worse things happening," the Chief says.

"No, Chief. He's manipulating us." Palfrey's face is a dangerous color and it looks like the purple bowtie is strangling him. He turns to Davenport. "You orchestrated this from the beginning. From when you gave them the fourth vote to take the appeal, when Carl wouldn't. When you refused to vote at conference—"

"What are you talking about?" Madeleine's scorn for Palfrey is unmistakable. "Do you also think Richard arranged Bernie's heart attack so he could become the swing vote on this?"

The Chief throws an angry glance at Palfrey. "I think this is a fine plan. Richard will discuss my opinion with me, and Herb's with him, and we'll see where he comes out. He got all of us to sign on to the assisted suicide decision. Maybe he can do the same here." He doesn't wait for anyone to challenge him. "Six o'clock Thursday, then. Agreed?

Davenport nods.

"Then we are adjourned until 10:00 a.m. Friday, when we will release our decision in Straubinger v. New York."

"Only if we have one," Palfrey says.

Madeleine is gone from the conference room before Davenport can catch up with her, and she is not in the corridor on his way back to chambers. In the courtyard, where he talked with her last week, the fountain is off and Harold sits on the rim of the basin, coatless, his hands jammed for warmth into his trouser pockets. He doesn't see Davenport come into the courtyard, and when he looks up his eyes are moist and red, his face swollen.

"This must be a real loss for you, Harold."

"I was just talking to him yesterday afternoon." A shiver rattles the clerk's voice. "This is going to crush Kevin. Mrs. Keane, too."

"Are you close to them?"

"I helped Kevin study for exams last year."

"That doesn't sound like something the justice would ask you to do."

"He didn't. Kevin and I met at a Sunday dinner, and he called me later. Justice Keane didn't know."

"From what I saw, his father was pretty rough on him."

"He was rough on me when I clerked for him, but I learned more from him than I ever will from anyone."

Me, too, Davenport thinks, even though it took a 2 × 4.

"You're wrong if you think Kevin isn't going to miss him." Harold removes a handkerchief from his back pocket and blows his nose. It is the display handkerchief with a stranger's monogram. "Kevin worshiped his father. He'd do anything for him."

What was there about this cruel, willful man that inspired such loyalty from his family and his clerks? "He couldn't have been easy to live with."

"The justice was a man of principle."

"You mean he wouldn't bend."

Harold says, "He'd bend, but no more than a degree or two, so you wouldn't see it unless you took the long view. Justice Keane was a greater believer in taking the long view."

"And that's why he joined my opinion in the assisted suicide case."

Shutters close behind the young clerk's eyes. "After my clerkship year was over, Justice Keane never talked with me about court business."

"But you talk with his current clerks."

"They're as loyal to him as I was."

"Then why do you think he joined my opinion in Clark?"

"It was narrow enough that he could live with it, and even he accepted that a 9–0 decision in a big case is not a bad thing."

"I don't buy that."

For all of his talents, Harold is young and Davenport is experienced at waiting out reluctant witnesses. Finally, Harold says, "I think his vote was Justice Keane's way of reminding Senator Nyquist that he wouldn't be blackmailed.'

"The senator was blackmailing him?"

"He tried." Harold looks away. Soot has darkened the icing of snow on the fountain. "In his last year in law practice, Justice Keane conducted an investigation for Cardinal McGowan into child sexual abuse by priests in the archdiocese. Nyquist thought it was a whitewash and he told the justice that he had documented information that the report covered up the most serious abuses. Justice Keane kicked the senator out of his office."

Davenport pictures the leprechaun-sized justice tossing the raw-boned North Dakotan from his chambers. He had been wrong about Keane from the start, with his suspicion that it was the justice who had given the inquest transcript to Nyquist. Keane had never seen the coroner's report, and had in fact deduced the senator's attempt to blackmail the new justice from his own experience with the man. "Who knows about this?"

"One of my co-clerks and me. I don't know if he told any of his other clerks."

"Why didn't you stay with him for a second term?"

"No clerk stays with a justice more than a year. I already had the offer to teach at Harvard."

"But you put that off so you could clerk for me."

"Justice Keane asked me to. That's the only reason I stayed. He said it would be good for the court if you had the benefit of my experience with him."

Davenport remembers Keane's judgment on him at their meeting yesterday. "Why would I be in need of that?"

"He said you had the makings of a great justice but, as much as he respected your rejection of ideology, he worried that, without some framework for deciding hard cases, you would turn into a lightweight like the Chief and waste your energy chasing after big majorities. That you would never get to see that it is ideas and principles that define the court's work, not majorities."

"That's a fine notion, but it's majorities that make the law."

"From day to day, sure. But, over the long term, what moves majorities? The Chief or Palfrey, or even Justice Bauman or Cardona, could be writing a majority opinion, but they were always looking over their shoulder at Justice Keane. They wanted to know what he had to say."

"And, apart from him, how does someone get to be a great justice?"

"Justice Keane hated what Justice Blackmun did with the abortion cases, but he thought Blackmun was as fine a justice as we've ever had. He told me to read Blackmun's biography, where he was deciding how he would vote in *Roe v. Wade*. Blackmun spent weeks in the main library researching the law. But late at night he'd go into the justices' private library, and not to study the law. He already knew that cold. No, he was studying himself, his own conscience. Justice Keane said that's what a great judge does. A good judge steals from other judges, from precedent, but a great judge steals from himself."

Davenport says, "Do you have any idea how much it would change constitutional law if the justices actually did that?"

"If a judge can manipulate the language and history of the Constitution to serve his political beliefs, what harm would it do if he twisted them to serve the cause of justice instead?"

Davenport considers repeating the brave belief of his confirmation testimony, that justice is a frail illusion, but he can no more do so with Harold today than he could with Keane yesterday. "The court is closed, Harold. Go home. There's no reason for you to stick around here."

"I rent a room. My people are all down in Tennessee. Up here in Washington, the court is the closest I have to a home."

The statement is, as Davenport would expect from Harold, matter-of-fact, not maudlin. He has to talk to Madeleine about her changed vote, and then with the others about reaching a compromise. But before he can do that he needs to sit with Harold for another moment to mourn the death of a justice.

18

Years ago, when he was still a young associate at his Manhattan law firm, Davenport's overcoat was stolen from the cloak room at the Harvard Club, and he never replaced it. He is brushing snow off the sleeve of his suit jacket—a blizzard had started in the afternoon—and is lost in thoughts about *Straubinger* when a movement at the door to his condominium startles him. The face that looks up from the hooded parka is Nola's. "I need to apologize," she says. "I have to talk to you."

Inside, Nola makes a tour of the apartment while Davenport boils water for tea. Her curiosity about the circumstances of his life pleases him, but it seems to Davenport that, now that she is here, she has second thoughts about talking to him. When Davenport comes into the living room, Nola is on the couch and takes the mug of tea he hands her. She says, "I'm sorry about the transcript. The senator lied when he told me he was going to use it to stop your confirmation."

Olivia never once apologized for the wreckage she caused, and it encourages Davenport that in this respect his daughter is different. Still, he has to work to keep the disappointment out of his voice. "Are you telling me you're sorry you gave him the transcript, or just that he didn't use it to kill my nomination?"

Nola studies the carpet. She is in no state to appreciate her father's irony. "When I went to see him—"

"Really, Nola, I don't need to hear this."

"Yes, you do!" Her voice is fierce. "It wasn't easy getting in to see him. His assistant wanted to know what I had before he would give me an appointment, but I told him I would only show it to the senator. When I finally got in to see him, he wasn't anything like he was at the hearings. He was nice and sort of clumsy, like a farmer. He took me through his big fancy office to a small room that had no windows and there was this weird smell, like mothballs. He took a long time reading the transcript, more than an hour, and he didn't stop to talk or even to look at me. When he finally finished, he said he needed to know everything about you and her."

"And you told him what I said after she tried to kill herself."

"That, and a few other things, but just day-to-day stuff."

Davenport lets this pass. He wants Nola to be done with the story and to be his daughter again.

"Then he said that if he was going to use the transcript at the hearing I had to put what I told him in writing. I said I didn't want to, but he said it was necessary to lay a foundation. He had to be able put the coroner's report in context."

"So you didn't just talk to him. You signed an affidavit."

"An affidavit, a statement—sure. The minute I walked into the hearing room, while you were talking, I knew he wasn't going to use the transcript. He even gave me a look like 'Do you really think I was going to use it for that?'"

"Nyquist knew that if he stopped my confirmation, the president would just nominate someone else like me. This way—"

"—he can blackmail you. That's what he's doing, isn't it? Getting you to vote his way."

"I told you in your apartment, that's not going to happen."

"This is about the case with the twin boys, isn't it? In upstate New York?"

"Buffalo," Davenport says.

"Am I allowed to ask how you're going to vote?"

Davenport shakes his head and when he sees that she misunderstands, says, "Of course you can ask. I just haven't made up my mind yet. How would you vote?"

"That's easy." She is glad to have the subject of the coroner's report behind her. "I'd vote for the transplant. I can see how it would be hard for the parents to decide which of their sons to put at risk, but I don't understand why it should be a hard decision for you."

"Well, there's a small matter of the United States Constitution that I swore to uphold—"

"I had a con law course in high school. I know all about federalism and the power of the states. But I don't see what right New York has to second-guess the parents' decision. If they were abusing their kids, sure, that would be a problem. But short of that, you have to trust parents to do the right thing for their children."

Nola sees Davenport's bemusement, and the look she returns is curious. They are not past the coroner's report, after all. She says, "It wasn't all a disaster, you know. We had some good times, the three of us. You just don't remember."

Now Davenport understands her expression. It is hard for him to accept, but on the difficult subject of family, Nola is more courageous than he is.

Nola says, "Remember that weekend she said that, if we didn't get off our butts, we were going to spend the rest of our lives in New York without seeing a single tourist site? I think I was ten. Do you remember where she took us—the Statue of Liberty, the Empire State Building—"

"The Bronx Zoo, the Botanical Gardens—"

"The Staten Island Ferry, even though we didn't get off, just turned around and came back."

"Why did you go to see Nyquist?"

Nola rises from the couch and walks to the window, where outside the snow is still falling hard. She says, "I never thought of Washington as a place where it snows."

Davenport fears that he has pushed too hard, and has lost her again.

Nola says, "I didn't think you really cared about people. Or that you had any right to judge what they did." Her eyes are on the falling snow. "I hated you."

"Because of how you think I treated your mother?"

Nola turns, and in that long, silent moment Davenport realizes he has not understood a single thing about his family. Not one. "Not her," Nola says. "Me. The way you treated me. Your job was to protect me, and you didn't."

Davenport remembers when Nola was four and learning to ice-skate. The beginner's class at the Wollman Rink in Central Park was full, so Olivia enrolled her in one more advanced, and as the older girls performed their glides and turns, Davenport watched in agony as his daughter struggled just to stay upright. His fury at Olivia's negligence, her casual indifference to their daughter's humiliation, receded only when, at the end of the lesson, Nola clambered out of the rink beaming, evidently without a clue that she had performed anything less than superbly. Davenport thinks, from what did this stout heart need protection? "Protect you from what?"

"From her! Your job was to protect me from her."

Davenport would not be more astonished if someone told him that Nola was not his daughter, or Olivia not his wife. "I always thought you were best friends. I was jealous of you. Going to lunch together. Your shopping expeditions. Going off for your walks on the beach at 'Sconset."

"Are you serious? She kidnapped me. That's what it felt like. She took me hostage and wouldn't let me go. Why do you think I went to Columbia?"

"You said you wanted to live in the City. I wanted you to go to Harvard."

"I wanted to go to Harvard more than anything in the world, but she said she wouldn't survive a day if I left. She said she would kill herself."

Davenport's mistake had been to ascribe to Nola every attribute of decency other than kinship to himself. He says, "She told me that if I divorced her, she'd kill herself, but I never imagined she would do something like that to you."

"I thought you were smart enough to figure that out for yourself."

"If she really wanted to kill herself, she would have, Nola. It had nothing to do with you or me. There was nothing we could do about it."

"How was I supposed to know that? I was a kid." Nola's eyes meet his and fill with understanding. "I think she did want to kill herself. She just didn't have the courage."

"You mean what happened on the ferry." If Davenport could rewind his life and undo his actions that night, he still doesn't know if he would. He chooses his words carefully. "I'm sorry I didn't do a better job of protecting you. But what could I have done?"

And there it is, hanging between them, the question to which both now know the answer, but themselves lack the courage or the recklessness to speak. Much as Davenport aches to share his secret with Nola, he knows that he will not.

Nola says, "Do you miss her?"

Davenport is aware that they have been speaking of Olivia as *she* and *her*, and not by name, as if she has become a ghost. Their ghost. "Do you?"

"Sometimes," Nola says. A fleeting smile, no more than a shadow, crosses her lips. "But mostly, having her gone is a relief." She lets their eyes meet again. "I'm not supposed to say that, am I?"

Davenport hears the question behind the question. "I feel the same way."

"It's like, after all the noise crashing around you, you find yourself in a big, empty, quiet room."

"Exactly."

"You're not going to let him blackmail you, are you?" Nola has moved back to the safety of the present.

"Of course not." Davenport still hasn't decided how he is going to vote. He wants to know if Nola has a boyfriend, anyone serious, but asks about her schoolwork instead. He is not surprised that his daughter, who spent so much of her high school years in the City's museums has decided to major in art history, and they talk for a while about which periods will be the most interesting for her study. "Would you like to stay over? The couch in my study folds out, and there's linen in the closet. I think I can find an extra toothbrush for you."

"I have to be back for an exam tomorrow. There's a ten o'clock flight to LaGuardia."

Davenport glances out the window. "If they're flying." In the boat harbor, the falling snow only partially obscures the running lights that bob and dip with the current.

"I'll take my chances. Can you call a taxi while I wash up?"

"I'll drive you." Davenport will do anything to prolong his time with Nola, but he feels a spark of resentment, for she has cheated him. He had wanted her to challenge his treatment of Olivia, and she has offered him only her own complicity. Whoever said that women are romantic and men are realists, never met his daughter or him.

Davenport ducks his head, a swimmer's reflex, as he takes the ramp down into the Harbour Square garage, back from the airport. He does the same in the morning when he enters the court's underground parking. This going down is like a dive underwater, a submersion at the start and end of his work day. Inside the garage, sodium lamps dazzle and bounce off yellow enameled walls, but otherwise, no light is squandered here. An incandescent bulb in a wire basket barely illuminates two or three square feet in front of the single elevator, and when Davenport opens the car door, a small pool of light spills into the darkness.

A stench of piss and beer swamps the usual residues of automobile exhaust. Ten feet away, a human shadow moves from behind a pillar and weaves across the narrow band of light. The man is stocky and about Davenport's height. Across his chest he holds a rifle at an angle, as a soldier would. Davenport's first thought is that this is a security guard from the complex, but of course it isn't, for the guards at Harbour Square aren't armed. A hand gun would alarm Davenport, but curiously the rifle does not. If anything, it appears comical; the intruder is playing at cowboys and Indians in this cloistered space lined with expensive automobiles.

As the man comes closer, Davenport sees that his khaki army jacket is unzipped, revealing bright block letters against a dark background, "U C" on top, "O" below. As if he is completing a crossword puzzle, Davenport finds himself trying to remember which University of California campus has an "O" in the middle of its location. Is there a UC Stockton? He says, "Can I help you?"

The youth—this close, Davenport sees that he is no more than eighteen or nineteen—crooks the rifle in an arm and with the hand that he had been using to support its butt, removes a folded sheet from a jacket pocket, shakes it open, squints at it and then at Davenport. "You're the judge, right? Davenport."

"I hope this isn't about a case."

"Of course it's about a case!" The boy's words are strained and come from high in his throat. "Why else would I be here?"

"Well, that's impossible. I can't talk to you about a case."

"Are you serious? Who else am I going to talk to? Do you know who I am?"

"It doesn't matter who you are." Davenport rapidly sorts through the criminal appeals on the court's docket, but the names of the defendants are an anonymous blur. "A judge can't talk to a party in a pending case."

"I'm going to die if I don't get a transplant, and you tell me you can't talk to me? You can't take one fucking minute out of your important day to listen to someone whose life is in your hands?"

Of course. This is Leonard Straubinger, Jr., for the past several days, a name as familiar to him as his own daughter's. Now that he understands who the youth is and why he is here, Davenport knows that no further conversation is possible. He starts toward the elevator, but Leonard is agile for someone so thick-bodied, and intercepts him, pressing the rifle muzzle into Davenport's chest to restrain him.

If the rifle doesn't frighten Davenport, Leonard's flushed condition does. His face is swollen, the skin mottled as if from fever. In an unheated garage on a winter night, perspiration streams down his cheeks. The garage is vast and, even this late, there are empty spaces, including Madeleine and Phil's, two slots away from his own. Before long, a neighbor will arrive and call the police who can take the boy to a hospital. "Look, Leonard—"

"Junior."

"There's a system, Junior. I didn't create it, but I'm a part of it. If judges started talking to the parties in their cases, the whole system would collapse."

"What kind of fucked-up system won't let someone talk to the man who has the power to save him? My lawyer told me you're the judge who's going to decide my case."

"Along with eight others."

"I know that," Junior says. "But he said your vote is the one that's going to make the difference."

This time, when Junior pokes Davenport with the rifle barrel, his jacket falls open, revealing a yellow-lettered message that Davenport has never seen on a shirt before. Like the rifle, the effect is absurd rather than intimidating. What are young men watching on television these days that this one would think that, by brandishing a rifle, he can make a Supreme Court justice vote his way in a pending case? Does he imagine this is a video game? Does he truly believe there won't be consequences? "How do you know I don't already plan to vote for you?"

"That's what my lawyer said, but he's not very smart. This is my insurance."

The clatter of metal floor plates echoes at the entrance to the garage and tires squeal from a car taking a turn too fast. Headlights careen off the shadowed corners close to where Davenport stands, and he is about to shout for help, but the lights veer off in a different direction. Davenport knows that no matter how many times he tells Junior that this conversation is impossible, he will not change the youth's mind.

Davenport says, "How did you find me?"

"You're kidding, right? Anyone can find you. Where you live. Your apartment number. That you don't use the court police. You drive yourself home." Junior's voice has turned reedy. He is fighting for breath. "Your daughter goes to school in New York. She lives on 113th Street."

Davenport reaches into his jacket and removes his cellphone. "Do you know what will happen if I call the police and tell them you're threatening me?"

A sharp crack from the rifle butt knocks the phone to the concrete floor. "The only person I hear making threats is you."

Davenport's hand throbs and he wonders how quick the police will be to get the boy to a hospital. Another set of headlights slashes through the darkness and disappears. Behind Davenport an exhaust fan switches on. "Look at yourself. You need to get to a hospital."

"Do you have any idea what it's like being chained to that fucking machine? I can't stay on it forever. I need a transplant now."

"How did you get here?"

"I drove."

"You came from Buffalo, right? That has to be an eight-hour drive. What about your treatment?"

"I've skipped nights before. I'm on a portable machine."

"Look, Junior—"

"You think you're some big fucking deal." He shakes his head unsteadily. "Lawyers think they can talk anyone into anything."

"And you think that's what I'm trying to do?"

The fever has sharpened the boy's eyes, and that or the alcohol makes them glitter. "Is your head so far up your ass you can't hear me? I need your help."

The sense that he is looking not only at Junior Straubinger, but also at his autistic twin, jars Davenport. "How much have you had to drink?"

"It doesn't matter. I piss like everybody else."

Young as he is, Junior has the caginess of a practiced drunk, and Davenport remembers how dangerous Olivia could be when she was like this. "People write to me. You didn't have to come here."

"Do you read their letters?"

"Some. I read your mother's letter."

"My mother wrote to you?"

Against his judgment Davenport had finally torn open the brown and gold express envelope, and then the letter on hotel stationery inside. This is a family, Davenport thinks, that doesn't believe that rules were made for them. "Do you have any idea what you're doing to her? How selfish you are?"

"I can't believe she wrote to you."

They could go on like this all night, but Junior needs to see a doctor. Davenport bends to reach for his phone but the boy's reflex is too quick and, depleted as he is, his grip on Davenport's arm is like steel. Junior's recklessness of his own welfare infuriates Davenport and he hurls all his force against the boy, driving him into the pillar behind him, pinning him there, each hand against a shoulder. The rifle drops. Junior crumbles under his hands like something made of paper. In his fingertips Davenport feels the pulse of grave illness. "How long have you been like this?"

Junior doesn't respond. The eyes blaze with fever.

"I've never seen anyone who wants to kill himself as much as you do. You don't want a transplant. You want to die."

"I would never do anything to hurt my brother."

"Let me drive you to an emergency room." With his hands, Davenport props up the falling youth. Headlights sweep the wall and Davenport prays that it's not Madeleine or Phil. "Stand up straight. Move away from the pillar."

Junior only glares at him.

"If you don't move, a SWAT team will be here right after that car."

With an effort, Junior shuffles two or three steps clear of the pillar and Davenport tentatively loosens his hold. Seconds later, when the car passes Davenport has one hand on the boy's shoulder, and with the other waves casually at the driver. He zips up Junior's jacket.

"I can drive myself. I don't need you." Strength has returned to Junior's voice. "I'm not leaving until you promise to vote for me."

"You know I can't do that."

"Then promise you'll think about it."

"I promise you, Junior, I think about nothing else." Davenport feels the boy's fever through his clothes. "Where's your car?"

"I have a van. I parked a couple of blocks away."

A jet leaves a trail that bisects the universe. A bicyclist in France turns right rather than left. An instant's decision to act or not can change your life forever. The lives of others, too. Mothers who write letters. Wives who sit on ferry railings.

Junior starts away, then turns. "But you're going to vote for me, right?"

"Get going."

"I'm doing the best I can. You know that, right?"

"Sure," Davenport says.

"Can you say that for yourself? That you're doing the best you can?"

This time Davenport has no answer.

19

Anne is at the open door when Davenport comes down the corridor on his way to Madeleine's chambers. "Senator Nyquist wants to talk to you."

"Tell him to put what he wants in writing."

"No, I mean he's here." She gestures behind her. "In your office."

"Why would you—"

"I'm sorry, but he was getting in my hair, asking about Nola—how well I know her, what she's doing now." Anne sees her mistake and, rare for her, becomes contrite. "He was talking with Edward when I left him."

In his alcove, Edward frowns in the direction of Davenport's office. Nyquist has taken the chair across from the rocker. "I see you've left Justice McWhorter's office as it was." He glances at the blazing fireplace. "Edward still builds a fine fire."

"I have a busy day, Senator. What can I do for you?"

Nyquist continues looking around to let Davenport know that he will not be rushed. This is the nearest Davenport has been to him, closer than in the hearing room, and it may be the absence of television lights, but the eyes seem even more deeply hooded, the senator's bearing cadaverous. Davenport thinks of the black-and-white woodcut villains in the children's books of his youth.

"Well, let's get down to business." The senator's voice is tight. "I understand that you're holding back your vote in the transplant case."

"Before a decision is announced, no one can know if the justices have even met."

"You know, Justice Davenport, it's curious how people make the mistake of thinking that the Senate exercises power over the justices only when we confirm you and when we convict you following impeachment." The senator's tone has become easy. "The public doesn't appreciate how deep an interest members of the Judiciary Committee take in the justices' activities between those two events."

Davenport doesn't know which is more absurd, the observation or the implicit threat of impeachment. "There is nothing I can tell you about the case."

"You're being foolish, so let me tell you what you already know. The vote going into this morning's conference was 4–4, with you abstaining. Justice Keane's death made it 4–3 in favor of overturning the New York statute. But then Justice Cardona changed her vote which, with your continued abstention, made it 4–3 to uphold the statute, and that is where the vote presently stands."

Nyquist's source had called him as soon as the conference ended, while Davenport was in the courtyard with Harold. Davenport realizes that his knowledge of his colleagues is so meager that the senator's informant could be any of them.

"As I said, Senator, I have a busy day, so you will understand if—"

"I am sure that at least one of your fellow justices has pointed out to you that, after the opinion you wrote in the assisted suicide case, it would be impossible for you to vote to overturn the New York statute."

Davenport considers whether it was Nyquist and not the Chief who engineered the trap for him to write the opinion in *Clark*. He also remembers Keane's unexpected suggestion at the conference that they disregard the opinion. "I'm very grateful for your advice, Senator." He starts to rise. "But as I said—"

"Please sit, Justice Davenport—"

"I already told your aide that I will not be blackmailed—"

"Just for a few minutes. In the interests, let's say, of senatorial oversight."

"Even if we voted, and even if your numbers are right, if I vote against the statute, the result will be a 4–4 tie and you'll still get what you want. The statute will remain in force and this boy will not get his transplant."

"I'm afraid you don't understand. I have devoted a good deal of prayer to this case, and a 4–4 draw is not what I had in mind. What

I need is a ringing declaration from the Supreme Court of the United States that the New York legislature did the right and moral thing when it enacted this statute. That to allow a transplant in these circumstances would violate God's will. That is why I need you to join the Chief Justice and the others and make this a 5–3 decision."

Davenport is tired of the back-and-forth, which could consume the rest of the day. It could, he realizes, fill the remainder of his time on the court. "The coroner's transcript is a sealed document. There's no way you can use it without committing a felony."

"Have you forgotten that it was Nola who gave me the transcript?" He cocks his head. "Or is it possible that she hasn't told you about our meeting? Legally, Nola had a perfect right to do anything with the transcript she pleased."

Like the senator's familiarity with his chambers, there is a creepiness about the intimacy with which he uses Nola's name. Behind this, Davenport feels the force of politics grinding forward. Impeachment would be a masterstroke, achieving for the senator not only a black mark against a Democratic president, but a warning to future nominees and a rallying cause for the far-right branch of his party. Also, and not the least, he would win Davenport's removal and another open seat on the court.

"You'll never get the House to impeach or the Senate to convict."

"Please, Justice Davenport, you misunderstand my intentions. I don't plan to initiate impeachment proceedings. It's been two centuries since a Supreme Court justice has been impeached. Unless of course you resign, you have life tenure."

Madeleine's boast. "What do you want from me?"

"As I said, for you to join the Chief and the others in this transplant case."

"And if I don't?"

"Did you know that my first job out of law school was in a district attorney's office? One of the great advantages of being a prosecutor in North Dakota is that there were so few of us and so much work to go around that, green as we were, they started us out with felonies. And once you've had your first felony jury trial, well, the taste never leaves you, and you just want more. Of course, my present responsibilities prevent me from prosecuting cases, but I'm sure there are plenty of hungry young lawyers in the district attorney's office in Barnstable County, Massachusetts. That's where your wife died, isn't it?"

"If you read the coroner's report, you know they went through all of this and concluded that there is no evidence of a crime."

"I also know that inquests can be reopened. There's no double jeopardy."

"And your new evidence?"

"Why, Nola, of course. Our conversation in my office."

Davenport's first thought is that Nola gave Nyquist more than she told him. But of course she hadn't, for what more could she know? "Any testimony about your meeting with my daughter would be hearsay."

Nyquist shakes his head. "It wouldn't be my testimony in court. It would be Nola's. I'm sure the prosecutors in Barnstable County will want to subpoena her. It would be gross misfeasance not to."

"You can't—" The words are a reflex. Of course Nyquist can do this. Davenport had warned Nola as much.

"I can't because she's your daughter? It's curious, isn't it, how the evidence code gives a privilege against testifying to spouses, but not to children. Nola will make a wonderful witness. A beautiful young woman. Passionate, but so disappointed in her father."

"You would do this to get my seat on the court?"

"I don't need your seat." He watches for Davenport's reaction. "Your president already promised me Justice Keane's."

Keane's deal with Locke would not have included Nyquist as his replacement. Keane would never allow this blackmailer on the court. No, this was a bargain struck directly between Locke and the senator. "Then why are you doing this?"

"You really don't understand, do you? I want you off the court. You are an immoral man. You are even worse than the liberal progressives like Bauman and Cardona. They at least have a philosophy to guide them. You, on the other hand, are a nihilist. You decide cases on personal whim. A trial will reveal you for the immoral man you are, and the publicity will force you to resign."

Davenport fights the thought that he can end this by resigning right now. He knows that this is only fatigue pulling him down. Exit was

Olivia's solution, not his. "And I can avoid a trial by letting you tell me how to vote."

"I know you see me as one of God's dark creatures, Justice Davenport. Some people do. But I see this as a fair compromise."

Davenport has never wanted his seat on the court as much as he wants it right now. He has a vote to cast in the transplant case and another's—Madeleine's—to maneuver as leverage for a compromise. "And your idea of morality is to blackmail justices into voting your way. Not just me. Others, too."

"I don't know what you're talking about."

"You tried to blackmail Justice Keane over a child sex abuse cover-up."

"That's ridiculous. It's inconceivable that Justice Keane would ever submit to blackmail."

"You know that only because you tried with him and failed."

Keane is dead and for Nyquist no longer a threat. Davenport understands that he has lost if he cannot come up with another name. He takes a leap. "Justice Cardona wouldn't have changed her vote in the transplant case if you weren't blackmailing her. She waited to see if I would vote your way and she changed her vote only when I didn't."

The former prosecutor's dead, hooded eyes give no clue whether Davenport has hit a target. "Where would a United States senator from North Dakota get the resources to dig up dirt on Supreme Court justices?"

Davenport remembers Edward's look on his way into the office. Difficult as it is to accept, it is not hard to believe that Justice McWhorter's sharp right turn in his later years on the court was the result of Nyquist's visits to his chambers. "You don't need resources. You're a magnet for every low-level aide with a grudge against his boss, every rejected mistress or personal assistant fired from her job." And, Davenport thinks, every daughter who resents her father for failing to protect her.

"You know," Nyquist says, "if there's a trial in Barnstable County, it won't be for manslaughter or negligent homicide. You'll be tried for first degree murder. I don't believe you just watched when your wife went into the water. I believe you pushed her."

This is what Keane predicted, and Davenport wonders what it says about him that, of all people, his blackmailer would understand the darkest corner of his soul. But it is only a corner, he reminds himself, and not the whole of it.

Nyquist says, "Do you have any concern for how this is going to affect Nola? Testifying at trial? The media are not going to be kind to her."

"Do you have a child, Senator?"

"We're not talking about my children."

"What would you do to protect them?"

"I would never put them in a position where they could be disgraced the way you have."

"I've done nothing to embarrass my daughter."

"You put her in the center of this," Nyquist says.

"No, she did that herself. What happens next is her business, not mine."

"Are you that immoral, that you don't care what happens to your own daughter?"

"Of course I care! But if my daughter is going to succeed in life, she's going to have to learn to take it on its own terms."

"I don't believe you. You're bluffing."

It may have started as a bluff—and Davenport isn't sure even of that—but the words fit his conviction perfectly. And his sturdy ice skater will survive just fine. "The difference between you and me, Senator, is that you're a coward and I'm not. Whatever happened with my wife on that ferry, I'm prepared to take responsibility for my part. I'll go to trial if I have to, rather than vote your way. You, on the other hand, are going to fold."

Their voices must have dropped to a whisper because Anne's voice on the intercom startles them both. "The president is on the phone."

It is not hard to guess what Locke wants. "Tell him I'll call back." Then it occurs to Davenport that it is always the president who calls him. "Get a number."

"Why would I fold?

"You may not be as smart as you think you are, but you're smart enough to know that a criminal case against me in Massachusetts is a long shot at best. You have the coroner's report weighing against you. All the rest of what you think you have is hearsay and speculation.

Even my daughter's affidavit. On the other hand, when word gets out that you've been blackmailing justices of the United States Supreme Court, your senate colleagues, who you think are going to confirm your nomination to the court, are going to vote to expel you from the Senate. I suppose, though, you will have the good sense to resign before that happens."

"And you're telling me that if I back off from you, you'll back off from this."

"No," Davenport says. "I'm telling you that if I ever hear even a whisper that you are pressuring any justice of this court to vote your way, I will inform the attorney general, the majority leader of the Senate and the chairman of the Judiciary Committee of your activities."

Nyquist says, "Before you make your decision, I think you will want to discuss this with your friend, the president. I have the impression that on matters like this you are not particularly astute."

Davenport rises. The fatigue has lifted and his energy overflows. "You will have to excuse me, Senator. As I said, I have a busy day."

20

Madeleine's office is as stylish and contained as the justice herself. The walls are hung with prints by Johns and Rauschenberg. Two couches of a rough weave face each other across a steel and glass coffee table on which is a framed photograph of a young Phil Bronson in hiking gear with snow-capped mountains in the background. The faint scent of forest is from the sheaf of spruce boughs in the fireplace. Madeleine looks up from the small writer's table angled across a corner of the office.

Davenport asks, "Was it you who told Nyquist about this morning's vote?"

"Why would I do that?"

"He was in my office just now. He knows everything that happened."

"I have no idea who would tell him."

"Why did you change your vote this morning?"

"The Chief convinced me that because I signed on to your opinion in the assisted suicide case, I couldn't vote one way in that case and the other way in this one".

"I find it hard to picture the Chief convincing you of anything. Nyquist is blackmailing you, isn't he?"

"That's ridiculous."

Davenport considers how cleverly Madeleine has protected herself. If she stays with the Chief, Palfrey, and Park, and if he votes with Bauman, Shell, and Cippolone, the court's order will consist of a single anonymous sentence: "The judgment is affirmed by an equally divided court." Nyquist will know that she voted with the Chief, but her friends in the abortion rights community will have no reason to think that she abandoned them. They will believe it was the new justice, a man unencumbered by ideology, who joined the Chief and the others.

"You're not the only one he's blackmailing," Davenport says. "He threatened to reopen the inquest into Olivia's death if I don't vote with the Chief and you. To have my daughter subpoenaed to testify."

"What did you do?"

At first Davenport thinks she means what he did on the ferry, then understands that Madeleine is only asking how he dealt with Nyquist. "I told him to leave."

Madeleine rises, as if that will be enough for him to go. "You must have misunderstood him. United States senators don't blackmail Supreme Court justices."

"Then how did he put it when he propositioned you?"

"This is completely out of line, Richard."

"Did you know that he tried to blackmail Bernie Keane?"

"Who told you that?"

"Keane told Harold and his co-clerk."

"I warned you about Harold."

"What does Nyquist have on you?"

"Nothing. He has nothing on me."

The evasion is subtle but unmistakable. "Then who?"

Madeleine withdraws into one of her silences. She could be considering the photograph of her husband because she turns that way, but she could also be looking deep into herself. Davenport realizes that what so infuriates him about Madeleine's silences is that, like Olivia's drunken blackouts, they place her beyond reach; she has abandoned him. "For just once, Madeleine, would you please stay with me and not go off to wherever it is you go."

"I'm not as quick as the rest of you." Her eyes glisten with hurt. "I need time to think."

"This is about Phil, isn't it?"

More seconds pass. Physically, Madeleine shrinks. Finally she says, "A couple of years ago Phil committed securities fraud. An SEC investigator discovered it when they were auditing one of his real estate companies. Instead of reporting it, the investigator told someone on

Nyquist's staff, and he came to me, and I made a deal. Nyquist would keep the SEC out of it if I got Phil to retire—"

"—and if you agreed to vote the way Nyquist tells you."

"Not all the time."

"Just the important cases." And, Davenport thinks, when you can't get me to do it for you.

"But never on abortion. That was our deal. I would never give up a woman's right to choose."

Only cases that undermine it. Davenport glances at the photograph of the sturdy adventurer. "And Phil goes along with this."

"You can't be serious! If Phil knew about the SEC he would have turned himself in." The dark eyes are still moist. "I know what you're thinking. What he did is a white collar crime and prison's a country club. But in Phil's condition it would have killed him. He wouldn't have lasted a month."

"You have to change your vote."

"What if it came down to protecting your wife? Would you have sacrificed her for this?"

Davenport thinks he once knew the answer to that, but he no longer does. "Phil doesn't want your protection any more than he wants you to push his wheelchair for him."

"Or any more than you want to take calls from your friend, the president. But you do."

Who had told Madeleine about the calls from Locke? "He'll stop calling when he realizes he can't touch my vote."

Madeleine says, "Do you know what the court's biggest secret is? Why every chief justice since the invention of television has refused to let cameras in the courtroom? None of them would say so, but every chief justice since Earl Warren was afraid that if they brought television cameras into the courtroom, the American public would quickly discover how ordinary we are. Feet of clay, and maybe a lot more. Better to limit our public image to the annual posed photograph, a postcard from Valhalla."

Or Magh Meall. "You need to talk to Phil. The only way you can show Nyquist you won't be blackmailed is to change your vote."

"Have you thought of what you're exposing your daughter to if you don't vote with the Chief and the rest of us? Her humiliation when Nyquist subpoenas her?"

"Nola can take care of herself, just as I'm sure Phil can take care of himself."

Madeleine says, "I'm not going to promise you anything."

Before she can fall into another of her silences, Davenport leaves.

● ● ● ● ● ● ● ● ● ● ● ● ● ● ● ● ● ● ●

Anne holds out the telephone receiver to Davenport. "The White House has been waiting for twenty minutes."

"I said I would call back."

"Apparently our president doesn't like to wait."

Davenport goes into his office, closes the door and waits for Locke's secretary to connect them.

"What's on your mind, Mr. President?"'

"I understand the vote is now 4–3 to affirm, but it's your vote that counts." The difference between a president and a senator is that a president gets right to the point. "I need you to join the Chief Justice and his wing."

As in everything he does, the president's pursuit of the religious right will be headlong and indiscriminate. To ask Locke who told him about the morning's vote would only prolong what Davenport wants to be a short conversation, and he already knows that it was Nyquist who made the call.

"You're unusually quiet, Richard. You know, one of the rewards of power is that I can use it to do good."

"We cannot be having this conversation." He had said the same to Junior Straubinger in the Harbor Square garage; there is no difference.

"The Chief Justice has told me he wants to retire at the end of the term. The job is yours if you want it. That will give you more opportunities to orchestrate big majorities the way you did in that assisted suicide case. The Chief Justice doesn't have the political instincts to put them together. You do."

Not the political instincts to persuade New York's legislators to defeat the Susie Briscoe Act, but apparently enough to corral eight Supreme Court justices. How could he have forgotten Locke's self-absorption, the banality of conversations with him?

Locke says, "If the statute was that bad you would have voted against it by now."

"This isn't about the statute, it's about boundaries. There's a line here that neither of us can cross."

The silence grows another layer before Locke says, "I hope you know why I didn't come to Olivia's memorial service."

"I hadn't thought about it."

"I was concerned that my presence would have turned what I'm sure you wanted to be a private occasion into a public event. Also, it may have given people the wrong idea about how close we are. How long has it been that I have depended on your loyalty?"

Davenport counts. It has been twenty-five years since what happened in Adams House.

"Olivia once told me you are the most loyal creature she knew, and she was right. Whatever she or I did, you would always come back."

"You make loyalty sound like a character defect."

"In your case it is. I dated Olivia before I introduced her to you. She never told you that, did she? She was an amazing lay, but completely nuts. That's why I dropped her. You should have divorced her the day you discovered how crazy she was, and saved yourself a lot of grief. But you had to be the loyal husband."

"My blind spot," Davenport says. And then it is gone. For whatever reason, or for no reason at all, the magnetic force that first drew him to Locke, and that bound him to the man for all these years, has abruptly shut down. "Nyquist is blackmailing you, isn't he?" Davenport imagines a line of victims, young and old, at the senator's door, offering up tales of Locke's indiscretions. Anyone as self-centered and reckless in his personal life as Locke would have a good many of them. "That's why you called."

"The man is an unscrupulous son of a bitch," the president says.

"But you're going to appoint him to the court."

"He has me by the short hairs, Richard."

"Why didn't you give him McWhorter's seat?"

"Bernie Keane wouldn't let me. He hated Nyquist. He said if I nominated him, he'd expose him as a blackmailer."

"That's why Keane agreed to resign," Davenport says. "He knew he was sick, and he was afraid that whoever was president when he died would nominate Nyquist for his seat. So he made a deal with you. He would resign because of poor health, and you agreed to pick anyone but Nyquist to replace him."

"But he died before he could resign, so I'm free to nominate whoever I want."

"No, you're not," Davenport says. "If you nominate Oren Nyquist to the Supreme Court, or to any court, I'll do what Bernie Keane can't. I'll expose him."

"You can't afford to do that. You need me."

"I don't want anything to do with you. I don't want your phone calls or your invitations to the White House—"

"You need me because I'm the only one who can stop the senator from exposing you."

And subjecting Nola to the press. "I already told you, I have nothing to hide about what happened on the ferry."

"I'm not talking about the ferry."

"Then, what?" The rush of ice to Davenport's heart is not because he doesn't know, but because he does.

"Do you have any idea how the media are going to spin what happened in Cambridge? A student-athlete assaults a helpless girl in his dorm room, and his best friend who saw the whole thing, doesn't report it to the university or the police? A best friend who, if I'm re-elected, is on track to become the next Chief Justice of the United States."

How typical of Locke to center the blame on him. "If this woman wanted to expose you, she would have told her story when you were running for president, or even governor. She wouldn't wait to talk to Nyquist until after you were elected."

"Apparently she didn't want to talk to anyone at all, even the police. But she told her daughter, who is a born-again Christian, and her daughter gave it to Nyquist."

"Then she must have told him that I was the one who stopped you."

"The daughter said you were there in the room, but she didn't say anything to Nyquist about you saving her mother."

"But you know."

"Why would I want to share that fact with anyone and lose my leverage over you? No, Richard, the world may never really know what happened with Olivia on the ferry, but this story, with this woman, is black-and-white. Nola's just about the same age that girl was. I can't imagine how you would try to explain this to her."

"Don't ever call me again." The president is still talking when Davenport puts down the receiver.

21

Junior's burning up! The ringing telephone snatches Gloria from a nightmare. "Junior's burning up!" The panic in her husband's voice is of a piece with the early morning darkness in the hotel room. Still, Gloria's first reflex is to thank God that, after almost a week without any word, her son is alive. "What do you mean 'burning up'?"

"He's boiling. His face is all red. He's sweating like a pig."

Dr. Hershberger had warned them about this. If Junior wasn't careful with the tubes from his machine, he could get infected. "Take him to Emergency."

"We're on our way. We just got in the car."

"Do you know where to go?"

"Jesus Christ, Gloria, how long have we lived here? We're five blocks from Buffalo General. I sell houses here."

A picture flashes into Gloria's thoughts. "What's he wearing?"

"Jeans. A T-shirt—"

"The black shirt, with the words?"

"Do you think I'd take him to the hospital like that? It's soaked."

Leonard could be calling from another planet, the conversation feels that unreal.

"Junior and I can take care of ourselves. That's your problem, Gloria; you think you're the only one who can take care of the family. If we took Denny out of that place when I said, Junior would be better now and you wouldn't be in Washington. No one would care about this damn case."

"At Emergency, tell them to call Dr. Hershberger."

Leonard said, "You won't believe where our boy was. What he did. He went to Washington. He talked to the judge. The new one."

"That's the fever talking, Leonard."

"No, he talked to him. He found out where the judge lived and he talked to him."

"Tell the emergency doctor that Dr. Hershberger needs to see Junior right away."

. . . .

Gloria doesn't want to be here in the overheated court room. She wants to be in Buffalo, at the hospital with Junior, but no airline has a seat until 2:00 p.m. Two days ago, when she was leaving the hotel, Christine called to tell her that one of the judges had died, and that the court wouldn't announce its decision until the next day. Christine called the next day to say that it had been postponed again, and maybe it wouldn't be until Friday. She said Gloria didn't have to stay in Washington, and that she would call her as soon as the decision was announced. But Gloria worried that her absence would somehow put the outcome of the case at risk. If the new judge got her letter, he would be looking for her. She spent the first day making plane reservations, then cancelling them a half-hour later, twice taking a taxi to National Airport, only to change her mind when she got there. She visited museums on the Mall in a futile effort to escape thinking about Junior. She had dinner in the hotel room and fell asleep lying across the bed, still in her clothes.

. . . .

Christine was furious when Gloria told her about the letter she sent to the new judge. "You can't do that, Gloria. It's against all the rules." "But it won't hurt our case?" Christine's reply—"Of course not"—was too quick and too filled with anger. It occurred to Gloria that Christine was less concerned about the infraction's effect on their case than about the new judge's opinion of a lawyer who would let her client do such a thing.

Sitting next to her in the courtroom, Christine pokes around in her purse and comes up with a skinny gold pen, then a small leather notebook. Christine seems less special than she did on Monday. Gloria's impression then was that the lawyer was one of those perfect women like Dr. Burroughs, but this morning, up close over coffee in the court's cafeteria, she could see where the makeup didn't go on perfectly and that the flesh above her lip was creased. Behind the perfume was a smell of cigarette tobacco. When Gloria asked her how she managed to remember all the cases and page numbers when she argued to the judges, Christine laughed and explained that there were usually only three or four cases the judges really cared about and she memorized only these. "Anyway, if I get the page number wrong, who's going to know?" Still, after Christine's blow-up over the letter, Gloria decided not to confide in her about Junior's trip to Washington or his return home.

A buzzer sounds, a voice from somewhere cries out a jumble of words, Christine taps the back of Gloria's hand to signal her to rise and, behind the long bench, the three sets of blood-red curtains part. Gloria observes that, despite his lion's mane of white hair, the chief judge is short, but that when he takes his chair and the others take theirs, he suddenly appears to be the tallest. They could be in the mirror room at an amusement park fun house. The chief judge waits for quiet as if he has all the time in the world, and when he finally starts, it is not about their case, but about the judge who died. At breakfast when Gloria asked Christine what effect the judge's death would have on their case, she said it wasn't going to hurt them because the judge was a definite vote against allowing the transplant. Christine said that four of the judges, including the one she worked for after law school, are going to vote for the transplant, so, if the new judge joins them, the decision will be 5–3 in their favor but, if he doesn't, the vote will be 4–4 and the lower court decision against them will stand.

The chief judge's voice rises. He is moving to a different subject. "In Number 15-1160, *Straubinger v. New York*, Mr. Justice Davenport will announce the decision of the court."

The effect on Gloria of her name filling the courtroom is that it no longer belongs to her, but has become public property, like a park or a swimming pool. She doesn't know what it means that the new judge is announcing the decision. She looks over at Christine, but the lawyer just touches the back of Gloria's hand again. The new judge adjusts the small microphone in front of him and Gloria realizes that, maybe because she wrote to him, she has come to think of him as her judge.

As he speaks, the judge's eyes search the room. "In light of the urgency that attends this appeal, we have agreed to enter our order and announce our decision today, but we will postpone to a later day the release of our formal opinion in the case. However, as I will be writing that opinion, it may be appropriate for me to make a few informal remarks now. I should add that these are my own, personal thoughts, and do not necessarily reflect those of my colleagues who have joined in my vote. Indeed"—for the first time, he smiles and Gloria's heart skips—"I believe it is safe to say that my colleagues will publicly endorse very little of what I am about to say."

The searching eyes come to rest on Gloria's. He could be reaching out to take her hand. "My vote was the last to be recorded in this case. In fact I didn't vote until shortly after midnight. I took that long because I believe that the faith this court demands of its nation's citizens requires in return that, in reaching our decisions, we as justices not only study the facts and the law governing the case, but also reflect on our own life experiences and our conscience."

Gloria thinks, how can one lawyer be so wise and another so foolish? If Mike Bossio's IQ was a percentage point higher, he would have known that there are states where the laws weren't like New York's, and they could have taken Junior and Denny there instead of starting this lawsuit. He could have warned them that, after the lower court ruled against them, there would be an order that stopped her from taking Denny from the Home.

"These reflections ultimately confirmed for me the fundamental truth that where youth or, as in the present case, incapacity prevent an individual from making the most consequential life or death decisions for himself, our Constitution commits those decisions not to the institutions of the state but to the individual's family, if he is fortunate enough to have one. I am authorized to say that Justices Bauman, Cardona, Shell and Cippolone join me in voting to reverse the decision below on the ground that the New York statute, the so-called Susie Briscoe Act, is unconstitutional."

Christine's hand squeezes hers, and when Gloria says, "Thank God," her lawyer nods but puts a finger to her lips. Gloria's next thought is of the towering, brightly lit Christmas tree in the Supreme Court lobby. She realizes that arrangements for the transplant will push Christmas to the side this year but, if she understands what is happening, the court's decision will let her take Denny out of the Home and into Arcade or anywhere he wants to see the Christmas lights. The meaning of the judge's words rolls over her like a gentle wave. She hears the individual words, but they are like water.

"To be sure," the judge says, "families may err when they make these life-and-death decisions. The great paradox of family life is that it compels us to some of our most wretched deeds as well as to our noblest ones. But, with all its many flaws, what institution in our society can do better in making these decisions than the family? Certainly not our legislators. No one who has spent even a day observing the legislative process would come away thinking that our legislators would do a better job than the family does. As counsel to New York's former governor, I had a front row seat at the New York State legislature's passage of the Susie Briscoe Act. I can report to you firsthand on the backroom deals that were made, not only to pass this statute but, even more intensively, to override the governor's veto after the statute was passed. I saw votes for the Susie Briscoe Act traded for state highway funds, for housing redevelopment subsidies and for the approval of a truck plaza at the Peace Bridge to Canada. I saw the needs of individuals and their families fall to the bottom of the political barrel."

The other judges are restless in their high-backed chairs, and Gloria doesn't know if this is because they are bored or because, as her judge promised, they would not agree with what he said.

"Who would you rather entrust with the life of a fireman suffering the last painful ravages of disease—his devoted family, who have only his welfare in mind, or politicians with little on their mind but re-election and fine meals with their favorite lobbyists? To whom would you rather entrust the terrible decision to administer the fatal dose—family members who will forever bear the moral burden of their decision, or a US senator impatient to get on to the next item of political business or to hobnob on the Washington social circuit? Ask the children who must make the decision whether to remove a parent or sibling from life support, and every one of them will tell you that, wish as they might for someone wiser or stronger to pull the plug, they will not give up the right to make that decision themselves. Consider the *Straubinger* case itself—"

In the thick air of the overheated courtroom, Gloria feels a chill. She studies the judge's fine face and troubled eyes and, just as when she observed Christine's imperfect makeup at breakfast, she realizes that the judge has escaped life's challenges no better than she has. Tears fill her eyes. He read her letter. She knows exactly what is coming.

"I have studied the record in this case, what there is of it, and I believe that I understand the situation of the Straubinger family as well as anyone. One son suffers an extreme form of autism, while his twin suffers a fatal kidney disease. May the one son donate a kidney to the other? Should we let the parents decide? Can anyone imagine how torn they are? How many sleepless nights they must have spent debating their decision, the quarrels they doubtless waged between—and within—themselves in reaching their decision?"

Is it wrong that Gloria is thinking about Denny, and not Junior? That time in Dr. Burrough's office, the superintendent spat out the word "ambivalence" as if it was itself the name of a fatal disease. Maybe this is why she feels connected to the new judge. Why would he be the last to vote, and after midnight, if their case had not torn him in two? And in the end, despite their doubts, they had both made a decision—Gloria to write a letter and the judge to cast his vote.

"Will some families make these decisions more lightly than others? I am certain that will happen. Will the motives of a parent or sibling sometimes be mixed—part selfless, part selfish—as he or she reaches the deadly conclusion? Undoubtedly they will. But ultimately no legislator or government official can consistently make a better decision than will these families, for none of these political creatures will ever suffer a life as regularly visited by remorse and doubt as will a family member who has so acted or failed to act. Nor do we do these family members a favor when we forcibly lift this burden from their shoulders and deliver it up instead to the indifferent institutions of the state. I say that because this burden embodies the very essence of being human."

Christine hurriedly writes something on her pad, tears off the sheet and, after a moment's deliberation, crumples it. She places her hand over Gloria's and clasps it. Gloria wants nothing more than to be home and with her boys.

The judge looks down along the bench before continuing. "The freedom of families, no less than the freedom of individuals, is of course bounded by the needs of civil society. Without such boundaries we risk anarchy, and it falls to the courts, and ultimately to this court, to locate these boundaries. This is inevitably our greatest challenge. But how well have we done as justices in meeting it?"

Christine's grip on Gloria's hand tightens. Something is wrong.

"Certainly, if freedom from political bias is the criterion by which this court's decisions are to be judged, this court has performed poorly, indeed. How many Americans would view it as a coincidence that at the turn of this century, in a presidential election that separated the Republican and Democrat candidates by only a handful of ballots, the votes of the nine justices of this court divided, five conservatives to four liberals, and handed the election to the Republican candidate?"

The judge's gaze so absorbs Gloria that, only when Christine squeezes her hand even more tightly does she see that the judge sitting next to the chief judge, the tall one with the bow tie sticking out from his robe, has risen. His face is flushed. He pulls his arm away from the chief judge who is trying to restrain him and in the next moment disappears through the red curtain. Christine is at the edge of her seat, her knees against the seat in front of her. She scribbles a note on her pad and hands it to Gloria. *This has never happened before.* The *never* is underlined three times. Voices around them buzz. The Asian-looking judge gets up and follows the first one through the curtains. The chief judge looks furious, but when he bangs his gavel for quiet, he does so only once, and almost gently.

If Gloria's judge has noticed the departures, they've made no impression on him, for he has not broken his pace. He could be a swimmer making his way purposefully against the current. "Court watchers warn that religion is the Supreme Court's fatal third rail, never to be discussed. But is it a coincidence that this court's votes on abortion have divided according to the dictates of each justice's announced religious faith? What, other than religious conviction, can explain the paradox that the very same justices who vote to outlaw abortion will vote to uphold the death penalty?"

Three other justices have left the bench now: the old one with the thick eyebrows who had been sitting next to the chief judge; the bald one; and the woman who Gloria had wanted to like because she looked so much like the girls in her crowd at Erie County Community College. Only the Spanish-looking judge remains along with the chief judge who looks like he would leave if only his job description let him do so.

Gloria thinks about how for the past two years these complete strangers, these judges, have stolen her life from her, and have shown nothing but indifference to her needs and those of her family. Junior's doctors and nurses have treated him better than this, and for a longer time. The orderlies at the Home have paid more attention to Denny than have these judges. Even Dr. Ice has.

It seems that the judge is done because the chief judge shifts in his chair as if he is about to leave. For the first time since he glanced down the then-full bench, the new judge looks about and appears puzzled by the absences. He fixes his gaze on a point in the back of the filled courtroom and says, "In the end, and hard as it can sometimes be to discover, justice is all that we have to guide us in the exercise of our transcendent power. But justice is not some will-o'-the wisp, a flickering light to be obscured by the heavy folds of doctrine and revealed only as the opinion polls and this court's perception of its relations with the public require. No, justice needs to be open and transparent. But what hope can we have for justice if this court, its decisions final and unreviewable, cannot rise above the easy pieties of politics, ideology and faith? Even if it requires us to steal from ourselves to do so, what hope for justice can there be if we as judges fail to search out every evidence of human frailty, aspiration and desert that we can?"

The judge seems about to say more, but he stops as if suddenly struck by the consequence of what he has said. The stillness in the courtroom is so deep that it seems to Gloria it might go on forever. The chief judge rises, then the Spanish judge and finally the new judge and, like a magician followed by his assistants, the three swiftly disappear through the tall curtains.

Even in late June, at 6:30 in the morning the Atlantic Ocean off 'Sconset is colder than the pool at the "Y." Nola will arrive this evening. She put the house on the market last month and the sale will close next week, so this is Davenport's last visit. After lunch, he will fill the tires of Olivia's ancient English bicycle and ride into the Village to shop for dinner. Over the past few months of living alone, Davenport has discovered an unexpected pleasure in cooking, and for dinner he has planned a green salad dressed with oil, vinegar and crumbled blue cheese; cioppino dense with clams, mussels, crab, lobster and cod, and fragrant of garlic and fennel; and apple pie from the new bakery he noticed in town on his arrival yesterday evening.

Davenport has not seen Nola since that December night in his apartment, but they speak over the phone as often as once a week. Their conversations remain stiff, and the closeness he had hoped for since the visit has not developed, but he has learned to be careful of his expectations and also—his great failure with Olivia—to be patient. Nola will spend August with friends in Provence, then take her junior year abroad in Paris, after which she will return to Columbia. More than once the odd image has occurred to Davenport of Harold and Nola meeting on the Morningside Heights campus, for Harold has declined Harvard's teaching offer and in the fall will join the law faculty at Columbia instead. He told Davenport that he wanted to live in a "real city," but the justice doesn't think of Harold as someone who is particular about where he lives, and suspects that in the end it was loyalty to his alma mater that explained his decision.

Swimming in the Atlantic, Davenport imagines the black line on the bottom of the "Y" pool. The trick in freestyle swimming is to become the black line, to rotate no more than a degree, never two, off its axis. Do people know that fear of drowning will sometimes overcome even the most accomplished swimmer? In cap and goggles, but like an astronaut detached from his capsule and adrift in space, the swimmer swivels in panic that he has lost the black line. Davenport believes that in the months immediately before and after Olivia's death, this is what happened to him, but now that the line is gone he doesn't miss it.

Impermanence hangs over the summer house and its contents, but not because of the sale. Only rarely has Davenport felt at home in this place that was in Olivia's family for three generations. Nor, if he thinks about it, did he ever feel entirely comfortable with her. One morning early in their marriage it struck him that the face asleep on the pillow across from him was that of a complete stranger. That distance never entirely disappeared—does it ever, for any couple?—and while Davenport once blamed its persistence on Olivia's growing illness, today he accepts that something is missing in him as well. He does not expect to marry again.

As he promised at his confirmation hearings, Davenport still carefully studies the law and facts in every case. He gives little weight, though, to the views of the other justices. He votes with the liberals more often than with the conservatives but, as in last month's school prayer case, he usually writes a concurring opinion to state his own view of the principles at stake. In working toward a just result, he continues to search as deeply in his own experience as he can bear. Madeleine, the asperity in her tone unmistakable, has observed to Davenport that he has taken on Bernie Keane's role as the court's lone wolf. Edward told him much the same, but in a manner that betrayed none of Madeleine's disapproval.

On Monday the court will announce its last decisions of the term. Officially one term doesn't end until the next one begins, on the first Monday in October, but most chambers have begun to wind down their work for the summer break. Davenport's bench-clearing observations about the influence of faith and politics on the justices' votes have produced a breach with his colleagues that will probably never heal.

Madeleine is alone in exchanging more than the necessary courtesies with him. The disruptive observations do not appear in the official version of Davenport's majority opinion in *Straubinger v. New York* released a month later, but they were widely reported in the press at the time, and of course the transcript of his remarks is still available on the Internet.

The incident has made Davenport a hero of sorts for letter writers from around the world and Edward now spends half his day sorting through the mail. One such letter, from the superintendent of the facility outside Buffalo where the autistic Straubinger twin is a patient, was extravagant in thanking Davenport for making it possible to realize the boy's wish to help his brother. The superintendent added that the transplant was a complete success for both boys.

For a few days in January the rumor floated that the president was going to nominate Oren Nyquist to fill Bernie Keane's seat, but the story abruptly vanished when the Senate Judiciary Committee Chair, Joel Mandeville, told the press that it was inconceivable that the Democratic Senate would confirm such an unusual choice. The next day, Locke announced his nomination of Raymond Tolliver, a politically moderate, African-American court of appeals judge, for the seat. The rapid sequence of events displayed, to Davenport at least, Bennett Jaffe's fine political hand: by advancing the prospect that the president would nominate Nyquist, Bennett had protected not only the president's right flank, but also his promise to Nyquist. At the same time, Bennett had delegated the president's protection from the left to Mandeville. The Senate promptly confirmed Tolliver, and his appointment has created a solid liberal majority of five, from which Madeleine has so far not repeated her defection.

The Chief talks of retirement from time to time but, staunch Republican that he is, no one expects him to leave before an election that, according to the early polls, his party's candidate may well win. From his high spirits and brisk manner, leading foreign visitors on tours through the halls of the court building and conducting the weekly conference of the justices, the Chief betrays neither fatigue from his duties nor loss of sleep at the thought that Oren Nyquist will be his successor. The presidential nominating convention is two months off, but Tony Locke is already running, and it is impossible to pick up a newspaper or watch the evening news without finding him at a factory opening, the site of some natural disaster or visiting the troops on a distant battlefield. Davenport has not spoken with the president since their telephone call in December, and while other justices have been to dinners at the White House, no invitations have arrived for Davenport nor would he have accepted them if they had.

Because they partake of his being, the other corners of Davenport's life are irreducible. The workouts in the "Y" pool remain as central to the meaning of his day as a monk's morning prayers, and he now understands that in the exhaustion of this daily routine, and of his work, he seeks the same oblivion that Olivia sought in alcohol. His taste in civic architecture is unchanged. When he debarked the Hy-Line ferry yesterday evening, he observed in the austere lines of Nantucket's Broad Street courthouse greater possibilities for the rule of law than he finds in the Supreme Court's towering colonnade, and most particularly at the magical hour when twilight first falls on the foursquare brick building. His circle of friends, always small, has grown smaller. Today Davenport knows no one who would throw a small dog from a second-story window. But if someone did, he is still the man who will race across a twilit lawn to save it.

Acknowledgments

At the Supreme Court of the United States, I am grateful to Associate Justice Ruth Bader Ginsburg, Matt Hofstedt, Rakesh Kilaru, and Kate Wilko for introducing me to some of the court's more private corners. Russ Feingold, Jeff Fisher, Tom Goldstein, Pam Karlan, and Alan Morrison have my thanks for helping to ensure authenticity of place and manner in and around the Court and the Capitol. Closer home, I am indebted to Rick Banks, Barbara Fried, Hank Greely, and Mike McConnell for answering questions; to Bruce Frymire and Adam Johnson for reading and commenting on all or part of early drafts; and to Lewis Haut, MD, for keeping the manuscript free of medical error.

For their astute editorial suggestions, I am grateful to Sarah Crichton, Jon Malysiak, and Carl Yorke and, as ever, I am indebted to Lynne Anderson for typing the manuscript through its several drafts, all the while keeping a sharp eye out for miscues and miscreancies.